RELIC OF THE DAWN

Exalted, Book 2

By David Niall Wilson

"No need to worry about making an impression," Dharni said. "The scruffier you look, the more you'll fit the role of messenger. I'm afraid they wouldn't credit a mercenary with the intelligence to concoct a story like yours. Those still on the council who remember the battle of Mishaka came away with some odd impressions."

Krislan glanced up sharply, searching the other man's expression for a hint of insult. There was none.

"I know, you see," Dharni continued. "I have served as the captain of their guard for seven years now, having served an equal number as lieutenant in a mercenary band. There are those among them who only see the mercenary in me and still have difficulty believing I can be trusted to tie off my own horse. Thankfully, they do not make up the bulk, or the leading factions, of the city or the council."

Krislan laughed. "It's better that way. They can be continually surprised by your competency, and you can be assured that they will underestimate you. It's a good plan."

"Oh, they know me well enough," Dharni mused. "Sometimes I think they only pretend not to trust me so they can have an excuse to underpay."

The two left the room together and walked down a long, rough hall. They exited through another back door, an apparent habit of Dharni's, and emerged onto a darkened street. Krislan followed Dharni's lead, weaving through the back streets and alleys until they came to another, wider, thoroughfare, across which a large stone building stood. There were lights seeping out under the cracks of the front door, and in the windows, shadows moved about slowly.

It Is the Second Age of Man

Long ago, in the First Age, mortals became Exalted by the Unconquered Sun and other celestial gods. These demigods were Princes of the Earth and presided over a golden age of unparalleled wonder. But like all utopias, the age ended in tears and bloodshed.

The official histories say that the Solar Exalted went mad and had to be put down lest they destroy all Creation. Those who had been enlightened rulers became despots and anathema, and the First Age gave way to an era of chaos and warfare. This harsh time only ended with the rise of the Scarlet Empress, a powerful Dragon-Blood who fought back all enemies and founded a great empire. For a time, all was well—at least for those who toed the Empress's line.

But times are changing again. The Scarlet Empress has either gone missing or retreated into seclusion. The dark forces of the undead and the Fair Folk are stirring again. And, most cataclysmic of all, the Solar Exalted have returned. Across Creation, men and women find themselves imbued with the power of the Unconquered Sun and awaken to memories from a long-ago golden age.

The Sun-Children, the Anathema, have been reborn.

Among their kind is Dace. Before his Exaltation he was a grizzled mercenary, a veteran of the petty wars of the so-called Scavenger Lands—the region around the great trading city of Nexus. Now, empowered by the Sun with unparalleled combat skill, he leads his own mercenary force and has become one of Nexus's protectors. But the weight of destiny lies heavily on his shoulders, and he fears great struggles are ahead. Already he has faced grim agents of the Deathlords and invading demons.

There is little rest for the chosen of the Sun.

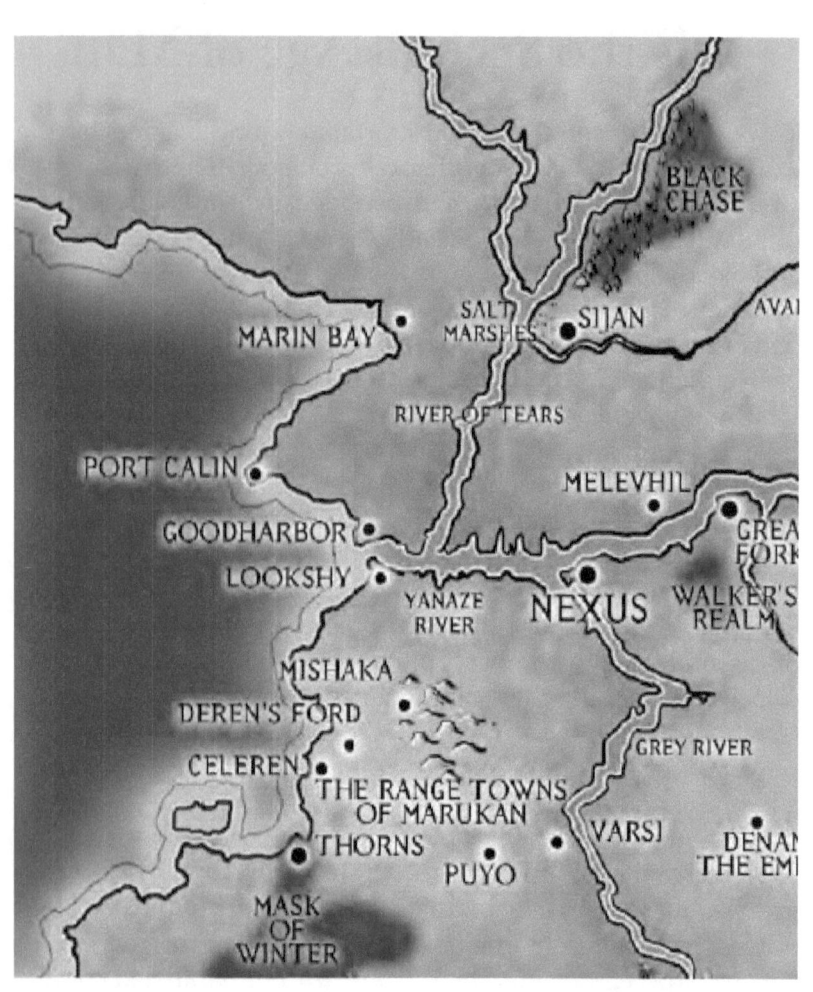

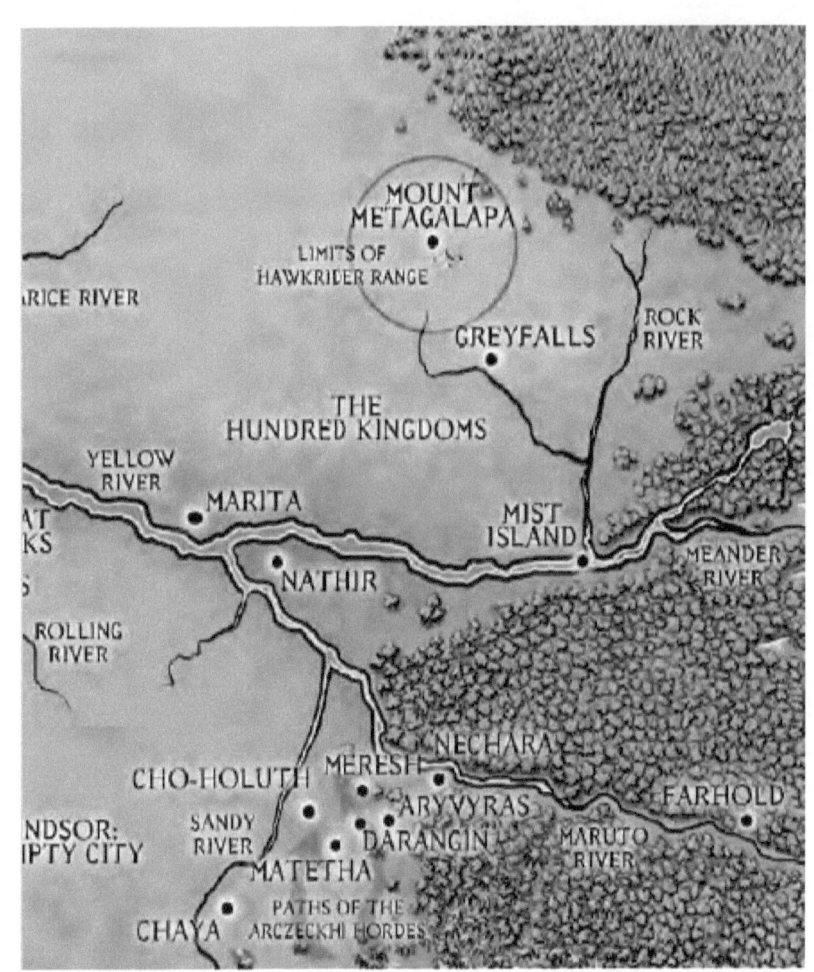

Prologue

The moon hung high and bright in the sky, casting shadows and blending white to silver to gray on the pale stone side of the mountain. Overlooking a sheer drop-off that fell so far away to the valley below that its base was lost in shadow, a gnarled and broken tree gripped the stone and loose soil with desperate, clinging root-fingers. On its highest branch, preening her feathers with her wicked, hooked beak, sat a great silver owl. Each time she moved, the branch that held her shook. The roots of the tree lost a little more ground. Irritated by the feeble nature of her perch, she sidestepped along the branch and dug her talons deeper, scoring the withered bark deeply.

Her head swiveled slowly, each motion haughty and cold. She fixed her gaze on the inky shadows below, her eyes darting from side to side, motions so swift her regal features blurred to silver in the brilliant moonlight. Then she was still as a statue, hewn of the stone of the mountain. The wind riffled through her feathers, rustled through the sparse leaves of the tree, and whispered along the slopes of the mountain, winding eerily through every crack and crevice and finding its voice in hollow logs and rugged stone.

She gripped the branch more tightly, raised her wings very slowly until they stretched to either side, a beautiful, impossible span of sinew and bone. A shiver ran through her frame. She raised her head, just for a moment, beak parted and eyes flashing with wild hunger, and she screamed. It wasn't the piercing cry of the owl—not exactly. It was more, pitched higher and slipping lower than any bird's nightmare would allow. With a lurch she was airborne. She did not release the branch immediately. Instead, she pitted the strength of her wings against its last, feeble hold on the mountain. She wrenched it free, and as she plummeted down the sheer slope, the tree groaned and released its age-old grip on the stone, falling at her back, too slow and clumsy to race her in her breathtaking dive.

Shadows parted. Her wings spread behind her in a rigid V and held her steady. She dropped like a stone, the tree spreading out behind her, nearly matching her speed. She never glanced upward, though the shadows would have told her of its presence. She focused downward, and, as the mountaintop grew smaller at her back, the ground spread beneath her, forests to the right and a long, sloping valley floor to the left.

Her eyes were so sharp they cut to the blades of grass, the dancing motes of dirt and dust whirling across the ground, the pulsing throb of hot red blood in a fur-encased throat. Unaware, breathing normally, the big cat hunkered in its own shadows. Other forms moved in other places, and it watched them with a hunger that mirrored the owl's in pale reflection. The cat's tail twitched; its claws gripped a fallen log as the desire to sprint shivered through its frame.

The dive was the act of moments. A thousand feet in the span of a breath, and as the owl reached the tips of trees, she whipped her wings down, arched her back and spread her claws, huge claws, large and sharp, screaming a second time. The cat froze. For a moment, it seemed to melt into the ground, unable to leap, or snarl, unable to rid its mind of its hunger.

In the distance, a hare leaped and pelted into the shadows. Dust and small rocks flew, and the ground thumped with each pounding beat of fur-tufted feet. The cat yowled, whirling too late. The owl, huge and terrible, struck like lightning, gripping the cougar by its neck and flanks and, with another terrible cry and a crashing of wings, lifted up, and away from the ground.

As the huge owl lifted her prey from the earth, the tree crashed behind it, a splintering, grinding final howl of shattered wood and clattering stone. The sound blended with the screeching yowl of the big cat, flailing and whipping its great head from side to side, trying to twist in the grip that held it fast, to snap and bite and rend the flesh just out of reach. Nothing could loose her talons from its flesh. She pounded the wind with her huge, powerful wings, and she and her prey rose steadily, until the trees below were nothing more than a blur. The cougar's struggles grew wild. Frantically it tore at the grip on its neck and skin, biting the air viciously.

There was no thought in its actions. It was no longer aware of the earth below, or the lost prey. Its world was pain that centered just beyond its reach. Blood gushed from the wounds, pouring down its flanks and falling away in deep dark droplets that glittered wetly and disappeared. Still the owl climbed. She banked, fighting the weight of the cat and the unbalanced pull of its struggles.

The tree had shattered, but she was returning to where it had stood, the highest point of the mountain, the solitary peak where no other dared climb, or fly, or dream of setting foot. Already she could taste its heart, the hot red blood and soft flesh, the sensation of red life spattering her face.

Loss of blood and the chill air of the heights were taking the fight from the big cat. It still rolled and snapped, but weakly, hanging limp in her grip. With contemptuous ease, she released her prey and watched as it plummeted through the air, too weak to react to the sudden shift in gravity. The cougar screamed, but the sound cut off with a wet thump as it struck the stone.

A flash of wings, and she was on him. Bones had broken in the fall, and the cat could move only weakly. She dove in quick and close, tearing his throat with the sharp hook of her beak, ripping it until the blood flowed freely and dodging back from the last weak swipes of its paws. She was careful. The cat was nearly dead, but nearly was not enough. It grew still, and with terrible speed, she struck, burying her beak in its chest and tearing at the cat's flesh. She ripped and shredded her way to the center—the heart. A final shudder rippled through the cougar and she stole the moment of death, dipping deep into the cavity of its ruined chest and plucking free the heart.

She threw her head back. Her prize was too large for a single gulp. Biting down, she parted the still hot, pulsing organ with a sharp snap. She caught the first morsel before it dropped to the ground, swallowed, and dipped for the second before it could begin to cool. Before the life had fully gone from it. Before the glorious, heated savor grew as cold and lifeless as the body from which it had been torn.

And then, as quickly as the hunt had begun, it ended. She shivered. The heart slid down her throat, and her thoughts shimmered. She saw the hare as the cat had seen it, saw the quivering, nervous motion of its whiskers flashing in the moonlight, caught the quivering muscles of its flanks, stuck between flight and cowering fear. She sensed its terror and felt the clench of unfamiliar muscles. She stretched her wings and her form rippled. Skin stretched, bone and sinew popped, and then she stretched her long, slender arms over her head. Leaning back, her white hair flowing over the stone like molten silver, Lilith laughed, though there was no mirth in it. Her laughter rolled over the stone and into the valley below, then faded slowly to a soft sigh of lament.

She had enjoyed the hunt, despite her constant melancholy, and the bright copper taste of blood from the big cat's heart distracted her thoughts. She felt the spirit of the cougar seeping into her being, felt the patterns of its muscle and bone blending with her own. The mountain felt good at her back. Solid and endless, it stretched into the earth as the moon bathed her in its brilliance. Lilith licked the last of the blood from her lips, savoring the difference of the sensation—bird to woman. Dreaming of the time when she would know that savor as the cat.

The mountain was the first of many. She was near. Somehow she knew she was near to what she sought, and this brought another ripple of wild laughter. It had been so long since she'd moved with a purpose that it was an alien sensation. Memories long dormant shifted to the surface of her conscious thought, irritating her in little ways that egged her onward.

She remembered him well enough. Desus. Bright like the sun and strong, so strong she had felt molten in his embrace. In lust, and in anger, she had felt him move upon the Earth, and had shared those emotions with him, his strength and passion, his anger and his dreams. Then, when he had burned out like the falling of a star, she had remained.

The end of those crazed final days had been a guilty release. He had grown cruel, and she had not fled. She had fought, but he was strong, and each day he'd slipped further over some inner edge she could not pull him back from. Their love had become a blaze of desire and anger, hatred and fire. Each and every time she was burned, she returned.

Now she lay back against the cool of the earth, bathed in moonlight, and he tugged at her. Across the years and miles, screams and smiles, she yearned for him. She knew he would return—not the when or where of it, but the certainty of it. It pulsed through the mountain at her back and itched at her mind.

"What?" she whispered.

Almost, the wind breathed an answer. Lilith rose. She was not far from the point where the tree had torn from the flesh of the mountain. Curious, she moved closer. A gaping wound had opened in the mountainside. She leaned closer. The roots had stretched more deeply into the soil than she would have believed, and clung more tenaciously. Sand and silt, loose soil and gravel, had tumbled behind her in her dive and crashed to the valley below.

Something glinted. She leaned closer still, reaching down and brushing loose dirt aside for a better look. It was gold, glittering and bright, trapped beneath a second layer of earth. Memories flashed through her mind. Leaning quickly, her movements still faintly bird-like, she snatched it up and stepped back.

It was a very old coin. It bore symbols she'd not seen in years upon years, etched into a surface of pure orichalcum. On one side it presented the sigil of the Unconquered Sun—on the other a great city. Lilith whirled it in her fingers hypnotically, and her thoughts wandered.

She thought of those final days, the days before Desus had left her. She thought of his words, which had been little more than mad ranting. Something—something she was to find. Something he would leave to her, to no other. Something important, as quickly forgotten and spit out with his jumbled insults and wild proclamations. Still, he had said it, and so she knew it was true. She knew there was a box.

She had been searching for nearly a year, ever since she'd become aware of the Solar Exalted and their return. She had spent those months slipping from shadow to shadow, listening where she could, buying answers where she couldn't. She'd learned a few things, but there was so much more. Somewhere, she knew, the essence that had been Desus would awaken in another skin, and only her own patience and perseverance could lead her to him.

She didn't know what was in the box, but she knew that things were changing in the world. The Solar Exalted were returning, and there were flurries of activity among the dark places. Deathknights drove their armies across the land, and even the cities were not as they had once been, rebuilding on the bones of what had gone before. She had felt the Solars, afire with the sun and crashing about the earth, lighting the lines of power like beacons. Desus would be back, she knew. What that meant, she did not know.

Memories can grow so dim over centuries that they become secrets, and she knew he had left a whispered secret in a box for her, if only she were clever enough to figure out where it might be located, and what it meant. There was time. There had always been time. It passed differently for owls, and wolves, and those who walked the wilder ways, but it was inevitable in its progression.

There were a few hours remaining before the moon would fade from sight, and the sun would rise to heat and glory. Lilith had miles to cover, and the sight of the coin—so bright, and yet so old, reminded her of her purpose.

She considered the cat. It would be wonderful to stretch out her limbs, to bound down from stone to stone, fighting for balance and depending on her instincts to keep her from following that dead, ancient tree in its plummet from the cliff, screaming her defiance to the night—but it would not be so swift. It would wait for another time. With a final silvery laugh, she tossed back her head and raised her arms. The air about her glimmered, just for an instant, and then the owl stretched its powerful, impossible wings to the wind and whipped down in a single beat that launched her to the heart of the sky.

A bright pinpoint of silver-white reflected against the darkness, she headed deeper into the mountains, disappearing from sight.

Chapter One

Tarsus slumped near the rear of his cage, knees drawn up to his chest, hunger eating at him like acid and his mind a blurred landscape of memory, pain, and despair. He had eaten only scant bites over the past three days; not because they didn't feed him, but because he couldn't keep it down when they did. The walking dead were filthy, and the living who passed near didn't bother to pay their prisoner any attention. The food they offered was the remnant of their own: old rotten and crawling with maggots. His water was tepid, swirling with a multi-colored oily film.

They had penned him near the animals, and the only question that remained unanswered was how he would die. Since his capture he had been beaten, half-starved, had mud kicked through the bars of his makeshift prison, but he had not been questioned. He knew his value in such a situation was measured in words, and so far those words seemed of little interest to his captors. Tarsus spent his hours contemplating ways of taking the answer to the question from their hands. In that camp swarming with those risen from death, he contemplated his own.

The nights were the worst. By day he saw little of the dead, and the deathknight, whom they called the Drinker of Seeping Poison, was not to be seen. His men worked, and they could be seen about the camp, readying things for the coming night and caring for the animals. At first Tarsus had believed this lack of activity by day might afford him a chance at escape, but the thought was short-lived.

One thing he had not known, and doubted that his own commander, Dace, would have suspected, was that the deathknight was served by a small number of the Dragon-Blooded. They were quiet, brooding, dripping with arrogant power in ways with which the Dragon-Blooded Tarsus was familiar with and those who served the Elemental Dragons were not. They did not seem to care for one another's company, but handled different, larger tasks for the deathknight.

One of them had begun to take an interest in Tarsus and this was something the scout wanted, beyond all things in the small remnant of his world, to avoid. The Dragon-Blooded was tall, taller than any other in the camp. His hair was slick and black, like a rain of silk. By day he was pale, but at night Tarsus would have sworn the moonlight rippled over the man's skin to reveal blues and deep greens woven into the flesh. Every motion was supple and smooth, almost too beautiful. The Dragon-Blooded was of the caste of water, and Tarsus had not seen many of his kind.

And the warrior watched him. This was the strangest thing. The others, human, dead and Dragon-Blooded alike, paid no attention to Tarsus at all. They appeared content to wait for him to die, or for the Abyssal to call for him. Beyond that he was of no interest, except to this one, who stood, staring from the shadows at him for long periods of time, silent as the rest, but—watching.

Tarsus sensed the warrior's approach before he actually saw him. The sun was high in the sky, and the dead warriors that made up most of the Drinker of Seeping Poison's force were dormant. There were a few soldiers moving about, and servants, loading and unloading supply wagons as they rolled into camp from some shadowed roadway Tarsus could not make out where he was caged. He knew from the position of the sun that they came from a general northward direction, and departed the same, but once they moved beyond his vision, he could not track them, and he hadn't gotten close enough before his capture to get a good feel for it.

He had had time to think about it, though. It was odd that the traffic was to the north. Assuming that the Deathlord the Mask of Winters was behind it all, to and from Thorns would be the logical route for supplies. There was nothing to the north for long leagues, and any traffic along that route would be open and easy to track with scouts. There had been no word from the north that Tarsus was aware of and, despite the hopelessness of his situation, he had spent some time worrying it over in his mind.

Thorns was almost due south. To the north, the trade routes in and out of Nexus would surely intersect any caravans moving this way, and yet supplies arrived daily, and other wagons departed. The numbers of the dead increased, though it was difficult to tell by what degree from his position near the center of the camp. That there was some attack or ambush imminent was obvious, but Tarsus could gain no clue of what it might be.

The Dragon-Blooded warrior had stopped across a broad path through the camp. He stood beneath the limbs of a gnarled, half-dead tree, blending gracefully into the meager shadow and glimmering with a pale, light-blue sheen in the sunlight. He did not smile, and those who moved about near him avoided catching his attention. He wore a long, slender sword with a hilt of black jade and intricate lines of script running the length of the sharp, curved blade. The lines of the weapon blended with those of his armor, which was lighter than most, allowing ease of motion. The man moved like a dancer.

Tarsus feigned sleep, laying his arms across his knees and letting his head fall forward across them. He didn't close his eyes, and he could still glance sidelong to where the Dragon-Blooded warrior held him fixed in his gaze, but he hoped the other would not suspect. He didn't want to attract attention, but he also didn't want to leave his guard, such as it was, down when the only person in camp who was paying any attention to him was so close.

The warrior stood unmoving for a long moment, then strode forward. Without a glance to the right, or the left, the man pulled a key from his belt, unlocked the cage where Tarsus cowered, and flung the door wide. He stepped inside, even as Tarsus, trying desperately to stand from the cramped, bent position he'd been sitting in, weak from hunger and lack of sleep, toppled to the side and fell heavily, cracking his head on one of the bars of the cage and bruising his shoulder.

The Dragon-Blooded warrior didn't hesitate. He leaned in close, gripped Tarsus by his hair, and yanked him to his feet. Tarsus struggled feebly. The man shook him.

"Be silent," the warrior hissed. "If you want to see another day of life, shut your mouth and listen to me."

Tarsus made no reply, but he bit his lip. He fought against the vertigo stealing up through his brain and reached out to brace himself, gripping the side of the cage to help right himself and relieve some of the pressure on his hair. His head was ringing from the crack on the bars, and his scalp screamed where the man's gauntleted fist gripped his hair tightly enough to yank it by its roots.

The warrior lifted Tarsus closer so that his lips were very close to Tarsus's ear. He spoke very low and repeated nothing, and the entire experience was over before Tarsus's confused thoughts could fully coalesce.

"There are horses tethered beneath the trees at the southern edge of the camp." The smooth, whispered words sank past the pain to register in Tarsus mind. He would have shown his shock, but the grip on his hair prevented anything but gasps of pain. "You will find your dagger planted in the earth beyond the bars of your cell after I leave. There is a clump of weeds to our left."

The Dragon-Blooded warrior shook Tarsus like a leaf when he started to turn his head. "Are you a fool?" the man continued. "This is all I can do for you. There are not many by day, and the knife is yours. If you don't make it, I suggest you put it to use before they bring you back here.

"One last thing," the man hissed. "They will attack Mishaka. If you win free, that is the message you must carry."

Then, before Tarsus could catch his breath, let alone form an answer, he was flung hard into the bars of the cage and his head struck the bars again. He gasped for breath, but at first nothing came. His breath had been knocked from him by the blow and he lay as he fell, crumbled against the wall of his cage in a stunned daze as the warrior spun contemptuously and stalked from the cage. The door was slammed back into place, and the lock snapped shut.

Tarsus took stock of his injuries and found that, despite the sudden violence of what had just befallen him, he had sustained no real damage. He was bruised and there was a knot of swollen skin pulsing on the back of his head, but he would live. Slowly he dragged himself into a more upright, seated position against the bars. As he did so, he was careful to move toward the spot where he'd been told the dagger would be. He had no idea why the deathknight's lieutenant would aid him, or why he should trust the man if he did, but there was no other help in sight. He knew that, even if the only purpose to which he could put the blade was ending his own life, it was a blessing.

He glanced surreptitiously around the area, but no one was paying him any more attention than they had at any other time since his capture. The dragon warrior who had accosted him was nowhere to be seen, and for a moment Tarsus wondered if he'd slumped into delirium and imagined the entire encounter.

Then he managed to glance over his shoulder into the weeds beyond his prison, and the solid, polished hilt of his dagger winked back at him. How had the man done it? How could it be there without Tarsus himself even realizing it had happened? Too many questions, but no answers presented themselves, and there was no time to think about it. Tarsus slowly scooted around so that his side was against the bars, and, in as smooth a motion as he could muster, he slipped his arm through the bars, gripped the hilt of the dagger, and drew it in close against his thigh, keeping it hidden from view.

His heartbeat had speeded, and his head still pounded with pain from the crack on the metal bars. He leaned into the pain, gripped the hilt of the knife more tightly, and began to run the situation through his mind.

Very soon they would send one of the men to feed him. It would be the same, stooped old gnome of a man who hobbled from pen to pen feeding the animals, as it was every afternoon. The first few times his prison had been opened, sullen guards had accompanied the old man, but they had long since grown bored with the task. Tarsus had made no attempts to escape, and if he had, where would he go?

Except that now he knew—south. He would go to the

southern side of the camp, and if the Dragon-Blood had told him the truth, he'd find horses there. If he could get mounted, and away from the camp, before sounding an alarm, there was a small chance he could make it to the trade route, or even to the city of Mishaka itself, before they could catch up with him. Dace and the caravan were on that route, and they needed to be warned about this camp, whatever its purpose.

Any action was better than sitting and waiting for the death-knight to grow bored with him, or worse.

In the end, there was little planning involved. He heard the shuffling steps of the old man and the creaking of the wooden cart he wheeled among the animals coming closer, and laid his head back against the bars. Willing himself as calm as possible, he kept his eyes closed and waited. He knew the sound of the door to his prison well enough, and there was no sense putting the old man on his guard by appearing to be awake.

The shuffling steps drew near, and the cell was opened. He heard the wheezing breath of the gnarled servant drawing near, but still he waited. His own bowl, a soiled wooden thing that resembled a trough more than something meant for a human, was about a foot to his right.

The old man wandered in, hesitated for just a moment, then, cursing to himself, turned to dump the contents of the bucket in his hand into the wooden bowl. In that instant, Tarsus sprang. His muscles were stiff and sore, but adrenaline and fear fueled his spring. He brought the hilt of his dagger down hard at the base of the man's neck. There was a sickening crunch, and the old servant fell flat into the bowl at his feet.

Tarsus quickly rolled him off and over to the bars of the cell. With a quick shrug he removed his travel-stained and half-shredded cloak, draping it over the prone form of the old man. Exiting quickly, he closed and locked the door and turned to the main trail leading through the camp without a backward glance. There was no movement nearby, and he slipped across into the growing, late-afternoon shadows of the buildings and tents on the far side of the trail. Moving swiftly, he slipped from building to building, avoiding any sound or sign of movement among the denizens of the place. Once he was nearly certain one of the slaves had seen him, but the man made no sign, and Tarsus passed on through the line of trees at the south side of the camp and continued on.

No sense in watching too closely behind him. If they discovered he was gone he'd have to run for it, and if they didn't, so much the better, but he needed to concentrate on the trail ahead. The horses would be near the far edge of the trees, he knew, closer to the road beyond. They would also be guarded.

Tarsus had no idea what the motivation of the Dragon-Blooded who'd aided him might have been, but he had no illusions of safety. He was on his own, and if he didn't find a way to get to these horses, get one free of the others and out past the tree line, he was a dead man and might as well begin preparing to end his life before they re-took him.

If he could get free of the trees, though, he knew they couldn't be too far from the main trade route between Mishaka and Nexus. Somewhere along that route, probably almost to Mishaka, Dace and the others would be found escorting the caravan Tarsus had been scouting for, and he had to try to reach them. Whatever the reason for allowing him to escape, the news of the attack had to be delivered if he could manage it.

He heard the whickering and stamping of horses ahead and slowed his pace further. He saw no sign of guards, but that meant nothing. He wound his way through the close-spaced trees and could make out a clearing, at last. It was getting late in the afternoon, and the sun threatened to dip beneath the sky line. He knew his time was nearly at an end.

Then a dark shape passed between where he stood, and the horses. Tarsus moved closer and saw that the clearing opened into a wider meadow that was fenced in as a makeshift corral. A soldier strode through the center of that clearing with a bucket of grain in each hand. The man did not look pleased, and grunted with the effort of carrying the weight.

Tarsus circled in the opposite direction, making his way to the point where the fence opened in a rough gate. It was held closed by a single loop of rope while the guard fed the horses. Tarsus took advantage of the moment and dropped to the ground behind a wheeled cart pulled up next to the gate.

There were racks of tack and harnesses and a lean-to off to one side protected saddles and other gear from the weather. Tarsus scanned the corral and the surrounding woods, but he saw no sign of any other guards.

The guard poured the contents of his two buckets into the feed troughs and swung back toward the gate. He moved more quickly now, and Tarsus suspected he was hurrying through tasks that should have already been finished. It was near to the normal time for a changing of the guard, and the man likely had chores to complete before his relief would assume the watch.

More reasons to hurry. The man swung the gate wide, dropped the two buckets beside him on the ground, and turned to latch it once more. Tarsus attacked. He didn't try to slip up on the man. He relied on the suddenness of his appearance to catch the man off guard. He tried to brain the man with the dagger hilt as he had the older servant, but this man was a soldier, and his instincts were better. He heard Tarsus's footsteps in time to jerk to one side. The blow that struck his head was only glancing, and he staggered toward the corral fence, already reaching for his blade.

Tarsus leaped. He whipped his dagger in a quick arc and caught the side of the man's throat before he could think to cry out for aid. The guard tumbled to the side, clutching his collar in both hands, and dropped heavily to the dirt.

Tarsus did not wait to see if he had killed the man. He dragged the gate open. He wished he had time for a saddle and bridle, but he did not spare the wish too much thought. He crossed the corral and stopped by a tall roan. The horse still had reins and bridle. The man must have intended to ride it out after his watch, or perhaps he'd just been too lazy to care for the animal properly.

It didn't matter. Tarsus grabbed the reins and, with a grunt of pain as his bruised muscles and head complained, he slid up and into place on the horse's broad back. He guided the animal out and turned into the trees immediately. Although he couldn't be far from the main road, he didn't want to chance meeting the guard's relief on the trail. He picked a way carefully through the trees, and, just as the shadows began to deepen to full dusk, he reached the outer tree line and the road beyond. Tarsus sat for a moment in those shadows, scanning the road in both directions for signs of motion. There was nothing. Leaning close to the horse's neck, he reached back and gave a sharp slap to the animal's hindquarter.

Moments later he was shooting down the road, then angling out into the wilderness and away at a gallop. He knew there would be pursuit, but with luck he had the lead he would need to elude them. If his strength held out, he could ride through the night and—if he made it through until the next day, and the light—he believed he had a chance.

The moon ascended over the forest and the camp, and the echo of the horses' hooves faded to silence. Deep in the trees, the Dragon-Blooded warrior Daedalus watched the rider's retreating form. When he was sure the escape was as complete as he could make it, he turned back into the trees and made his way to camp slowly, arriving just as the alarm was sounded. He moved swiftly to the center of camp, arriving just as his master, the Drinker of Seeping Poison, strode into view from the opposite direction.

"What has happened?" Daedalus called out. "Why did they sound the alarm?"

The Abyssal stood very still, eyeing his lieutenant coldly, then turned away toward the empty cell, where the body of the old servant was being dragged out by its feet.

"It seems we have an escape on our hands," the deathknight replied.

Daedalus spun to several men who'd come up on his left and barked quick commands.

"Spread out," he told them. "He can't have gotten far. He is half-starved and weak. Drag him back here."

"Do not kill him," the deathknight added. "Bring him to me."

"Why not kill him?" Daedalus asked, spinning back. "Why keep him at all?"

The Drinker of Seeping Poison came as close to a smile at that moment as Daedalus had ever seen him. The effect was both chilling and fascinating, as humor and the dead, empty stare of the Abyssal's eyes warred, and the death won.

"Because a quick, merciful death teaches no lessons," he replied. "Come with me." He gestured to Daedalus. "We will make our own arrangements to stop him. We can't count on stopping his escape until we know how it happened, and how he is traveling."

Daedalus nodded and followed the deathknight deeper into the camp. The rest of those who had gathered spread out. Two of the other lieutenants had arrived on the scene and had taken charge of organizing the search.

Chapter Two

Daedalus felt as though ice slid through his veins. He followed as calmly as he could manage behind his Abyssal captain, and he kept his face rigid in its practiced mask of hard cruelty, a mask that seldom, if ever, cracked, but he was petrified. He did not believe that there was any way his treachery could have been discovered, but he knew that his own belief was not enough to make it so. He had been in the camp of the Drinker of Seeping Poison long enough to know that things were seldom as they seemed. He might be following his captain in his position as lieutenant, or he might be walking calmly to his own slaughter. The only way to find out which was the truth was to follow, and to wait.

He knew the prisoner was long gone. He knew, in fact, all of the things others were about to find out, because he had orchestrated them. What he did not and could not know was just how much of it his captain knew. Daedalus glanced to the north again and took a deep breath. He had come here, and he had done as he'd been ordered to do, but would it be enough? Would it work? The irony of it was that he might not be alive long enough to find out.

They entered a wider clearing slowly, and as they did so, all activity ceased. The deathknight stopped at the edge of the clearing, scanning the downcast faces of his followers, and smiled cruelly. Then he stepped to the center of them all, Daedalus at his heel.

As he walked, he swayed, side to side, the undulating motion of a great serpent. The Drinker of Seeping Poison felt the flow of essence and reached out to it, soaked in it. The center of the circle was positioned perfectly, as he'd known it would

be. He lowered his head, letting the energy fill him, and he did
not raise his gaze from the ground at his feet until he heard
the first screams. Daedalus, who had been watching the deathknight curiously, could not suppress the quick jerk of his head
and tightening of his shoulders the first scream brought, though
he controlled himself quickly.

Turning, the Abyssal watched a young man being dragged
into the clearing. The boy had long golden hair, falling nearly to
the center of his back. His hands were bound behind him and
his ankles were hobbled. His arms were held tightly by grinning, rotting corpses, their leers more a product of decay than
mirth. They moved with mechanical precision to their lord's
side, throwing the boy to his knees at the deathknight's feet.

Their prisoner tried to dart to the side, lost his balance, disoriented and blindfolded, and fell to the ground, his chin digging a short furrow. The Drinker of Seeping Poison stepped forward and placed a booted foot on the boy's back.

"Move again," the deathknight said, breaking his silence for
the first time, "and I will kill you and bring out your sister. It
makes no difference to me, or to the ritual."

Tears streamed from the boy's eyes, but he lay still, shaking. The two of the dead dragged stakes from the shadows and
pounded them into the ground, a pair of them, spread a yard
apart and driven deep. The Drinker of Seeping Poison watched
in stoic silence.

The boy was lifted, dragged back to his knees, and turned
so that his ankles could be bound to the stakes. His wrists were
cut free, then bound once more, crossed and bound to the same
stakes as his ankles. Arched like a strung bow, he shivered in
the cool air. The Abyssal Poisons watched with dead, uncaring
eyes.

The deathknight turned to Daedalus. "At the side of the
clearing there is a leather bag. Bring it to me."

Daedalus strode to the clearing's edge, rummaged around
among the equipment, and found the bag. He returned unhesi-
tatingly to his captain and held it out. The Drinker of Seeping
Poison nodded. He took the bag, slid his hand inside, and drew
forth a long, pointed spike. It sparkled, dark obsidian against

the shadows of the night. The moonlight glittered up and down its length and the deathknight twisted the spike, concentrating, his gaze centered on some point beyond the object in his hand. His nails were sharpened to wicked points and painted to the same black as the stone blade, and as he gripped more tightly it became increasingly difficult to tell where his flesh ended and the obsidian spike began.

He moved like lightning. One moment he stood, the black stake held loosely between the palms of his hands; the next, everything changed. It was not a sequence of motion that could be followed and catalogued, but a blur. The boy's eyes grew wide as his hair was gripped and dragged back. It was a mistake, this widening of his gaze, opening the target to the spike.

The Drinker of Seeping Poison chanted, a steady, ominous stream of sound. No words were discernible to those who were close enough to hear, but energy crackled through the hastily cleared glade, dancing up the deathknight's legs and swirling about him. The obsidian spike glinted, and just as the boy grasped the situation in a final moment of clarity, sharp stone bit deep. The boy's twin blue eyes were forever parted as one disappeared. The spike slid through lens and iris, stopped just short of the brain, and was dragged free.

The cadence of the Abyssal's words shifted with a subtlety so precise it seemed he repeated himself. The words had transposed, their order reversed. His grip tightened still more on the boy's hair. Though the scream was long and terrible, the boy's features remained motionless. The spike bit a second time. It sliced through the second eye, the first a pouring fountain of blood and fluid, flowing down to stain the boy's tunic.

"And so," the Drinker of Seeping Poison spoke so softly his words might have been a whisper, "the blind grant their gift of sight to me."

He tossed the boy's head back, ignoring the mind-bending screams as though they were wind whispering through the trees. He held his hand out without glancing back, and Daedalus placed another instrument in his hand. The Drinker of Seeping Poison bent close to the boy's writhing form, slid the gory spike down his captor's chest, scratching swiftly. A bloody network of symbols formed, the blood from one cut flowing into that of the next, working its way downward until, in a quick stroke, the deathknight plunged the spike into the earth between the boy's legs and released it.

Completion was close, but there was no room for error. His features revealed no emotion, but the rigid set of his shoulders and the uncanny continuity of his voice, rising once more to chant, betrayed his level of concentration.

The others, all but Daedalus, had withdrawn to the edges of the clearing. The dead stood like rotting statues, awaiting their next command. Those alive and mortal and unfortunate enough to be present stood nearly as still as the dead themselves. Daedalus remained at his captain's side, standing like a stone, his arms clasped behind his back.

Daedalus was spellbound. He had seen necromancy before, but never so close, nor so powerful. It was intoxicating, and he found that even the tortured body of the boy at their feet meant little. Daedalus's lips were parted, and he watched in spellbound fascination as his lord worked. His expression was hard, but his muscles were too taut, his rapt attention forced almost to the point of parody.

The Abyssal paid no attention to Daedalus or any other in the clearing. He knelt before his victim. With his right hand, he clamped onto the boy's throat and pressed. The young body bowed yet further, blind bleeding eyes cast skyward as a new blade was brought to bear. The deathknight held a wicked blade, the hilt set with multi-colored stones set in an intricate pattern, hidden by the grip of his palm.

He struck, slicing down the center of the boy's chest. He dragged the blade to the right, back left, then zigzagged it downward. The Abyssal stopped the blade short of the boy's navel, coming so close that the skin rippled at the rim before he spun his hand deftly and moved upward again.

He gripped the skin to the right side of his incision and dragged back with an almost casual flip of his wrist. Flesh peeled away from ribs with a wet, sickening sound, followed by a nearly identical sound as he released his grip and took hold of the left side.

The captive boy's heart pulsed in the open cavity. Each heaving breath caused the uncovered lungs to expand. Without the skin to help with the restraint, they pressed between the boy's exposed ribs, their expansion continued beyond its normal bounds. The Drinker of Seeping Poison worked slowly and carefully.

As Daedalus watched, his throat grew dry. His heart pounded and his eyes watered with the need to blink, but he allowed himself no such weakness. His skin was hot, as if it were he, not the boy, being eviscerated. His tongue had swollen so that he knew, were he required to speak, that he could not.

He had never witnessed this ritual and, though he strove to catch the words and the motions, he knew that the result would be the only memory he would carry from this clearing. He kept his gaze fixed on the ritual before him, but his mind slipped back to the prisoner in his hog-pen cell, and the sight of his escape.

The Drinker of Seeping Poison gave a final jerk of his wrist, leaving the blade of the knife poised, dangling from the boy's quivering, dying flesh. He pulled back, pressed the palms of his hands together, and lowered his head. He spoke only three words, each so low in tone, or so soft, that they could not be heard, and yet they burst from him in a wave of some other vibration—a deep, resonant, staggering power. The clearing rang with the all-encompassing force, and the deathknight thrust his palms forward. They slammed into the base of the obsidian spike and drove it into the boy's heart. The Abyssal focused on a point beyond his victim, in the soft loamy earth, and the blade punched through as the boy's blood burst out around the deathknight's wrists and hands.

His face splattered in blood, the Drinker of Seeping Poison rose. He raised his gaze to the star-strewn sky and uttered a final sound, more curse than word, more breath than any human articulation of sound.

The Drinker of Seeping Poison stepped back. He turned, his arms soaked and dripping with the boy's blood. Daedalus watched in silence, daring neither to speak nor to move. He breathed, but only because *not* to breathe would cost him the strength he needed in the moments to come.

The Drinker raised his bloodied hands anew and red and white fire bloomed in them. With a precise movement he hurled these bolts of primal essence into the pool of blood and viscera gathered about the boy. The fluids immediately took to a strong boil, sending a vile charnel smell into the air. The Drinker then reached to his belt and removed two large gems. They caught a glimmer of the stars as they dropped into the boiling flesh pit.

The Abyssal was eerily calm throughout. He moved languidly, as if he slid through liquid instead of air. His lips curled slowly in the mockery of a smile.

"How long," the deathknight asked softly, "do you think it can be avoided, Daedalus?"

Daedalus listened to his captain, but his gaze was drawn to where the ground behind the deathknight had begun to shake. Tremors rose and quivered up his legs. The earth shivered, stilled, then shook again. A crack split the sod and followed the Abyssal's approach, threatening to burst between his legs and send him sprawling. Energy hummed in the air, bonding with the vibration from below, and Daedalus felt it tremble through his frame. He fought the urge to turn and bolt.

"I… don't…" Daedalus fell silent, unable to form an answer that made sense.

The vibration beneath them blurred Daedalus's sight. The deathknight stepped still closer, and his smile lost even the mocking pretense of humor. Daedalus fought to still the tremors shifting through his muscles and jumping across his nerves. The Abyssal was so close that the scent of the blood coating his arms wafted up through Daedalus's nostrils and sat, bitter and acidic, in the back of his throat. They stood so close together that their cloaks brushed in the wind, and the impossibly chilled depths of the deathknight's eyes threatened to draw Daedalus in, headlong, the world forgotten. Now even his breath was forgotten.

"There are no second chances," the Drinker of Seeping Poison whispered. "There is no room for error in my world."

Behind him, the ground split. The bone-white tips of huge claws rent the earth. The scent of musk filled the air, but it was rotten. It reminded Daedalus of rodents, or stray cats, but there was something—wrong—in the scent, something missing at its core that turned the stomach and left an etched scar across the senses. It did not belong.

"Sir," Daedalus spoke, finding his voice at last. His traitorous body took a half-step back before he could regain control of it. "I..."

"The bone lion will stalk its victim for a hundred days, plus one," the Drinker of Seeping Poison intoned softly. "It will stop at nothing; no river or mountain can stand in its way."

"The prisoner will reach the city," Daedalus gasped. He hated his own weakness, hated the way his skin was coated in a sheen of hot sweat and how his pulse raced, and he hated that the Drinker of Seeping Poison read every nuance of it. The only reaction in his captain was that the empty smile widened.

"I have no doubt you are right," the Abyssal said, speaking very softly, reaching out to drag a long, black nail over Daedalus's cheek. "I have no doubt you knew that when you set him free. What I don't know is why you would do such a thing. Even more curious is why you might think you'd get away with it.

"I expect very little of those who fail me, and though I'm uncertain why I offer it, you have one chance. You have one hundred and one days to prove you are worthy, and that you are loyal to me alone. If and when you return, we will discuss who might have sent you into my service, and why. I will find out, you know, with or without you.

"If I were you," the deathknight hesitated and glanced over his shoulder. Two huge, skeletal paws gripped the earth, strained, and a bulge of soil, leaves, and branches began to rise between the deathknight and his lieutenant. "I would be running. I believe he is hungry."

The mound of earth erupted, sending them both staggering backward. The Drinker of Seeping Poison threw back his head, dark laughter pouring out and blending with the crunch of bone and the spill of broken earth.

Daedalus backed away, the lethargy in his limbs departing like smoke. He watched the thing drag itself free of the earth in horror, the scene blurring to surreality with the backdrop of the deathknight's laughter. He was dimly aware of the Abyssal standing, blood still dripping from his arms and head thrown back in booming, echoing laughter, but the sound confused itself with his heartbeat. He fell back another step, gasped for air, and found it. Thought departed. He tried to speak, found no words, clamped his jaw shut and spun. With a scream, he launched through the unflinching line of the dead. They fell back before him like toys.

Daedalus drew deep and called forth what stored essence he could muster for the sprint. They were not so far from the corral from which Tarsus had made his escape. Without a horse, he knew he stood no chance. Even if he stood his ground and managed to kill the bone lion, what then—forgiveness?

There was no immediate sound of pursuit, and Daedalus plunged through the trees and on, making it to the corral in scant moments. There were several guards on duty, and one was about to depart, the reins of a large, dark stallion gripped in his gloved hands.

They had no reason to suspect him, and Daedalus willed his features into a scowl.

"The horse, man," he cried out. "Give me the horse."

The man stood, gaping in horror as his Dragon-Blooded lieutenant bore down on him. The reins dangled loosely in his hand, but he didn't move quickly enough. Daedalus kicked out viciously, sending the man sprawling, and leaped into the saddle without a downward or backward glance. He sent the animal caroming through the trees at a gallop.

In the clearing, not so far behind, but still well out of sight of Daedalus's fleeing form, the bone lion reared back, claws digging into the soft earth of the forest floor, and gave a silent roar. Devoid of lungs and throat, the terrible construct could only open its fiendish maw wide and show the endless rows of teeth it would use to rend its prey. Long, talon-shaped spikes of bone protruded from its skeletal joints, like the blades used on the wheels of battle wagons or chariots. Two large diamonds blazed with dark essence in its pitted eye sockets. The guards near the corral slunk into the trees in fear, staring at one another wide-eyed and trembling.

The Drinker of Seeping Poison leaned down and scooped up the bag that Daedalus had carried. He lifted it to the lion, holding it in one steady hand. The scent of its quarry wafted from the soiled leather. The lion reared again, flexing the bones and sinew of its form, and then leaned down more closely. The Abyssal met the eerie beast's gaze and held the leather bag very still.

"Go," he commanded. "Go and drag him back to whatever pit spawned you."

For a moment, the lion did not react. Its head inclined to one side and it ran its ruined muzzle over the leather. Then it sprang. The motion was so sudden and powerful that even the deathknight took half a step back as it passed. The lion had leapt straight him, the huge, vicious claws of its rear paws near to grazing his head.

He watched until the sound of the bone lion's passing had faded, and he stood alone in the clearing with his troop of walking dead. In the distance, behind him now, Daedalus rode for his life. Despite the exhilaration of the moment, the Abyssal was not pleased. The attack was to have been quick and unmerciful—and a surprise. There was little he could do now to preserve that surprise. It would take thought, and a revised plan. He would also have to give thought to who lay behind the events just past.

He had a momentary pang of regret. Daedalus had such promise, and had served so faithfully—until now. Then he shook it off. There were others, and he was done with Daedalus. Soon the world would be done with him as well.

Turning, the deathknight strode back through the trees the way he'd come. He walked quickly. He had less time than ever, and an army of the dead to gather. The Drinker of Seeping Poison could spare no further thought or time to either the escaped spy or his fleeing lieutenant. He needed to make a report to his own commander, and that was almost never a pleasant task. Behind him the dead moved at their own pace, covering the ground like a mass of skeletal insects, moving without thought or emotion, following where he led. Only the moon observed their passing.

Chapter Three

Dace rose with the dawn. He always watched the sun rising to fill the sky, and he was particularly fond of that view when he was on the road. Though his tent was large and comfortable, he slept fully clothed and it took only moments to don boots and weapons and step out into the camp. The first rose tint of sun was illuminating the horizon beyond the line of wagons and the soft shuffle of booted feet moved slowly about changing guards and preparing the camp for the days travel. They should reach Mishaka in less than three days at the speed they'd been maintaining, and for once the journey had been relatively quiet. One scout was unaccounted for—Tarsus—but there had been no raids. Not like the last time he'd made a similar journey and encountered a newly seeded shadowland for his trouble.

Dace stood, watching the rising sun in silence. There was a hint of destiny in that sight, a sense of accomplishment at having survived to witness it once again.

When Dace's Exaltation had come upon him, he had been nearly fifty. Many of those years he'd spent as a mercenary in the employ of whoever held out the most silver dinars to him, risking his life daily at the whim and vision of others. In those years, he'd known little fear. There had been the battles, the work, the hours spent with his men, but there had not been the impending weight of eternity. Not as there was now.

The Solar Exalted aged only very slowly. His power, rather than waning as time passed as was the natural course of nature, was growing steadily. Every day, every hour and minute that passed, he drew further back from the others. He could not control it. They watched him and they watched one another. Time left its mark on most, though some, like Risa, held power of their own. For Dace, time left no discernible marks.

The sun rose, and Dace watched it in silence. He thought, as he did so, that it was very much like his own rise. Steady, filled with light and power. He remembered the sunset the night before, and he considered it all. His power was not corrupting him, as he had feared. He did not take it for granted, nor did he take those who served with him for granted. It could end as quickly as it had begun, though, admittedly, it would take something, or someone, very powerful to make it reality. A man of action, Dace took the Exaltation as he took a good fight, or a draught of wine: head on and without hesitation.

Another would live on then. Another would bear the power and the burden of Exaltation, vague memories of Dace floating in the background of their mind as he had witnessed flickers of those who'd gone before.

Dace couldn't shake the impression that there was more to this simple caravan support than was obvious. It was the scout, Tarsus, that worried him most of all. Dace did not choose scouts without careful thought—they were his best, strong, quick, and silent. They also knew how to take orders, and Tarsus's orders should have brought him back a full two days earlier.

Still, there were a number of reasons the man might be late. Horses went lame. Any rider could be thrown. Risa had sent riders to find him and they would return soon enough.

As the tent flap closed behind him, deep, luminous eyes watched his back from high in the branches of one of the few trees scattered about near the road. Lilith tilted her head, preened the feathers of one wing, and thought. Dace was much as she had been told he was: tall, strong—different. She knew he was newly Exalted, but even without that knowledge she would have appreciated the way he carried himself. He was a warrior.

Lilith fluttered her broad owl-wings briefly, lifted from the branch that held her, and floated to the ground, shifting in mid-air and coming gently to rest on a lower limb in the form of a sparrow. The owl was her preference, but by day it was conspicuous, and too likely to draw attention. Moments later, when a woman warrior entered Dace's tent, she launched herself and flitted to land at the top of one of the poles that held the tent aloft. Voices floated up to her from within, and she cocked her head, listening carefully.

"There is no sign of him, Dace," the woman was saying. "It's as if he disappeared from the face of the earth. if he'd been within the range he was supposed to keep to, the riders would have returned with news by now."

"He may have found something worth looking into," Dace replied. "It isn't the first time one of our scouts has been late reporting, Risa."

"It's not just one of our scouts," she returned hotly. "It's Tarsus. This is not like him, and you know it."

There was silence for a moment, and Lilith twitched her head from side to side. It wasn't likely anyone would take notice of a single sparrow perched atop their commander's tent, but she had not lived so long by being foolish.

"We'll decide what to do when your riders return," Dace said at last. "Right now we have a caravan to move, and we should be moving."

"Yes sir," Risa replied.

The tent flap rippled again, and the woman departed. Lilith watched her with curiosity, then launched into the air once again. She had seen two riders depart the night before, as she watched from her perch above the camp. They had been riding toward the north. Without hesitation, Lilith circled higher, stretching her tiny wings near their limits until she had nearly reached the lowest of the morning clouds. Then, shifting to the form of an eagle, she cut through those clouds and away.

When the black velvet air of night wrapped about her and the silver light of the moon glinted off the ice-chips of her eyes, Lilith felt free. Flight was a gift, and freedom of form her destiny. Daylight depressed her. The overwhelming heat of the sun beat down on her wings and heated her form, making breathing more difficult and replacing the sweet cool air with waves of oppressive heat. Lilith ignored the discomfort and flashed onward.

It would take her most of the day and part of the night to reach Thorns, and she wanted time enough to be out of that place before the light rose again. Lilith was old, and her power was great, but she had no inclination to face a deathknight with a full force if she could avoid them. They were a tricky lot, and their power was a warping of the night she loved—making darkness a thing of death and pain. She had no personal quarrel with them, or their filthy minions. What she sought was information.

If she could find this missing scout, or perhaps learn his fate, then she would have a reason to present herself to Dace, and would be more likely to be received well. They would not know her immediately for what she was, but they would suspect, and she wanted every advantage she could get in the days to come.

She thought briefly of the coin she'd found, and the last time she'd seen such a coin. There was something about this Dace that drew her, something familiar and she was fairly certain she knew what it was. He was part of the circle, one of those who'd been close to her lover in the First Age. His memories would not be complete, but they might be enough to help guide her on her quest. She wanted to bring information that would help her gain his respect.

Lilith had learned plenty about respect from another Solar, so many years in the past that the razor edges of pain he had left in his passing had dulled to coarse, scratching aches, irritating her at the worst possible moments and snatching at her concentration.

While Lilith had been Desus's lover, his consort, and his companion, it had gone much further than that before the end. She'd become his plaything, a toy he could abuse at will as his mind disintegrated and the impossible strength that coursed through his being lashed out, uncontrolled. Lilith had taken many of those lashings. The bones of her left wrist would never heal perfectly from where Swan had broken it with the butt of his axe.

That incarnation of Desus was gone, but the essence of the Solar Exalted that he had worn so well when he walked the earth had risen once more and Lilith remembered. If one fell, another rose. Another Desus? Word of the Solar's return was spreading. It had reached her, even in her exile, traveling in rumors carried by traders and refugees fleeing into the wilds.

She flew onward, increasing her speed until she was nothing but a dark blur against the white clouds and the sun-bright sky. Too soon to think of that. Too soon to think of the future, when memory was blurred and secrets itched at the corners of her consciousness. First she would solve this puzzle, this odd itch in her mind. To do so, she would need to get her head straight. It was too long since she'd been near a Solar, and fortuitous to have found Dace. He intrigued her.

Early in her flight she passed over the small party of horsemen that Risa had sent after the missing scout. She paid no attention to them. The sun slipped down through afternoon to evening, and Lilith flew on. She skirted the road to Mishaka and wheeled off to the southeast, past Celeren and on toward the heavy forests surrounding Thorns.

Chapter Four

The forest teemed with activity. The dead rose from the ground of their fathers and from the death-soaked soil of ancient battles. They clawed free of clinging roots and gravestones tumbled, cracking and crumbling as the army of bones and clinging flesh, putrescent filth and dry, rotted blood massed, swelling the Drinker of Seeping Poison's ranks and threatening to burst beyond the lines of trees and spill to the plains beyond. The force mustered there before Tarsus's "escape" was large. They poured into the city from the north road, doubling and then tripling in number in only a few days.

There were men, as well, and Dragon-Blooded captains, but few. They were not the main force of the army. The plan was a simple flood of dead flesh, smothering every living thing in its path until nothing moved or breathed in Mishaka. The city was a good one to defend, but sheer numbers would bring it down. The city had nothing to defend against such a horde.

The Drinker of Seeping Poison sat, drinking deep red wine and watching his men organizing the vast army. Now and again he glanced to the horizon, beyond the activity and the planning, the loading of wagons and the sharpening of blades. The wine was rich and strong, burning through him with velvet heat. The evening was young, the night stretching before him.

He thought of the escaped prisoner, Tarsus. By now, if he had managed to survive the hunger and the thirst, the man would have reported the coming attack to his master. He would be filled with stories of the dead, of the cage where he'd been kept like a dog, and the army massing for the attack. Tarsus would have some idea, from what he'd seen, of the numbers that had been present, and he would have questions, as well.

Next he thought of Daedalus. It was a shame when one who served so well had become such an example of betrayal. The prisoner should be lying dead, or better still, raised to join the Abyssal's army. Instead he was free, and only the passing pleasure of thinking how the bone lion would dismember Daedalus remained to bring a smile. The deathknight had been certain to keep word from spreading back to his own commander. The few among his men who actually knew what Daedalus had done would say nothing, and the rest, while they might suspect, were happy to see the issue laid to rest along with the bones of another.

The thought of bones brought another smile, and the Drinker of Seeping Poison held out his goblet. Without a word from her master, a young girl stepped from the shadows, clad in dark silk, refilling the cup. She was gone as quickly and silently as she'd appeared.

The bone lion had been a masterful performance. The thing's silent cry had actually rippled through the Drinker of Seeping Poison's hair. Its musk had rivaled the stench of the entire army of the dead, and the power... Images of Daedalus's rent frame and torn flesh rose to the forefront of the deathknight's mind. Such power.

He wished that he could be present when the hunt ended. Daedalus was not weak. He bore his weapons proudly, and the blood of the Elemental Dragons flowed through his veins, gift of his father. He was probably no match for a creature such as the lion, but he would fight, and the battle would be fascinating. Who knew? Maybe their paths would meet again. The Drinker of Seeping Poison was fascinated by anything relating to death, and the harder that death was won, the more intriguing it became. In any case, the lion would keep Daedalus busy long enough that any information he might carry would be of no consequence. It would soon be no secret that an army of the dead marched on Mishaka, and the rest of the Drinker of Seeping Poison's plans he'd kept to himself...

Another sip of the wine and he grew restless. Rising from his chair, he stepped down, holding his goblet to the side. It was removed before he'd gone a pace, and he strode off into the night toward the east edge of the camp. He passed through rank after rank of decomposing warriors. They shuffled aside as he passed, but they would not grow truly animated until it was his will that they do so. They did not acknowledge him. Only his lieutenants and his men and bowed low as he passed. None spoke, the expression on his face warning them away.

He skirted the camp and came to a break in the trees. It was the border of a graveyard. Beyond it, stretching into the woods, the ruins of a large keep crumbled and fell to ruin. Here and there the cobbles of what had once been a street poked through the overgrown weeds. There were walls, some stretching to twice the height of a man, with the stones crushed from their upper reaches in some past battle.

Just beyond the far wall of the graveyard, which had held up against the years better than most of the place, a single wall stood with a tombstone-shaped window above high, arching doors. It was a temple, broken and remaining only as a façade, its single eye staring out over the final resting place of a people whose families were long gone. The Drinker of Seeping Poison breathed deeply as he entered. Beneath the ground and the graves there were currents of essence, and, as he stepped farther into the place, he felt them coursing toward the center, meeting and meshing near the center of the cemetery.

A large stone mausoleum stood dead center, and the death-knight strode toward it with even, measured steps. His gaze never wavered from that stone, marking the death of one long crumbled to dust. The structure was solid, marking the last resting place of one Alden Den, a man who had died rich enough for the stone that covered his bones, and poor enough that the only inscription he had been given was his name, his date of birth, and that of his death.

The ground was carefully desecrated. Symbols had been notched into the stone with crude implements. Blood stained the stone and the bones of both men and animals littered the nearby ground. The graves surrounding that stone hut might have belonged to the good and the just, but after they and their descendants had departed, others had been very busy. The deathknight had built on this, having grave markers broken and burning what could not be crushed to dust.

The deathknight had been tasked with invading the outlying city. He had been told to take it at whatever cost, and to hold it. Nexus would not send troops so far South, and the Abyssal's scouts had reported that the field forces of Lookshy were unlikely to come to Mishaka's aid. It seemed there were trade disputes. Not so many years in the past, those same Lookshy forces had helped to turn back the last attack from Thorns, but the memories of men are short. Greed was the best gauge of how a thing would turn out. That left the city all but defenseless.

The plan the Drinker of Seeping Poison had devised had been a simple one until the damned scout had been captured. Even after the capture, things had been well in hand until Daedalus had interfered. Now the city would be warned. This would have troubled the deathknight more had he only been counting on the frontal attack. He was not. The Abyssal believed that no good leader told his followers everything.

Stepping close to the dark gravestone, the deathknight held his arms out, palms to the center, one to each side of the stone. He closed his eyes and dropped his head back so that his face was to the star-studded sky. The air was infused with a sudden flicker of—something. It wound and twined around his fingers as he drew it from the ground, from the dead and decomposing flesh and bones. He held that connection for a beat, then concentrated it on that stone and drew it to the point between his palms. The energy sizzled through his being and his mouth opened in a wide rictus as the air before him shimmered.

The tomb hid a small shadowland, an area where the land of the living and the dead met. Through it. he would lead his men from the Underworld, using it as his private doorway to Mishaka. This night he did not want to step through. He wanted a window, not a doorway, a view of what awaited him on the far side.

The stone monument vibrated with energy. Slowly, like a gambling counter being turned to a different number, the stone grew hazy. Focus was lost and then, with a snap, returned, and the Drinker of Seeping Poison lowered his head, gazing through the doorway of a mausoleum. The stone was nowhere to be seen, and though the moon and stars beyond that dark doorway were the same as those beneath which he stood, the place upon which he gazed was absolutely different.

The gravestones were taller and more evenly spaced. The weeds and grass that grew up around the edges of the graves near his camp were gone, replaced by well-trimmed stones in neat rows. Here and there among the stones, baskets of fruit, flowers and small talismans rested. There were well-worn paths between the resting places of the dead.

At one of the graves, not more than ten stones from where he stood watching, the Drinker of Seeping Poison saw the form of a young woman. She was shrouded in black cloth, darker than the backdrop of the midnight sky. Her shoulders slumped, her head bowed, she knelt before a white, carven stone monument. She held a small book in one hand, and in the other a bundle of fresh wildflowers, muted to chiaroscuro shades of gray and white in the silver illumination of the moon.

He stood very still, gazing on the woman as she placed the flowers on the grave before her. Holding the book close, apparently so that she could see well enough in the moonlight to read, she spoke. The Abyssal could not hear her words, and for just a moment he considered stepping from his place of concealment and taking her. He could watch the life flow from her eyes, leave her on the grave of her lover. He could take her book, its verse, or prayer, story or lament to be his own and study it at length, remembering her face and the emotion rippling across it in the moonlight. He did not.

Just at that moment, though, as if drawn by some energy, or sound, the woman looked up. She glanced straight at the mausoleum door, and shuddered. It was a dark place among the bedchambers of the dead. Iron spikes, rusted and neglected, surrounded it and cut it off from the main body of the cemetery. The words and the name that had been carved into the stone before it was buried solidly in the earth had been defaced, chiseled away by many hands on many nights, braving the sprits who had gone on beyond the world to rid their burial place of the words, and the name. None had the courage to break the stone, or to remove what lay within, but neither did they pull the weeds, or wash the green fungus from the stone walls.

The remains of the dead were safe, if only out of fear, and the remains of the man who was buried in that place lay beyond the courage and strength of those who would see it pounded to dust, his bones burned and scattered, and the earth sanctified by prayer and years. There was a curse, and a curse is more powerful in the words that describe it alone than the forces of righteousness at their peak. Whether there was power behind that curse to reach out and break their tiny lives was not important. They believed and so they shunned. Shunned, the mausoleum fell to ruin within those ruined walls. The Drinker of Seeping Poison gazed out with eyes blazing.

The woman rose, her hand rising to her breast. The book fell to the earth, forgotten. She reached out toward the deathknight as though she saw—something—but she did not speak. With a small cry, the woman turned and ran.

The Abyssal watched her retreating form, silhouetted against the walls and dim lights of the city of Mishaka. Easing his mind back from the sight, and the essence, he let his vision leave the distant shadowland, and closed his eyes at the same moment, standing still as stone. Without a backward glance, he turned and exited the cemetery. The dark, solitary gravestone stood as silent sentinel, saluting his retreat.

There were surprises in store for the citizens of Mishaka, the mercenaries, and even those who awaited his return. It was a good night to be alive, and even better to be so close, skirting on the thin film of death.

As he moved back toward the camp and his tents, there was a flutter of wings against the silence of the night. He grew still, stopping and gazing through the trees toward the moon. He saw nothing, and the sound was not repeated.

The spell of his reverie broken, the deathknight stalked back to his quarters.

From the upper branches of a half-dead tree, gold-glowing eyes watched the Drinker of Seeping Poison's retreat with interest..

Launching into the sky, the great owl circled, her gaze locked to the gathering horde, counting, memorizing, stealing the moment and wheeling away into the darkness. None noted her passing. The night was dying.

It was enough. Lilith could see the preparations, could feel the earth releasing her dead. Whatever information Dace had, it would not include all of this. The numbers of the Drinker of Seeping Poison's army grew steadily. There were no more men or Dragon-born than there had been before, but the dead were so thick they clotted on the ground like congealing puddles of blood. And they were restless. It would not be much longer before they would take to the road, rolling and spilling across the landscape in a dark tide.

Lilith flew the miles to Mishaka, calculating, She thought of the forms and aspects that were part of her, those she could assume. It was difficult for her to calculate the days of travel for an army of the dead. She had traveled in the form of wolf and owl, hawk and cat, but none of these would help her in this. The dead did not rest. They had no need for common supplies—no food, nor water. Only the Dragon-Blooded who led them and the men who followed required these things, and they could hang back, sending a wave of the dead onto the city in numbers so overwhelming that there would be no way to defend against it. In years not long past, this would not have been true, she knew. The city had withstood armies much greater than the one assembling below, but they had grown complacent in Mishaka, and they had defaulted on old debts. That was the word Lilith had heard on the road, and she had no reason to doubt it.

Lilith wheeled past the outskirts of the city and turned toward Nexus once more. She had something, it seemed, that might be worth bartering for. Lilith's trail led straight into the forests she now left behind, among the dead and the decay, and in the shadow of the deathknight's camp. She was not really worried for herself—she had met the dead and their masters before—but times change, the world shifts. Dace had met and defeated such enemies recently. Besides, he had known Desus, if not in this time-frame. His memories were buried, but not gone.

Her task complete, she let her mind drift. The box. She didn't know exactly where it was, but the image of it grew clearer in her mind with each passing day. It sent itchy, crawling fingers down her spine, even across the miles—how many miles? Whatever was in that small, intricately carved box called to her with a voice she could not resist, calling her back to days long fallen to dust, and ahead to the twin promises of power and change. She caught glimpses of its location, of the designs adorning its lid and sides. One of those sides was a bas relief of the sign of the Dawning Sun—a sign she had seen in Dace's camp. There was more, but what she knew was enough. She tried to visualize the clasp that would seal it, but for some reason it would not surface.

She knew that box, and she had the feeling that if she could get close enough to speak with him Dace would know it too. He would know what she sought, or would be able to feel it. Desus had been a Solar, and Dace would understand

But would he help? Even now that she had valuable information to barter, she was not sure. It might be that he would take the information, turn away to the task at hand, and pay her no more mind than he would one of his men. That would of course be a mistake on his part, but he might do it.

Lilith was old. She was old as the spirits of the animals she shared, old as the hills and the trees, which she had known as saplings and ushered into full growth. She had slipped into the shadows and away when the Solars were put down. With Desus dead, and the strength of the Wyld Hunt scourging the land of all trace of his return—or that of any Exalt that did not conform with their own beliefs—she'd been alone with her animals and her thoughts, her memories and her regrets.

Now the Solars were coming back, and Lilith had slipped back from her shadows to be a part of it. What part, she did not know, nor was she inclined to waste valuable thought on it. What mattered, for the moment, was to convince Dace to help her in her quest for the box. If it led beyond that, there would be time to make decisions along the way.

The first rays of the sun flickered over the horizon, and Lilith arced into a swooping dive. She had spent long hours in the form of the owl, lived in its world, and when the sunlight threatened, she felt the tug of deeper, cooler places. She felt the shadows calling to her, large crooks between heavy, hollow branches, the mouths of mountain caves. Deep, dense foliage that could eclipse the heat and the light.

There would be time to find Dace when the sun had lowered itself. His forces were moving slowly, held back by the plodding progress of the caravan. Lilith thought that, with the number of the enemy, and the importance of the information she had learned, the Solar might want a look himself. If he did, and she could convince him she might be of use, then maybe he would assist her along the way. His scouts might discover the dead army, but they would not know of the hidden shadowland, and Lilith suspected that, many as they were on the land, there was more waiting in the Underworld.

With a last screeching cry that reverberated through the fading darkness and on into the dawn, Lilith landed, climbing slowly toward the trunk of a huge oak set back from the road and miles ahead of where Dace and his men wound through the hot son, following the road to Mishaka. She found what she'd seen from the air in moments—a deep crevasse, dark, cool, and large enough to hold her easily in the owl's form. Without hesitation she slipped in and ruffled her wings. In moments, she slept, and she dreamed.

In the dream, the sun was high in the sky. She stood in a corner, as far back in the shadows as she could press herself, as he paced across the room. It was a tower, far above green fields and a road winding off into the distance. She could see this through an open window, and with every tenth or eleventh step he stopped to stare outward, gripping the stone of the window frame so tightly she feared it would crumble beneath his fingers.

His long robes swept back behind him as though the sunlight pouring in the window had been absorbed by the material, only to leak back out in an incandescent glow that trailed after him and shimmered along the ends of his long, golden hair. He wore only a ceremonial dagger as weapon, and the supple leather of his boots creaked when he moved. He reminded her of an image impressed in polished glass.

He did not speak. Lilith tried to control her breath, but his footfalls insinuated themselves into her heartbeats, and his pacing sped slowly, drawing her along with it. She was frightened, but could not tell why. She wanted to go to him, but knew she should not—possibly could not. He did not look at her, and she knew that, in such a state, she might as well have not been there. A toy, a cast-off plaything in the shadows, marionette strings dangling and waiting for the next time he would acknowledge her. Her desire to be near him warred with stark fear as she contemplated the directions that the next moment of contact might take them.

He spoke, but it was difficult to make out the words. He shouted, then muttered, whirling with each pass up and down and up again across the floor. He screamed from the window and leaped to the sill and flung his arms to the side, leaning out precariously into the void. Then he dropped back to the floor and resumed pacing.

Words and phrases caught in the filmy dream-web of her mind. Stone. Dying. Heat. He said something about a box, or "the" box. Hidden. Where sun and moon collide.

He spun, and Lilith would have screamed at the horrible light in his eyes, but she could not. She stood in the shadows as he stalked toward her. He spoke, but the words became hot breath, flowing around and through her, too hot. His eyes blazed, and the cold, solid stone at her back was a funeral slab.

Then another memory crashed in and the world flickered. He was seated at a table, staring out the window in silence. Lilith came up behind him and, though she screamed silently, fighting against her own forward motion, it was beyond her control. She lived in the midst of a memory that terrified her though she could not remember why. He was very quiet. She could not see the expression on his face.

Gently she placed a slender hand on his shoulder, meaning to massage. Her fingers barely grazed his skin, so hot to the touch, on fire with strength and energy. When he was turned away, and so still, like a statue, you could only sense it, but it was there, always. Year by year, and now by the day and hour, it strengthened. Lilith sometimes suspected that no body once human could possibly hold it. Only flashes of the Desus she'd known remained, and those were tucked away carefully, shared rarely.

She touched him and he spun. A lightning flash of flesh and swirling hair, the sharp whip-crack of limbs moving at the speed of instinct, thought far behind. She backed away, or tried to, but she was far too slow. She tried to shift form, to will herself into something with flight, or so small she would slip through his grasp, but her hand was suddenly in his. With a cruel, almost casual flick of his wrist, he snapped back her index finger. The bone might have been a small twig for all the resistance it gave, and Lilith, her mouth rolling into a scream shaped of a single silent "O" fell back and away, her shift forgotten, the soothing words she'd meant to offer lost in a wave of white-hot pain.

Desus stood over her and gazed down as if uncertain what he had done or how he felt about it. She saw his eyes focus, saw recognition slide across his features, and as he knelt beside her, reaching out, she backed away, clutching her ruined hand to her chest.

"Wait," he said. His words floated between them. She wanted to bat at them, drive them from her like a bubble to float and pop on the wall, but they hung in place and held her. "Wait. I have to tell you. There is a box...."

For a moment, she saw her Desus in those cold, burning eyes.

Lilith awoke with a start. She was in the hollow of the old tree, shivering. The sun had dropped beyond the horizon and the heat of day was draining into the earth beneath her. She shook her head gently, dream cobwebs shaking free to catch in the evening breeze and drift away. Stretching, she moved out along the branch slowly, talons gripping deep through bark and wood.

She knew where it was. The box. The dreams left her weak and lonely, but she remembered. She nearly slipped from the limb as one talon refused her order to grip. Where her finger would be, a throbbing pain remained. Residual dream essence, she wondered, or a message from her past?

With a cry, she launched herself into the night sky and banked toward the caravan. She could just make out the lights of their campfires below and farther up the road. She hadn't been too far off on her estimation of their travel.

Chapter Five

Dace sat across from Risa at a folding canvas table in his tent. To either side were the scouts, four in all, who'd been dispatched and returned. Dace was not without contacts, and some information had been gathered, but they had not found Tarsus.

Nothing was certain except that there was a massing of the dead, and that they appeared to be gathering in the direction of Thorns. From the scouts' reports, the numbers would be somewhere near twenty-five hundred strong. Not a huge force, but large enough to be significant.

Dace frowned. There had been no intelligence from his scouts in Thorns, and if such a force had been gathering there, there should have been something. He didn't like the fact that they were on the road, open to attack, or that this army of the dead gathered so near to Mishaka. The city was not the same as that he remembered from the last foray out of Thorns. The defenses were weakened, and a good, solid attack might topple them for good.

There would have to be leaders. There would be nemissaries, perhaps men in the service of the Mask of Winters. Dace was a mercenary, but he never would have fought for a deathknight, nor would he have taken up arms with the dead at his flank and rear. It was unnatural to Dace's way of seeing the world. Combined with a force of zombies and nemissaries, the resulting force could be wildly unpredictable and dangerous. And still, there was the matter of who was behind it.

"We have to move more quickly tomorrow," Risa said, laying her hands flat on the table. "If we don't, we take the chance that this force will move on Mishaka and catch us at the gates— or worse still, already be there."

The scouts remained silent. They'd already delivered what information they could, and only remained because they had not been dismissed. Dace wanted them back in the field, but he hesitated. There were a number of ways he could use them, and he hadn't brought his full force on this mission. Guarding a caravan was hardly a major battle. Now he had to use those forces he had most wisely, and that meant spreading the scouts thinner than he liked. They had been chosen for their speed, and their mounts were Marukani horses, the finest and fastest in the land, bred for strength and endurance. They could cover a great distance in a very short amount of time, and he wanted to be certain he chose their destinations well. Intelligence about one's enemy, or the lack thereof, could make or break a campaign.

Beyond the tent the sun was rising, and the caravan was awash in activity. Beasts were fed and harnessed, quick meals were taken on the run and where they could be found. Weapons were checked and donned, clanging and clanking against light armor.

"We need to get going," Dace said. To the scouts he snapped, "Find yourselves some food, and prepare to ride. I will send final assignments within the hour."

The scouts rose as one and filed from the room. Risa remained for a moment longer.

"You are worried," she said. It was not a question; she'd read it in his eyes.

"I can't shake the notion we're headed into the jaws of a trap," he replied. "It's all too simple. If it were marauders, or even a troop of Dragon-Blooded outcastes, I'd feel differently. At least I'd know what enemy might be at my doorstep. This dead army, if that is what it is, is not there without a purpose, and not knowing that purpose makes planning difficult. I want to know who is behind it."

"Thorns?" Risa asked, her question almost a statement. "They are the logical source of such a force, and the location seems right, placed between there and here. I wonder," Risa mused. "Surely the Mask of Winters, if he's behind it, wouldn't know that you might come to the city? It's as if they are out there as bait, but who is he trying to entice?"

"I don't know," Dace replied. "Lookshy, perhaps? Still, they won the last encounter—it hardly seems a good idea to bait them into another."

Risa smiled then, and her warrior-tough features softened in that instant. She was a truly beautiful creature, beyond the elemental strength and lithe figure. The smile was gone as quickly as it had flickered to life, but not before Dace managed a smile of his own.

"Blind or eyes wide open," she said, "whoever is behind this attack is making a mistake if they fail to take notice of this force. Twenty-five hundred dead, or twenty-five thousand."

It was true, and Dace knew it, but it did not remove niggling doubts that itched at his thoughts. While it was true that he, Risa, and the others were more than a match for what appeared to be the threat, *why* would anyone test it? Knowing they were on the road, and any real force would be preceded by their own scouts, why would the enemy make themselves known so blatantly?

"Let's hope that the dead are all we're facing," he replied, "and that the time of the attack, and the numbers, are not too far from the truth. We'll find our answers on the road.

"Go ahead and get them moving."

Risa saluted and turned, striding purposefully from the tent. Just as she reached the door Dace called out to her, and she turned back.

"Get Krislan and give him a small unit," he said. "Send them ahead to Mishaka. Have him tell them they must prepare for a possible attack, and to explain to them about the dead gathering. If we are too late, I don't want to leave them without warning."

Risa nodded, turned, and slipped out of the tent.

Dace was about to rise and leave the tent so it could be stowed for the road when he heard the flutter of wings closer than he'd expect any bird large enough to make the sound to fly. Moments later he heard the light pad of footsteps, not from within the keep, but from the balcony running along the outside wall, beyond his windows.

Instantly alert, he glided to where his huge orichalcum

daiklave leaned against his bunk. He hefted it quietly, fingers gripping tightly. His senses were keen, but he could not place the footfalls. They weren't loud enough to be the crunch of boots, and there were few children with the caravan, none who'd approach his tent uninvited.

A slender shadow passed along the wall of the tent. The scent of jasmine, mingled with the odor of—what? A bird? A whispered question slipped in on the wind.

Dace hesitated. Then, weapon still gripped tightly, he replied. "Enter."

Lilith slipped from the shadows with the grace of the ages. Her eyes flashed, just for a moment, silver and glowing like those of an animal caught in the gaze of the moon. White hair swirled back over her shoulders, and her well-muscled form rippled beneath her armor. Her breastplate, and the armored guards at her shins and forearms, seemed to glow with a pale, silvery light.

Dace stared at her, taking a defensive stance. He knew she hadn't ridden into camp: She would have been announced. The meaning of the sounds of a huge bird slipped easily into place. Lilith stopped in the doorway, watching him, as memories of his last encounter with a Lunar Exalted shifted through his mind.

He'd seen one Lunar in a battle long years past, bursting from the waves like a sea serpent. It had been powerful enough to rip the mast from a ship with one swipe of its arm. The savants he had consulted since then all agreed that Lunars bore no good will toward men or sun-children like him. Now, one had walked calmly into his tent.

She smiled, but from the tension in her shoulders and a slight hesitation in her step, she was as uncertain of her welcome as he was of the reason for her visit.

"Who are you?" he asked, not letting down his guard. "Why did you just walk in here without being announced?"

She did not answer immediately. She stared at him, taking him in. Dace stood still, waiting. He had done no less with her, and he feared nothing from her, though he knew she must be ancient, powerful, and dangerous.

"I am Lilith," she replied at last. "I am sometimes called Owl Woman."

Her voice was musical. It purred with the resonance of a big cat and chimed with the songbird's lilt. Dace was fascinated, but he remained where he stood. He wished they weren't in such close quarters. If he took a full swing with the daiklave in the tent he'd end up slicing canvas, poles, and all. So far there was no threat, but appearances were often deceptive.

"You are Dace," she said. It was a statement, not a question, and Dace did not acknowledge it.

"I have come to seek your help," she continued. "I would have come in, as you suggest, through the front door, but I doubt that your men would have received me well. I did not believe that killing them would be the best introduction."

Dace allowed a half-smile to play at the corners of his lips, but there was nothing genuine behind it. He was calculating the distance to the door, other means of extricating himself and giving his people more room, should they need it. He was worried that at any moment Risa or one of his other men would come to the door and drive this creature into something rash.

He stepped forward and faced his guest. "A wise choice," he acknowledged. "I hadn't thought of that. In my defense, you are the first Lunar Exalt I have met under peaceful circumstances. That is, you are if you're really here to ask for help, and not for some other purpose."

"I have been in the wilds for many years," she replied. "I have not felt welcome among men for a very long time."

"If you have come in peace," Dace replied, "then I have no quarrel with you. I have no quarrel with any I am not paid to quarrel with, and the Council has said nothing of the Lunars. I would be surprised, in fact, if they were aware of your presence."

Dace fell silent for a moment, studying her features. Something in her name, the tilt of her chin, and her voice itched at his memories, but he couldn't place it with any certainty.

"As would I," Lilith replied. She stepped farther into the tent, moving slowly, and held out a slender hand.

Dace took it with a nod, then released her and nodded toward the canvas table and chairs where he and Risa had sat only a few moments before. Lilith moved with him easily and seated herself. With no hesitation she crossed one leg over the other and leaned back to gaze up at him in curiosity.

Dace returned her gaze. He wanted to ask her again why she had come. He wanted to ask her a great many things, in fact. If she were as old as he believed she must be, she might have known him—before. She might have known the Solar within that had walked in other forms. Why else would she be here, sitting in his tent? Why would she seek him out? He said nothing.

"Sir?" A young soldier's voice called out from the door and Dace whirled. Catching himself, he steadied his voice.

"What is it?" he barked.

"We need to get this tent down and stowed, sir. The caravan is ready to move out."

Dace glanced at Lilith, then back at the door. He hesitated. He knew he should call out to them and alert the camp, but he held back. For the moment, the threat was only a potential.

"Work around me," he called out. "I have some things to finish up here. If I have to, I remember how to stow a tent."

There was a moment's silence, then the young man called back, "Yes, sir."

The man's footsteps retreated. The sound of the caravan creaking into motion around them; wagons rolling along the outer lines of the camp; the Ravenous Wolves, Dace's mercenaries, spreading out and taking point and rear, following Risa's direction. It was strange to sit motionless as the camp moved on, though Dace knew he could catch up easily enough. With the wagons and stock they moved slowly.

"At least one other will check in on me before they move on," he said.

"The woman?" Lilith asked.

"Risa, my lieutenant," Dace nodded.

Lilith's expression did not change. She watched him, and she waited. Moments later, as Dace had predicted, Risa pushed aside the tent's flap and entered. Before she could speak, or ask him what he was doing, she caught sight of Lilith and stopped, framed in the doorway. Her hand was on the hilt of her spear in a blur. Dace still held his daiklave.

"Leave two men and a wagon," Dace said. "I'm not sure why our visitor has come, but I won't be long. Get the caravan moving, and I'll catch up shortly."

Risa continued to stare, not moving toward the door. "But..." she said.

"Go," Dace told her. "I will tell you what I learn. Get the caravan away from here."

Risa stood just a moment longer, taking in Lilith's young, lithe form. She wasn't fooled. The woman had not walked in through the camp, and Dace would not be so tense if this was just woman. What other answer there might be, she could only guess.

"Yes sir," she said at last.

Dace breathed a sigh of relief. There could have been trouble. Risa would not like leaving her commander alone in such a situation, but she would not disobey his orders. He wanted his men, and the caravan, as far from Lilith as possible in case he learned that her visit was somewhat less friendly than it appeared. He wasn't worried about his ability to protect himself, but a battle with a Lunar would be a danger to those around them.

Dace turned back to Lilith and strode across to the table. He stood over her for a long moment, then shrugged and took the other camp chair.

"You have come at a bad time," he said at last. "I have to get this caravan to Mishaka safely, and I've already lost one scout."

"I have seen things that may be useful to you," she said softly. Her eyes were not soft, however. They searched his features, probed his thoughts, sought purchase on his form. Dace felt as if she were trying to find a way to open him and read some inner text that she alone was aware of. Very suddenly, he grew irritated.

"What do you know?" he asked. "How do you know? Have you come from Thorns, or are you here on your own?"

She raised a hand, palm out.

"I'm not your enemy," she assured him, "but I have seen one who is. He gathers an army of the dead"

Dace waited.

"I need your help," she repeated.

"You haven't told me what you know," he said, half rising. "If all you are here to tell me is that the dead are gathering in force, I already know that. I have a caravan to escort."

Before he was out of his chair, Lilith uncrossed her legs and put out a hand to stop him from rising. He tensed, but she did not attack. "Wait," she said.

"I don't have time for games," he replied. "If you are right, and an army is gathering this close to the city, then I need to get there and warn them."

"You would protect them?" she asked.

"If they paid me, I would," he replied simply. "If not, then I need to get my men out and back on the road to Nexus before the battle is joined. Either way, I don't have time to sit here and chat with you."

"I am seeking something," she replied. "It lies in the same direction as the threat you speak of. It has been a long time since I came across a gathering of the dead, or those who control them. There are a number of things in the world that are not what they were when I knew… in the First Age."

Dace caught the skip in her words.

"When you knew who? What? And what would you fear among the dead? Not the darkness, surely, or the night."

"What I seek was hidden by a Solar," she replied. "He was one I loved, and his name was Desus. We spent many years together, and he left me with a riddle."

"You need me to help solve a riddle left to you by your lover?" he asked incredulously. "If I was inclined to do that, which I'm not, what makes you believe I'd be any help?"

"You are of the Undying Sun," she replied. "Desus was, as well. I believe he has returned, or that he *will* return, but I have no idea where, or when, or in what form. He could be a woman, for all I know. Just before I last saw him, he spoke of a box. This box is what I seek. It haunts my dreams."

Dace gazed at her in wonder, considering what dreams might be like after a thousand years or more of life. He wondered who she was beneath her cool, fluid exterior. He wondered why she had come to him.

"I can't help you," he said, rising. "I have an obligation to fulfill, and you have already distracted me from that obligation."

"Where sun and moon collide," she whispered. The words

were spoken so softly that Dace was uncertain he'd actually heard them.

"What?" He asked.

"Where sun and moon collide," she repeated. "That is where he has hidden the box. I don't know of such a place, but I assume that when he spoke of the moon, he spoke of me. That would make me one half of the solution to the riddle. I thought…"

"That if you came to me we might complete the focus," Dace finished for her impatiently. "You thought that if you found another similar to the one you lost, everything might slide into place like the many shapes of a puzzle."

"No," she countered, surprising him. "You are no more like Desus than I am. I doubt that the two of you would think alike, or act alike. But my journey leads me toward the army of the dead, your enemy as well as mine. They are led by a deathknight that is called the Drinker of Seeping Poison. He is a necromancer of great power. As I have said, my experience with the dead is old. Very old.

"I hoped," she said, "that if we were together, that we could be of mutual benefit. I know where the deathknight gathers his army, and you may be more likely to understand what he will do if we encounter him. You could retrieve your missing scout, or word of him, and return with the information he should have brought you in the first place. I know some, but not enough. I don't know, for instance, where he will attack, or why, but I can help you find out."

"And in exchange for this, you want me to wander around in the woods while my men go on without me, helping you find some lost box. I said it before, and now I will say it again. I can't help you. I have to catch up with my men."

"One of the symbols on the box is of your caste," she said quickly. "Desus knew many Exalted before he grew—strange. It is possible that the box contains things that will jar your own memories, as well."

"You have no idea what he meant?" Dace asked. "You have no idea where he might have hidden this box, or even why?"

"He was fond of the heights," Lilith replied, glancing at the window to detach her gaze. "I believe it will be on a mountain, though he might choose otherwise to put me off the trail."

"If you were meant to find this box," Dace asked, "why would he put you off the trail?"

"I don't believe he left it for me to find. I was just there to hear him speak of it. I'm trying to find Desus, who- or whatever he has become. I believe he left the box for himself, or for those of his circle, to find. I don't know what it might contain, but if it were not important, why hide it?"

"You said he'd grown strange," Dace reminded her.

"But not stupid," she replied.

"No," Dace replied. "I guess he wouldn't have been. 'Where sun and moon collide' could just be a reference to his caste. There has to be more."

"One side of the box has the image of a mountain," she replied. "There is a mountain, not far from here, where Desus went from time to time. It is not far from his ancestral home, or what ruins are left of it. That is where I believe the box will be hidden."

"But you don't know?" Dace asked.

"No," she admitted. "I don't know, but I believe. Sometimes that is all you have. We will have to figure it out on the way."

"We?" Dace replied. "There is no *we*. I have told you, I will be on the road to Mishaka with my men."

"You will not be needed," she told him. "The dead only gather. It will take them several days' forced march to reach the city, if that is their goal. If you come with me, we might learn more than any ten of your scouts. The city can hold off an attack, if they are prepared, until you return."

"Then I must go, as I have said," Dace replied, though he considered her words. It would be good to have more intelligence. If the force came from Thorns, and was directed at Mishaka, he needed to know, but if there was a different purpose, that was equally important. Those he served in Nexus would want information on any movement of the Abyssals this near their own walls.

Dace wasn't really worried about the city, or the caravan. Risa was a seasoned leader, and his men were veterans. There was plenty of time for them to reach the city and prepare for what might come. If he rode out alone, or with this Lunar, Lilith, he could return to the city far in advance of any army of walking dead this Drinker of Seeping Poison might raise, and the information gathered might prove invaluable.

"What is it that you want from me?" he asked. "What will I gain from it? I have no time to play guessing games with you, as intriguing as your company might be."

"I have told you what I know," she answered quickly. "The box is a thing from the First Age, before Nexus was called Nexus and a time when you were not Dace, and yet you walked the earth. I walked the earth, and I walk it still. It may prove nothing more than the trinket of a crazy man, and then—it might be more. I am in search of my past, and what it might mean to my future. I believe you are tied in with this box as well."

"Why would we go together?" Dace asked. "Perhaps my question was worded incorrectly. What is in this for you?"

"I don't know," Lilith answered, turning to gaze thoughtfully at the wall of the tent. "That is why I must find it. I know there is a box, and I know whose it was, but I don't know what… or why—not exactly."

"Desus was a powerful Solar. Whatever is in that box, he didn't want just anyone to find it. I doubt that he wanted me to hear him speak of it, but as I have said…"

"He grew strange," Dace finished.

Lilith nodded, and Dace remained silent. He had a lot more questions, but Lilith had grown very still.

Then she said, "I fell under that title myself. Inconsequential. You see, Desus was slowly going mad."

"I am sorry for your pain, and the loss, though it was long ago, but I still don't see the connection to myself. I thank you for the information you have given me. It will be helpful. If there is a battle to be fought, I will remember that you helped me."

"For you, it would be no conflict at all," she replied, unperturbed. "Unless there is more to this gathering of the dead than what we see on the surface, there is no danger you can't easily handle. If the deathknight himself were to ride into battle, it would better if you were nearer to where he is and could meet him as far from the city as possible.

"What Desus has left must be of great importance," Lilith went on. "What he would consider important would not necessarily be important to me. It would be of importance to himself, or possibly to another Solar. Even if it is just memories I seek, they may be yours as well."

There was that dark flicker again. There, then gone. Dace frowned. He felt the growing distance between his life, his thoughts, and those of others around him. Her words cut deeper than she knew—or did she know?

"I am not Desus," he said softly. "I am not a thing, or a person that you know, or that you can predict. Whether or not I can be trusted is something you may have to learn on your own, as I would have to learn the same of you. You'll admit," he added, "that the reputation of your kind is not a good one."

Lilith smiled at him. "It has been a long time since I have been this near to a city," she said. "I prefer the wilds, other places—other forms. I do not seek company—only your assistance. If it was the favor of a city I coveted, I could save Mishaka myself."

Dace stood watching her. His frown deepened. "You are very sure of yourself, and I wonder why," he said at last, turning away from her and walking to the tent flap. He brushed it aside and stared out into the open expanse of the road. "Twice I have told you that I will not go. I am needed, leading my men into Mishaka, and yet you continue to speak as if I will not."

"I have not told you everything," she said softly. "I will never tell you everything. I know a part of what we will find, and it could be of use to you. I believe we will find things that were Desus's—artifacts of the First Age."

Dace considered. If all she said was true, then there was really no desperate need for his presence on the road to Mishaka, though he would not be able to delay for long. If she were wrong about the growing force of dead warriors, or their leader, she was right about one thing. The deathknight was something for him to handle, not for Risa, or the others. It might actually be for the best if he made a quick scouting run, intercepting them if he could.

"If we succeed, you could be on the road and caught up with

your men by the time they reach the city, or very soon after. I am not asking you to go to the ends of the earth, only to grant me two days, three at most."

"I will discuss it with Risa, and the others," he replied, suddenly turning back from the doorway. He stared at her openly, taking in her form, the odd tint of her skin, her long hair, and the deep, unflinching eyes. She was an enigma, and her age was not something to be taken lightly. Dace had half-memories and stories, this woman had walked the roads of the First Age.

He found that he wanted to go with her. He wished she had come at a time when duty and responsibility were not so pressing—not that many such times occurred in the life of a mercenary.

"Come to my tent tomorrow morning," he said. "I'm going to get out of here and catch up. I have duties to perform, and I have sat here for too long already."

Lilith nodded and rose. She brushed very close to him in passing and he caught her scent, though he couldn't place it. Then she was past, and stepping into the light of early morning. Dace followed.

Dace stepped back, startled, as Lilith hopped lightly to the canvas roof of his tent, then launched into the sky. Her body rippled, and he saw the essence well up and burst free. She shimmered like moonlight, bright enough even against the dawn sun for him to see clearly. The owl cried fiercely as it soared into the sky. Dace watched until she was gone from sight, and then he watched a bit longer.

He stared after her and whispered, "What do you have in store for me?"

Then, turning, he gathered his gear. The two men Risa had left behind struck the tent and stowed it quickly, not saying a word to their leader. Both had seen Lilith's transformation, and they knew what it meant, but neither could understand why their commander had met with her. He offered them no answer as he mounted his horse and wheeled toward Mishaka.

Chapter Six

Dace stood before the mustered troops he'd led out to escort the caravan with his hands behind his back, and watched as they gathered. Risa rode up and down along the front rank, her eyes dark, and her mood darker. Dace had told her just after sunrise that he would not be continuing with them directly to Mishaka. As the men gathered, he ran the meeting over in his mind again and frowned.

"But why you?" she'd asked. "With all due respect, Dace, your place is with the men. If those dead warriors descend on us before we reach the city, it's going to be pretty hard to explain."

"They can't get here that quickly, Risa. You know that. They are the reason I'm going. I don't want to send any more men into that area until we find out what happened to Tarsus, and what is going on in those woods. I can handle whatever I run into and at least get out to warn you. I don't know that about any of the scouts, or the men."

"I can go," Risa had said promptly. "I can take care of myself, sir. You should be with the men."

"I don't want you leaving alone with her," Dace said firmly. "I don't know this Lilith well enough to trust her, and certainly not with you. If she turns out not to be what she says she is, again, I am the one to handle that. On the other hand, if she is telling the truth, then we need to know what's about to happen with those dead soldiers, and who or what is behind them. A deathknight can be dangerous, particularly when you are ill prepared."

When she hadn't answered, Dace had continued. "I'll be to the city before you are, or almost as soon. I won't spend any more time on this than is absolutely necessary."

Risa had not looked convinced, or happy, but she'd let it drop.

He wasn't ready to tell Risa, or anyone, any more about Lilith. He wasn't certain how he felt about the situation, but he had a pretty good idea how they would feel. They would feel betrayed, angry, and they would advise him against trusting the Lunar with anything, particularly when his entire force was facing the possible attack of an army of the dead.

Now, watching his men prepare for another day on the road to Mishaka, Dace remained stone faced, hiding his uncertainty behind a mask of confidence. He knew he should tell Risa, if no one else, but he held back. He would see her within a few days time, and that would have to suffice. With luck, he would have a tale to tell her by the time he rejoined them on the road to Mishaka.

His men fell silent and Dace stepped closer, sweeping his gaze up and down their ranks. They were an impressive lot. Many other commanders allowed their companies of mercenaries free rein, but not Dace. His unit was one of the smoothest in action and most loyal of those serving Nexus. The formation he watched falling into place was tight and precise. Their blades were honed and polished, and their eyes sparkled with anticipation.

They were his men. They had not come to him as they stood before him—he had molded them. Risa had trained them, drilling incessantly and instilling precision and pride where they had once felt only the desire for money. Most were hardened veterans of more battles and wars than Dace could count.

Dace nodded to Risa and she raised her dire lance in salute. The weapon was tipped with jade and glittered in the morning light. Her eyes were cold, her lips drawn back in a sneer. Dace frowned at the obvious anger and disdain in her expression. His brow furrowed, and he nearly stepped forward to grab her reins, draw her down, and explain himself. Nearly. His pride prevented it, and her arrogance raised his own ire.

Dace addressed them, speaking loudly enough that Risa and the other officers who rode up and back along the lines of his men could hear.

"I have intelligence," he said, "that indicates the dead are gathering. I don't know exactly why, but I intend to find out. I am going to do this scouting mission myself. We lost one man already, and I don't want to send any of you into something you can't handle. I will join you farther down the road, or in Mishaka, and whatever I find out, we'll make our plans to face it then."

He fell silent, wondering if he'd said enough, too much, or if it mattered. The men shifted in their saddles. Some performed last-minute inventories on their gear. All were attentive, but it was obvious that he held their attention only by the force of his will. They were ready to move. It wasn't an easy task to keep a large caravan moving, and the knowledge that they were doing so with the threat of more than ordinary bandits made it that much more imperative that they get started.

Sensing this, Dace nodded to Risa and raised a gloved fist over his head.

Risa spun her mount, raised her spear overhead and barked orders to the lieutenants, who whirled in turn and rode along the lines of soldiers. The clatter of weapons and clopping of hooves filled the air. Men cried out and the merchants, gathered at their wagons, watching the meeting of their escort with curiosity and a mixture of anxious fear and impatience, quieted their animals and waited.

Then, as a single entity they spun, guiding their mounts to the road and spreading out along the perimeter of the caravan. Risa rode toward the front without looking back, and the wagons began to groan and creak as they rolled into motion. Dace stood, watching. He did not speak or move until they had faded into a drifting cloud of raised dust on the horizon.

"They are very impressive."

Dace whirled. He'd not heard her approach, but she stood close behind him, and he could tell from her expression she'd been there, and she'd seen Risa and the others depart. She was watching the road, but as he turned to her, she turned as well, meeting his gaze.

"I should be with them," Dace said, facing away from her and striding toward his gear, which he had left piled neatly near his mount.

Lilith did not reply. She followed behind, watching him move, studying him. Dace did not look back.

Dace stopped by his mount and turned, regarding her somberly and with not a small amount of distrust. Lilith was taking in his equipment, worn saddlebags neatly packed, the scabbard that held his daiklave close to hand mounted near the pommel of his saddle. The gear was compact and solid. Though Exalted, the mercenary in his makeup shone through in his preparations for the journey. He had not said it, but she had seen his men ride on toward Mishaka, so she knew he was going with her.

What she did not know, and what she knew she would have to be careful in discovering, was why. She had no way to know how long or how far she could trust in his company and his companionship, and she had to learn from him what she could, in case he veered off and left her along the way. Still, the proximity of a Solar was—comfortable—in ways she would have found difficult to put into words.

He sized her up in a glance, then took a slower look, letting his gaze linger on her form, catching her eyes. It was unsettling, as though he were memorizing her, reading her like a map of some place he thought to conquer. Lilith frowned slightly, and the flush crept higher up her cheekbones and spread to her throat.

"We should go," she said softly. Her voice was deeper than she'd intended, throatier, and inwardly she cursed herself. "There is little time, if you are to catch up to your men."

"We can travel swiftly enough," he replied, still gazing at her. "I can't work your magic of shifting to the shape of birds, or whatever else you can manage, but I can ride, and I don't tire easily."

Lilith nodded. Suddenly she did not trust her voice to serve her as it should. She wanted to be moving, to shift to the owl, or the hawk, and soar. She could not. She knew that if she were to travel with Dace she would have to match his speed. For all his power, he was bound to the earth, and they would need to ride.

"I need no mount," she said.

Turning, he gathered his things. He slid his daiklave into its scabbard and slung his saddlebags onto his mount. The sun was beginning to creep up toward its zenith, and the day was getting no longer.

They were on the road in only a few short moments. Lilith ran easily in the form of a tall rust-colored mare. She had slipped forms as Dace cinched his saddlebags in place, and he noted the change only when she snorted, pawing at the road with one hoof.

Dace rode well, but he was hard pressed to keep his mount at Lilith's pace. She moved with a freedom and grace denied a rider, and it was obvious that she enjoyed the form, the rippling muscles and sleek glide of the gallop.

She felt an elation that buoyed her energy and spirits. It had been so long since she'd spent time in the presence of one touched by the Unconquered Sun. She had been too long among the mountains and the animals. Her social skills had suffered, and she was glad for the time in horse form to gather her thoughts without the necessity of speech.

Mountains loomed in the distance. It would be past nightfall before they could draw near to them, and though she didn't know exactly what made her believe it, she didn't have to guess which mountain would hold the key.

Rising above all the others, a single plateau overlooked the entire range. It was the highest of the highest points, a flat expanse atop a tall peak. From where they were, it looked slender and fragile, but she knew that it would be different up close.

Dace stared alternately at the peaks in the distance, Lilith herself, and the road behind them, stretching out to Mishaka and beyond. He showed no signs of turning back, but his expression was troubled. He didn't like leaving his men, particularly in the middle of a mission, and the necessity of doing so wasn't sitting particularly well with him.

Lilith slowed and pulled up, waiting for Dace to ride up beside her. The air shimmered around her form, and the release of essence flickered in the afternoon sunlight, shimmering along the length of her as it receded with a crackle, leaving her standing beside Dace in her own form. She reached into a pouch hanging at her side and pulled free the coin she'd found after killing the big cat.

"Dace," she called softly.

When he turned to her, raising one eyebrow quizzically, she flipped the coin through the air. It spun in lazy arcs, catching the sunlight in a series of golden winks. Without thought Dace reached out, snagging it from the air deftly.

Dace stared at the coin for a long time. He turned the orichalcum disk over and over. Turning back to her, he frowned.

"What is it?" he asked. "Where did you get it? It feels very familiar to me, but I don't believe I've ever seen its like."

"It is a Solar coin," Lilith replied. "From the First Age. There weren't many of them. Desus, my companion, carried one. Each of his circle did, as well. There were others, but I have seen few. It is orichalcum."

Dace nodded and glanced back at the coin. He walked it deftly across the backs of his fingers, a trick he'd learned from an old conjurer after a battle. The coin disappeared between two fingers, then reappeared between thumb and forefinger to walk across once again.

Lilith felt a catch in her heart as she watched. Desus had had a similar trick, though he'd flicked his fingers randomly as the coin walked, sending it spinning through the air and catching it on the next knuckle. She closed her eyes. When she opened them again, she averted her gaze.

Dace still stared at the coin.

"What do think we'll will find?" he asked. "What is it that draws you to this box, and whatever is in it? Is it him? The hope he lives again in another, and that you might find him?"

Lilith didn't answer at first. She walked at his side as he turned his mount back to the road. She studied the ground, deep in thought.

"I'm not sure," she said at last. "I have been alone for a very long time. In those years, the Solars were hunted and killed. I was an outcast. Desus may return, but he will not be the one I loved, and may never be again. Yet his memory haunts me.

"When he walked at my side, I was his. There was never a doubt of that, and it is not a thing easily forgotten. He was very powerful, and he fills my dreams.

"What we seek might lead me to him, and if I can find him I think I can get the answers to questions I have held in my heart through the centuries. There may be nothing there for you—I don't know. Perhaps there are secrets of your own past that you might find useful. Few things in life are interesting enough to label significant."

She lifted her gaze to meet Dace's eyes, her own dark and defiant.

He smiled down at her and she met his gaze evenly, with sudden heat.

"You are a beautiful woman," Dace commented, keeping his tone matter of fact. "It's a shame for you to have been denied to the world for so long. A shame to be denied one you love, as well. You have such a past...."

His words trailed off and she remained silent, waiting for him to finish.

"I have power," he continued at last. "I have power that I never dreamed possible. I have memories that hover just beyond my reach, memories that are not truly mine, but that belong to the Solar, or Solars, who have come before. Sometimes it feels like I should know those things, that there are secrets I am meant to uncover, and others that I will have to fight for. Probably there are some I am better without.

"I've gained the world, but I've lost things as well. Bits and pieces of who I was—who I am. Friends who feared me as I was and run in terror from what I am.

"I feel that there is a great deal left to discover, things I must learn if I am to survive, and things that I must forget if I am to learn.

"As a man, I was a captain. I was respected, often feared, strong but aging. Now I don't seem to age much at all. If I ever grow infirm, or die of some rotting disease, if will not be for centuries. I am still a mercenary, and still a captain, but it all seems to be for different reasons entirely. When my men have withered and gone to their graves, I will remain. This is a difficult concept to understand, even more difficult to witness through the eyes of others."

Lilith waited, but when he did not continue, she steeled herself and spoke.

"You are certainly not the first to feel the things you feel," she told him softly. "You are part of a great legacy."

"Yes," he replied, "but you knew most of the generations of that legacy, if not all of them. While I am learning, you're just living. For all I know, you knew me in another time and place than this one."

Lilith met his gaze with her own, her features sharp and shrewd. He was a familiar stranger, comfortable and disconcerting all in the same breath. She wished in that moment that she could take to the air, soar to the heavens and float among the evening breezes. She needed to think. He was asking questions that he thought were cleverly tucked into the spaces between his words, and his eyes sought things from her that brought back memories. Not all of them were pleasant, and part of her wanted to place the anger she'd once felt toward Desus onto Dace.

"I'll tell you what I can," she replied. "My memories are not complete, nor are they likely to follow the same lines as your questions. I have spent long years with the animals, as an animal, flown with the owls and run with the wolves. They have taken hold of my mind and my memory, and the longer I spend with them, the more reluctantly they release me."

Dace glanced back at her, another piercing, deep-seeking glance, then turned and stared into the deepening shadows. He thought of Risa, saw the flare of anger in her eyes when he'd told her his plans. He saw Krislan's weathered features and wondered how the party he'd sent to Mishaka had fared. Thoughts of strategy and the taste of battle stirred his senses.

"Do you need to camp?" he asked.

"I prefer to travel by night," she replied. "I don't need much rest. We can ride through the night and camp at the base of the peak, then scale it when the sun is bright to light our way."

Dace grunted in answer, but she could tell he was pleased with her answer. She smiled. She'd expected his reaction—so like Desus, and yet, so different.

Without a word, Lilith shifted forms, and the mare stood beside Dace's mount. He stared at her for a moment, then gripped his own mount's reins hard and kicked in his heels. Within moments there was nothing to mark their passing but the distant sound of hooves.

Chapter Seven

Daedalus knew his mount would die beneath him if he continued as he was. He'd already stolen a second horse when the first began to falter, leaving it in the path of the beast as a distraction—one that failed.

He'd allowed himself only one short rest, long enough to water his horse. Daedalus himself remained in the saddle, half-turned and watching his back. There was no way to flee from the lion for the full 101 days. He might survive such a ride, but on foot he wouldn't last a minute, and the horse was near to death. He couldn't hope to change mounts often enough.

His options were few. He could continue as he was until he was forced to fight the creature on foot. He could wheel his mount, make a stand, and hope to cut the thing to ribbons before it could tear his heart from his body and feast on it; or he could find help. The latter seemed the best hope, but his problem was simple. Daedalus served a dark master, and had done so long enough for his reputation to precede him throughout the Scavenger Lands. None would be likely to help him. More likely, those who knew his name would cheer.

His thought blurred as he caught sight of a stand of trees ahead. He had no idea how long or how far he'd ridden. His stomach screamed with hunger, and his throat was parched and dry. A mortal would have fallen from the saddle long since, but he was more than that. The blood of the Elemental Dragons flowed through his veins. Even in this condition, he was strong, and angry.

Hatred of the Drinker of Seeping Poison fueled his flight. He had to survive. He had to find a way to disembowel the wheezing, bone-crackling demon on his heels and return to his own master, who would be waiting for a report. If the Drinker of Seeping Poison or the Walker in Darkness were to suspect the truth behind Daedalus's betrayal, then the bone lion would become the least of his problems. Still, it was distracting to let his mind wander down the road toward revenge.

Then his thoughts were shattered.

The lion burst through the shadows, hot on his heels. It was moving fast, gaining on the sweat-lathered horse with each step. Daedalus heard the crashing, terrifying sound of the thing's bones, cracking like breaking ice, but moving as though covered in sinew and muscle, imitating life even as the spell that drove it hurtled them toward a collision with death.

The horse's eyes rolled back, and it fought for breath. The animal sensed their pursuer as sharply as Daedalus himself, and it grew more and more difficult to control as that fear threatened to burst its heart.

Daedalus glanced at the trees ahead. He knew they would not stop the lion, but if he wove his way between them quickly enough he might pick up a few yards. Then he saw it, the flicker of flames between the low-slung branches. Someone was camped in those trees. His heart gave a quick leap. Hope is the last of man's follies to die.

With a wild cry, he kicked his boots into the horse's flanks in a futile effort to gain speed. He also wanted to warn whoever it was ahead. They would surely have sentries posted, and if they did, there was no way they could miss the sound of his cry, or the sight of his pursuer, loping tirelessly at his heels, eyes smoldering like pits of burning coal.

As they approached the tree line, the thing redoubled its speed and leaped. A natural beast would have roared, but the bone lion was silent. Deadalus could hear its footfalls and the gnashing of bones that accompanied its every move, however. It seemed to echo as loudly as the cry of any fleshed beast he'd encountered. With another scream, Daedalus leaned into the neck of his mount, prayed for it to miss the trees and not to brush him off, and gripped the hilt of his sword. Braced for one impact or the other, he was determined to go out a warrior, not a coward.

The thing was so close now that Daedalus felt it pounding on the road, heard the rushing of wind through the skeletal body and smelled the fetid stench of death in the air. . He did not look back. He would make it to the trees, or he would not. Someone would come from that camp and aid him, or not. If they knew the lion for what it was, they would know it posed no threat to any but him. Daedalus was counting on them *not* knowing. He was counting the seconds left to his life.

Many things happened at once as he burst through the first line of trees. He felt the rear legs of his mount swept from beneath him and, with a surge of fear-charged strength, he catapulted himself from the saddle and in among the trees.

He cleared the horse as it screamed and fell beneath the bone lion's taloned claws. Daedalus spun once, tucked his stiff knees close to his chest and gritted his teeth for the impact. Somehow, he did not fall. His feet struck the ground and he lurched into a run, dodging from tree to tree, never continuing in a straight line for more than a few yards.

He was aware that there was movement around him. Shadows flickered among the trees, and not all the sounds he heard were those of the lion. Daedalus was more aware of his surroundings than he'd been in any single moment of his life, but he could spare neither time nor thought to the others. They would aid him or they would avoid him. Either way, he would fight this night, and he would win, or die.

The trees opened into a clearing, and he saw a group of small campfires, more in the distance, stretching out as far as he could see without tapering off. Horses were tethered near the edges of the clearing. There was no sign of those who were camped, but one thing was certain: This was no small scouting party. He wasn't sure what exactly it was.

The clearing was the best chance he had. If he couldn't maneuver, he would die quickly and painfully, and all the miles and hours of flight would be so much wasted effort.

Daedalus planted and spun. The lion gave another silent roar. It broke into the clearing, crashing through trees and driving the tethered horses into a screaming, bucking frenzy.

Daedalus remained still. He fingered the jade hilt of his

sword and reached within himself. It was difficult to find his center with his heart beating like festival drums and his eyes burning with sweat, but he had faced many enemies on many battlefields. All of them lay dead, buried and forgotten, and he remained.

The beast lunged, and Daedalus leaped. He sprang straight up, anticipating the lion's hunger, knowing it would go for the quick kill and banking on his own speed to avoid the attack. He came down on the thing's head, whipped his sword back and drove it down, planting it where the creature's brain would have been.

He sliced dried sinew and the blade cut bits from the thinly knit bones, but there was no connection. He nearly lost his balance as the blade sank into nothingness, and barely managed to launch upward again as it spun, snapping its jaws up toward his legs.

Daedalus spun when he hit and whipped the blade backhand, feeling a solid connection as he sheared through the tip of the lion's front paw. Bones flew, glittering, into the clearing. The lion reared back, seemingly unaffected by the loss of two claws, and swiped its other paw toward him, aiming its claws at his throat.

He ducked, and, grasping the only hope he had, spun the sword overhand and brought it down on the thing's wrist. The bones cracked and part of that foot fell away, but the effort nearly cost him the precious seconds he needed to roll out from beneath its clamping jaws. There was no sign the beast felt pain. He was hacking it apart slowly, bit by bit, but it felt nothing, and it was no more tired or less quick than when they'd begun their chase days and miles in the past.

Using the nearest tree as a momentary shield, Daedalus ducked into the shadows, cursing himself seconds later as the beast whipped its paw in a backhand swipe that nearly decapitated him. Its gemstone eyes glowed with unholy power, and he wondered what had made him think he could hide from such a thing in the shadows. He dodged once again, spun around the next tree and lunged, hacking with the blade, no finesse in the attack, but the heat of battle bringing him his balance and his center. He felt the throb of the stone in the sword hilt burning into his palm, felt the glow seep into his arm and through his being.

Everything slowed. He spun again, leaped and flipped his legs up and over his head, landing and whipping the blade in a glittering arc. The beast met his speed and lunged, but Daedalus did not stop his motion, merely redirected. He launched straight into the air, as he'd done in his initial attack, but this time he flipped neatly. The lion reared up and he gripped the sides of its neck with his legs, keeping back behind the head where it could not reach him.

Then he hacked and slashed, using the sword as an axe, chopping away at the rear legs, the haunches, fighting all the while to remain in place, out of reach and moving. Always moving. He knew the moment he was still, he would cease to move forever, and very suddenly he was not ready to die.

The beast lunged, trying to smash its unwanted rider onto a tree or whip about fast enough to loosen his grip. Daedalus clung fiercely, smashing his hand down in a knife-edged slash that drove his fingers between bones. Gripping the thing by its own dead frame, he reared back, hacking down and to the left, aiming for the upper right leg.

The bone lion reacted too slowly, and the blade bit deep. Daedalus felt bone give, and the beast stumbled as its foot separated from its leg. It wasn't enough. The lion regained its balance with stunning ease, rolled into the missing limb, and hurled its shoulder, and Daedalus, to the ground. He tried to maintain his hold and lift himself up and away, but when the lion whipped back upright, he fell sprawling.

For a long, empty moment, Daedalus heard no sound. He tried frantically to raise his sword, but it was trapped beneath his body, and he knew that, quick as he might be, he could not roll off it and do any damage before the thing was on him.

Already the lion's snapping jaws and the burning gems that were its eyes were hurtling through the shadowy moonlight toward his throat. Releasing his sword, Daedalus rolled back, placed both hands flat on the ground and arched, kicking his booted feet straight into the thing's maw.

He managed to slow it, deflecting the snapping jaws to the right, and that was enough. He spun, grabbed his sword, and was up, stepping back and bracing himself for the next attack.

It never came. In that moment there was a loud cry from his left, and a figure hurtled into the clearing. It was difficult to make out the features, but from the strength and speed of the leap, Daedalus's mind flashed *Exalted*, even as a long wicked jade spear tip bristling with jade thorns pierced what should have been the lion's heart.

"It has no organs," he cried. "It must be broken to bits."

He couldn't tell if the woman, for he now saw that it was a woman, heard him or not, but her intent was suddenly clear. The spear pierced the lion, catching in the ground beneath, and with a sickening crunch of bone and gristle she launched on past it, never releasing the spear's hilt, using it as a lever between dead ribs. The lion was nearly torn in two by the attack, and Daedalus whistled low, admiring the attack.

Then he was moving again. There was no sense in running. If he ran she might let it go, and if the lion defeated her, it would come after him anyway—not to mention those who traveled with the woman, whoever they might be. It was time to end this and let the Five Dragons decide the rest.

Daedalus came in low. The lion had lunged after its new attacker, leaving its flank unguarded, and Daedalus struck. He drew back and whipped the blade in an arc, running it parallel to the ground and slicing cleanly through at least two ribs. Without hesitation he reversed the swing and swung it back with all his strength, cutting through three more ribs before he dropped, kicked off the ground, and rolled off to the side. The lion was trapped between the two of them, unable to attack one without opening itself to the other, unable to retreat because Daedalus was its destiny.

On his next attack, Daedalus drove his blade in a final, devastating swing, crying out the moment of impact and launching a shot at the beast's rear leg. With a crumbling, dust-choked explosion, the leg gave, and the creature was down.

The next moments were a blur of motion, sound, and concentrated essence. Far from finished, the lion was rolling, trying

to get purchase with its remaining claws and snapping at anything that moved with bone-crunching clamps of its huge jaws.
Daedalus concentrated on the legs. He managed to take off the
second rear leg and, with a cry of rage, kicked it away from the
floundering beast on the ground.

With a cry of her own, the woman warrior ran and leaped
as if she would vault over a wall, driving her dire lance down
through the bones of the thing's throat and into the ground.
When it caught, she twisted her body, swinging around the hilt
of the spear and driving toward the ground with all her weight.
For a tense moment it seemed the spear would bend and then
flip her back toward the beast.

Daedalus started to move to her aid, but in the next instant
he fell back. The woman gave a last harsh cry. Her shoulders
rippled and the spear bent down low. Another explosion of dead
flesh and chipped bone, and the lion's head popped cleanly
from its body, rolling to the side of the clearing. The lion moved
erratically about with half a claw to drag it but, with its head
removed, the beast seemed to have lost its sense of direction.

Daedalus fell against a tree, the exhaustion overwhelming
him. He tried to balance himself against the tree, missed, and
toppled toward the ground. He just managed to catch himself
and slump against the trunk of a tree. Risa approached, standing a safe distance from him.

"Easy, stranger," she said softly.

Daedalus lay very still, not answering her, and, for the first
time since he'd leaped to the back of the horse that lay dead a
few yards away, he closed his eyes. It took all the force of will
remaining to him not to drift away and let the darkness swal-
low him. He spoke to dispel his weariness.

"Who are you?" he asked. As his mind relaxed, his survival
instinct was in full control. He was already beyond the lion and
on to the next challenge. Daedalus opened his eyes as he spoke
and stared up into her face. She was beautiful. Her hair was a
light auburn, her skin the greenish tinge of the wood-blessed.
Dragon-Blooded, he thought, waiting for her to answer.

"I am Risa," she answered. "The camp you dragged your
friend over there," she glanced at the still-rolling carcass of the

bone lion, "is mine. My men are waiting for me to tell them it is safe to return. Now, you tell me. Who are you, and how safe is it?"

"If you mean," Daedalus replied, managing to sit up and lean back on the trunk of a tree, "was that the only supernatural creature trailing me and threatening to shred me into carrion for the vultures, then it is safe."

She didn't smile, but he saw the ghost of it slide through the depths of her eyes.

"You didn't answer the question," she said flatly. "Who are you, and why are you here? And don't lie to protect yourself, because it won't work. I have men with me from nearly every province from the Scavenger Lands to Nexus. One of them will know you, or of you. Don't take it as a compliment, but one of your power is not easily forgotten."

He almost laughed, then bit down on his tongue and shook his head, trying to clear his thoughts.

"I fear I may have won my life back, only to forfeit it, then," he said softly. "A deathknight put that thing on my trail, one I was serving at the time. No doubt he believed it would be the last he ever saw of me. I let one of his prisoners escape—he was less than pleased."

"Prisoner?" she said, her face creasing into a frown. "Who, and where?"

Daedalus glanced at her, gauging the wisdom of disclosing anything further. "A scout," he answered. "We had captured a scout, and I released the man so that he could get to the city of Mishaka and warn them."

Risa stepped back, her hand on her spear, and stared at him.

"Mishaka?" she asked. "Who was this prisoner, exactly, and why did he need to warn Mishaka?"

Warily, sliding his hand toward the hilt of his sword, Daedalus watched her, and answered. "His name was Tarsus. I released him so that he could warn the city that the Drinker of Seeping Poison is marching on their gates with an army of the dead at his heels."

"This Drinker of Seeping Poison," she asked, her eyes glittering, "you say he's a deathknight?"

Daedalus nodded. "Very powerful. He's the one behind the attack, though he's under orders himself."

"From who?" Risa asked. "The Mask of Winters? Thorns?"

Daedalus did not speak, but shook his head slowly. "Not him. The Drinker of Seeping Poison answers to the Walker in Darkness."

She stood very still, staring down at him, her face pale. "How did he gather a force so large under the nose of Thorns? If you know anything that will help me decide why I should not kill you, I'd speak now. My men guard a caravan bound for Mishaka. There are bows trained on you from all sides, and I believe I can drive this spear through your heart before you can draw that sword you keep fingering. Tell me why I should believe you."

"My purpose is to get the caravan safely to Mishaka," she told him. "Our scouts report that, though the attacking army is large, they will be at least eight days in reaching the city. We will be there in four, and my own captain, Dace, will have rejoined us by then.

"Now you show up." Risa turned, began to pace, and cursed under her breath.

Daedalus sized up his situation in an instant. He had information they would desperately need. They had him. While he was fairly certain he could defend himself against her, there was something in her steady gaze and the way she'd handled herself against the bone lion that gave him pause. Then there was the matter of his exhaustion, and hunger—the matter of his having nowhere to return to until things had played out.

"There is a graveyard in Mishaka, a shadowland that touches the Underworld," he said slowly. "The Drinker of Seeping Poison will use it to enter the city. He will send an overland force to distract you, or any others thinking to defend the city, but he will bring another force through the Underworld. It wasn't his initial plan, so it will take him some time to gather enough of a force to pull it off. He did not count on my releasing the prisoner, or defeating the lion."

Risa cursed again. With a quick, almost careless motion, she raised her spear and then struck. It crashed into the ground, so close to Daedalus's face that he could feel the razor edge of the tip kissing the flesh of his cheek.

Turning, Risa brought fingers to her lips and whistled. Voices rose in answer, and there was a sudden motion within the trees. Her men, coming at her call, emerged from the trees, skirting around the bone lion's still animated carcass. The first of them circled Daedalus to stand and glare, awaiting their captain's word.

Controlling her anger, Risa returned. "If you are telling me the truth," she spat, the sparks in her eyes making it clear that she did not believe he was, "then we are nearly out of time. You will remain with us until we reach the city. You will tell me everything you know about this Drinker of Seeping Poison, his army and his plans, on the road.

"You have the time between now and our arrival in Mishaka to convince me not to kill you. My inclination, so you know, is to kill you now and take my chances."

She glanced at the head of the beast she'd helped him to slay. It glared up at her, the malevolence in its burning, lifeless eyes not cowed or lessened by its defeat.

Turning, she waved an arm at her men.

"Get the pieces of that thing into a fire and burn it. Leave no trace. Then I want all lieutenants at my fire for a council. We may be on the road sooner than we thought."

Glaring over her shoulder at Daedalus, she growled. "You come with me—and pray we are not already too late."

Daedalus did as she bid him, grabbing his sword as he rose and slipping it into its scabbard. She showed him her back, almost in contempt, and walked through the shadows toward her fire. With a soft curse, Daedalus followed.

Chapter Eight

Krislan and his men pulled up a quarter of a mile short of Mishaka, and the sergeant cupped a hand over his eyes to shield them from the sun. There was little movement on the roads outside the city, but he'd not expected much this time of day. The heat baked both earth and road, and the air shimmered with it.

Krislan glanced back over his men. Their horses were lathered in sweat, and the men were not much better. They had ridden hard and made good time. Now that their goal stood so close at hand, however, he found himself wishing they still had some distance to ride.

There was no particular love lost between Nexus and the cities of the Scavenger Lands, Mishaka in particular. Though the two had formed an alliance in the battle of Mishaka, Nexus supplying a force of mercenaries that, along with soldiers from Lookshy and fighters from other nearby points of the Confederation of Rivers, had helped to stem the tide and end that bloody confrontation, there was little communication between the two.

Despite this recent alliance, no more than eight years in the past, the elders of Mishaka considered Nexus as likely an enemy as ally. Nexus until recently had considered Mishaka and its surrounding cities unimportant and far enough away to pose no immediate threat, but there was no way to guess how the elders of that great city might proceed if their mindset shifted.

Now here they sat, weary and tired, thirsty from several days on the road, poised to bring word to the city of a possible impending attack, and Krislan had to wonder what kind of welcome they might expect. His news should be welcome, but how could one predict such a thing? They might think he was a liar, or that he himself came from Thorns, an emissary of the deathknight, ready to trick them into defending against an attack that would never come, only to weaken their defense on another front.

They might just want nothing to do with mercenaries out of Nexus, and send them on their way. This wouldn't sit well with his men, nor would it bring a smile to Dace's lips when they returned to the caravan. It was up to Krislan to smooth-talk the city elders into cooperation, and to help organize what defense he could before Dace, Risa and the caravan arrived.

They were days ahead of the others, and that was a blessing, if for no other reason than that after such a time on the road he was hungry, thirsty, and tired, and could use a rest before the coming battle.

"Let's go!" he cried, turning his horse toward the city once more and taking off at a trot. The others fell in behind him, a tight, coordinated group. When they neared the gates of the city, they slowed to a trot, then to a walk.

Sentries watched them from two short towers that stood by the main gates of the city, which were open. As they approached, one of the guards disappeared momentarily, and then returned to his post. A squat man, not fat, but broad, stepped from behind the left-side tower and stood in the center of the road, facing them. He held a pike, point up, but dug into the dirt at his feet. His head was covered by a thick, leather-lined helmet. His eyes were bright pinpricks of piercing blue.

"Who is it?" he called out, stepping forward a pace. "Who are you, and what do you want?"

Krislan knew they would not have accosted a merchant wagon in this manner, but a group of well-armed soldiers riding up to the gate was an incident worthy of note. He rode forward alone to meet the man, dismounted, dropped the reins in the dirt so his horse would stand and stepped forward, offering a gloved hand to the shorter man.

"My name is Krislan," he said. "I bring important counsel to the elders of your city from my captain, Dace. He and the rest of our force are on the road, escorting a caravan of supplies from Nexus."

"What counsel?" the man asked. He was glaring at Krislan, and he did not take the offered handshake. "We weren't told to expect anyone."

"And yet," Krislan replied, keeping his anger in check, "here we are. The information I have for your elders is important, and I don't have time to waste. There is a force of the dead gathering near Thorns."

"We don't need the help of a pack of mercenaries from Nexus," the short man said, spitting in the dirt to one side. "We did not ask for your help."

"The army that is gathering is large," Krislan said, picking his words carefully. "It hasn't been that long since the mercenaries of Nexus helped you defend against attack."

The short man obviously had more to say, and none of it complimentary about Nexus or her men, but at that moment another man strode down the street. He was taller, wore well-fitted leather armor with a sword dangling from one hip, and wild iron-gray hair fell back over his shoulders in waves.

Krislan looked up as the man approached and the short guard, sensing he was no longer alone, spun quickly. When he saw the newcomer, he snapped a quick salute, more precise than Krislan would have given him credit for, and stepped aside, disappearing back around the left tower.

Krislan stood still, watching the newcomer's approach with interest. When they were about three feet apart, the stranger's eyes creased in a smile and he held out his hand.

"Welcome to Mishaka," he said, gripping Krislan's hand with surprising strength. "I am Ashish Dharni, captain of the city guard. My men signaled me of your approach hours ago—I would have been here to meet you myself, but you have come at a busy time."

"Krislan, Sergeant Krislan of the Bronze Tigers." Krislan replied. "I was just explaining that my men and I have been sent by my captain, Dace, to warn your city of an impending attack."

Dharni's eyes glittered. He held Krislan's hand a second longer, as if gauging his honesty, then released it.

"Come," Dharni said at last. "You have ridden long and hard indeed if you have come from Nexus, and you will be weary from the road. We have been waiting for a supply caravan from Nexus. I assume you are part of the escort? In any case, I will find you quarters and food, and then we will speak of this.

"The road is full of ears and eyes," he added, glancing over his shoulder to see that Krislan was leading his horse through the gates.

Krislan's men fell in behind their sergeant and led their mounts past the sullen guard, who now stood just out of sight behind the near wall of the tower, glaring at them as they passed. None of them paid him any further attention, but he watched until they had entered the city and moved away down the street, turning toward the central square.

"That lot will be trouble," the guard muttered to his companions when the group was out of earshot. "Mark my words. There's not a man in Nexus who gives a damn about us, and if they march all the way out here to say they do, there's more in the bargain than they're letting on."

The others nodded but said nothing; then, with a shrug, turned back to their posts and the watching of the road stretching out beyond the city.

Captain Ashish led them down one of Mishaka's wide, central streets through the shimmering heat and around a corner that led into an alley. At the far end they found the entrance to a large stable.

"This is the rear entrance," he explained. "It is the one that my men use. The front way is clogged with merchants and travelers, and often too busy to accommodate those who are not—known."

Captain Ashish spoke quickly with a tall, thick man who stepped out from within the stable, and moments later several stable hands appeared, taking the reins from the road-weary mercenaries. Krislan moved to grab his bags, but Dharni stopped him with a light touch on one arm.

"Your things will be brought to your quarters," he explained. "You are to be my guests while you are here."

Krislan nodded. The offer sounded sincere, and his attempt to offer the aid of the Bronze Tigers to the city would be off to a poor start if he managed to offend the captain of the city guard in his first few minutes in the city.

Krislan gestured for the others to follow, and they left their horses in the care of the stablemaster and his helpers. Dharni had already turned away and was walking back into the main street, turning the opposite way from which they'd come.

A few doors down and across the street, they found a small tavern with green and gold awnings over the doors and windows in front, deepening the already murky shadows beyond. It was too early in the day for lamps, but with the awnings blocking the midday sun, it took a few moments for Krislan's eyes to adjust to the shadowy interior.

Dharni directed him to a large table.

"Your men can remain here and share food and drink," he said. "You and I should talk, and quickly. Your news is disturbing, and it is likely I will have to leave you and act quickly to increase my efforts to bolster the city's defenses when I have heard all that you have to say."

Krislan nodded. His men fell into the seats wearily, and from a shadowed alcove in the rear of the place two young women appeared, watching the men with shy curiosity.

"Bring food!" Captain Ashish called to them. "Food for hungry men too long on the road—and wine. You may send the bill to the city in my name. Now hurry. Don't keep them waiting while you gawk like school girls."

With a quick titter of laughter, the two disappeared into the shadows once again and Dharni, guiding Krislan with a hand pressed to his back, moved toward a second doorway. Krislan stepped through and found himself in a smaller room. There was a large table in the center of the room, which was bare, but off to the side, by the room's one window, a second, smaller table sat. On it were two goblets and a bottle, and it was to this that Captain Ashish led him.

"I waited for you here," the man smiled. "It is close enough to the gate, but there is shade, and I had this wine. Much more pleasant than standing out on the towers, and the company, even when there is none, is better."

Krislan looked the man over. Somehow Captain Ashish did not strike him as the type of man to be lounging in the shade, drinking wine, when his city was in danger. "I was beginning to wonder if your guard would let us in or not," the sergeant admitted. "I believe he was about to launch into a speech about the evils of Nexus."

"That was Warryn," Dharni laughed. "He takes his position as chief of shift very seriously, and he is a man of very distinct beliefs. He is also overly fond of sharing those beliefs, and it is good that I came when I did. I suspect you would either be standing there still, listening to a harangue about his particular views on the history of Nexus and Mishaka. While there are others who share his concerns, most of the citizens remember your aid in the battle against Thorns. He also has some pretty deep-rooted thoughts on mercenaries."

Krislan's laugh became less tentative. "I'm afraid I'll do little to change Warryn's opinion of Nexus, then," he replied. "My captain, Dace, is a mercenary in the employ of the Council of Entities. We are all mercenaries, but we would follow Dace wherever he led. Nexus pays us well enough, but in a life such as mine, you get few chances to follow a true leader. Right now, he is bringing your caravan, but if there is a battle at hand, I'm sure something can be worked out."

"I look forward to meeting your captain," Dharni smiled. "Now, tell me why you've come ahead of the rest of your force. You can talk while you eat—my time is limited."

Krislan nodded. "There is an army gathered near Thorns," he began. "We lost a scout near there, and Dace sent others out to check on him. They didn't get close enough to find out anything definite, other than that the force that gathers is large. We believe they are led by a deathknight, and we assume that to mean that the Mask of Winters is gathering his forces once again."

"You are certain of this information?" Dharni asked, leaning closer. "I have heard of no traffic in and out of Thorns, and I don't know of any shadowland in the area you describe. Without such a borderland to the Underworld, how could the Mask of Winters gather such a force without the knowledge of my men?."

"I'm sure of the information that I have," Krislan replied, "but it isn't much. For what it's worth, my captain found it important enough to send me ahead."

"What can you offer us?" Dharni asked. "How many attackers do you expect, and how many of your own men to fend them off?"

"I have no definite numbers," Krislan replied. "We believe they number in the thousands, but as I said, our intelligence is scanty at best. Dace sent men back out, and I'm sure he'll have more when they arrive with the caravan. For now, the best I can do is the warning.

"Of our own, we can offer about five hundred men. The escort for the caravan isn't that large, and we didn't plan on a battle when we got here, just a simple escort, here and back to Nexus. Our force is Dace, the captain, one Dragon-Blooded, Risa, and the company of mercenaries."

"That is an odd way to put it," Dharni replied. "Why would you mention your captain as if he were a separate force?"

Krislan hesitated, eyeing Dharni carefully. "He is Exalted," the sergeant replied at last. "Solar Exalted. He is—powerful. I have yet to see just how powerful, I think. He will lead those who come. With Dace at your side, you need not fear the dead."

Captain Ashish stared at him for a moment, stunned.

"A Solar," he said at last. "I knew that they were returning, and that some had revealed themselves, but..."

Krislan waited. He'd seen a variety of reactions to his captain's Exaltation, and few of them had been wholly positive. Most still felt that those who had been touched by the Unconquered Sun were power mad and crazed, as much a danger—or more— to those they were near to as to those who called them enemies.

Then, very suddenly, Dharni was moving. "I must send my scouts out again and see if we can get a better fix on the numbers of this dead army, and on their leaders. I'll send someone to take you and your men to your quarters. Eat, drink, and rest.

I will want to speak again this evening, and by then I may have news."

Krislan rose, and Dharni hesitated, meeting his gaze. Then the man extended his hand and Krislan gripped it tightly.

"It will be good to fight again," Dharni said softly. "I have been cooped up within these walls, listening to the squabbles of elders and the petty complaints of the guards until I'm ready to kill them all myself, or die in the attempt. I think this is turning out to be a good day."

Krislan rose, regarding his companion grimly. He had to wonder at the sudden glint in the man's eye.

Then Dharni turned and was gone. Lifting the bottle of wine and one of the goblets, Krislan made his way into the main room, where the scent of hot food and the cheery voices of his men warmed his heart. It was a good start.

Chapter Nine

It was late evening when Krislan was awakened by a knock at his door. He and his men had been escorted to rooms behind the very establishment that had fed them, and it had taken very little time for the wine and the miles to drive him into deep slumber.

Shaking his head groggily, he rose and opened the door. Captain Ashish stood outside, smiling thinly.

"I am directed to bring you to a meeting of the elders," the man said, stepping inside. "I don't think they trust my judgment. They want to hear the warning directly from you."

Moving to a washstand in the corner of the room, Krislan splashed water over his face and hair, making himself as presentable as possible in a few moments' time. Dharni watched in silence, his expression unreadable.

"I sent scouts out toward Thorns," Dharni said. "We should have initial reports as early as tomorrow. I also sent messages by pigeon too, both to warn them and to ask for intelligence. We could get answers on those sooner."

"Good," Krislan said, feeling slightly refreshed. He ran his fingers back through his hair, then buckled on his sword belt and straightened his clothing as well as possible.

"No need to worry about making an impression," Dharni said. "The scruffier you look, the more you'll fit the role of messenger. I'm afraid they wouldn't credit a mercenary with the intelligence to concoct a story like yours. Those still on the council who remember the battle of Mishaka came away with some odd impressions."

Krislan glanced up sharply, searching the other man's expression for a hint of insult. There was none.

"I know, you see," Dharni continued. "I have served as the captain of their guard for seven years now, having served an equal number as lieutenant in a mercenary band. There are those among them who only see the mercenary in me and still have difficulty believing I can be trusted to tie off my own horse. Thankfully, they do not make up the bulk, or the leading factions, of the city or the council."

Krislan laughed. "It's better that way. They can be continually surprised by your competency, and you can be assured that they will underestimate you. It's a good plan."

"Oh, they know me well enough," Dharni mused. "Sometimes I think they only pretend not to trust me so they can have an excuse to underpay."

The two left the room together and walked down a long, rough hall. They exited through another back door, an apparent habit of Dharni's, and emerged onto a darkened street. Krislan followed Dharni's lead, weaving through the back streets and alleys until they came to another, wider, thoroughfare, across which a large stone building stood. There were lights seeping out under the cracks of the front door, and in the windows, shadows moved about slowly.

Most of the city was silent, and it felt eerie to Krislan. Nexus, with which he was much more familiar of late, was abuzz with activity by night. There would be vendors hawking wares, taverns spilling their trade over into the street, entertainments of every type conceivable and some the sergeant would rather not think of. Here, it was the opposite.

As they'd moved further from the rooms Krislan and his men occupied, they'd left the night-life of the city behind as well. Where they now stood, the building directly ahead was the only sign of life. The buildings here were larger and more ornate. Doorways were surrounded by bas-relief carvings and the colored awnings that he'd noticed in other parts of the city grew more expansive and complex, framing doors and windows with what would likely be colorful splendor by day. By night they created a webwork of filigreed shadows dancing up and down the smooth surfaces of the walls.

There were banks, temples, larger business establishments,

and officious buildings with flagpoles and large shields hung on heavy wooden doors. Dharni explained that this central square was generally alive and bustling by day, but grew quiet at night.

The two of them crossed the street and mounted the stairs, entering through large wooden doors at the top, nearly twice Krislan's height and carved with strange, staring faces near the center—at eye level for a grown man.

Inside, shadows danced over the floors. There were lanterns lit, but the light seeped from deeper within the place, and did not emanate from any readily apparent source. The sound of their footsteps echoed loud and ominous on the stone floor.

"Not a friendly place," Krislan commented.

Dharni grinned, and the dim light caught the bright white of his smile in an eerie parody of mirth. "Not at all. They don't meet often at night, and they tend not to care for the interruption to their daily routines. They are all here, though. I don't want one of them chasing me down tomorrow, or you, for that matter, with a lot of questions we won't have time for."

"Good to see you are taking it seriously," Krislan replied.

"I find that taking everything seriously greatly reduces the opportunities for underestimating a situation. If you can believe it, I'm sometimes thought of as downright taciturn."

Krislan laughed once again. They entered a large hallway lined with doors on either side, and moved to the centermost of those on the right. It was ornately carved and slightly larger than the others that flanked it. The doorway was arched, opening to either side from the center. The right side was propped partway open with a stone wedge and Krislan grabbed the handle, drawing it the rest of the way open. There was a loud creak, and the room beyond grew silent.

Krislan and Dharni stepped into that silence to meet the glare of twenty pairs of eyes. The center of the room was dominated by a large oak table, very thick and mounted on a pedestal base that must have been three feet in circumference. Seated around the far side of the table were a number of people, none smiling or offering greeting of any kind.

Captain Ashish closed the door behind them slowly, and turned to stand at Krislan's side.

"So," a wizened little man spoke up immediately. He couldn't have been more than four feet tall, and his hair stuck out at the sides of his head like flurries of snow. He would have appeared comical if it weren't for the dark glitter in his eye and the ice in his voice. "You have come to help us in our time of need, have you?"

He stared at Krislan in open hostility, and the sergeant began to see what Dharni had meant about the council and mercenaries.

"I have come with a warning," Krislan answered, "and if there is a need, to offer aid."

The answer seemed to be the right one. The small man's icy stare melted a few degrees, and he nodded.

A tall, slender woman to his right, dressed in a white robe tied at the waist, her long dark hair pulled forward in a single braid that hung over her shoulder, spoke up next. "Are we to understand that an army of dead warriors may be marching on our walls as we speak?"

Again, Krislan nodded. "That is the information I was sent to relay," he answered. "My captain bid me to offer any assistance possible, and to advise you that he and a strong force of his men are en route, but they are held back by the speed of the caravan they escort."

"How do we know," the woman asked, staring at him coldly, "that your captain is not trying to swindle us out of money? Why should we believe that Nexus would send us aid unrequested?"

Krislan colored but held his tongue. After a moment he spoke, keeping his voice low. "My captain is not one of the rulers of Nexus," he replied slowly. "He is captain of a mercenary guard based out of Nexus. If money changes hands, it will be by your own choice.

"An army of the dead means only one thing," he continued. "A Deathlord. Someone, we believe it likely to be the Mask of Winters, wants a stronghold closer to the borders of Nexus, or possibly closer to Lookshy.

"We would gain nothing by attacking your city, other than an enemy we can ill-spare."

Krislan looked directly at the woman as he added, "My

captain is an honorable man. *I* am an honorable man. I did not ride all these miles to be insulted."

"No insult is meant," the tiny white-haired man assured him, smiling now. "You will admit, though, that such a story is not the sort one hears every day. Armies of the dead? Deathlords? Then there is the fact that there has been no indication in years that Nexus remembers we exist, except when it comes time to send caravans of merchants to cart off our money. I hope you won't think us foolish for having our doubts."

"No," Krislan replied, lowering his eyes for just a moment. "Of course not. I know how it must sound. But the danger is very real, and closer than I would like, in the interest of mounting a suitable defense. My captain will arrive ahead of the attackers, but by a slim margin, and though he is—formidable—there could be great loss of life and property if we do not act swiftly."

"It is *we*, then, is it?" the woman cut in again. She was smiling, as well, but there was little humor in the expression. It was more a subtle twist of the lips than any show of real emotion, and her eyes betrayed her lack of belief and trust.

"*We*," Krislan replied, "would like to see your caravan delivered safely, at the least. Beyond that…"

Captain Ashish stepped forward.

"I didn't call you all together to grill our visitor, but to plan our strategy of defense. I have already dispatched scouts, so we will know the truth of his words soon enough, at least those pertaining to the attack.

"As all of you well know, spending has dropped off on the defense of the city. The repairs we began in such earnest after the Mask of Winters was turned away from our doors have gone incomplete, and our forces are spread out too thinly for good defense. The city, in other words, is not what it was the last time we withstood a siege, nor are our men as ready. One of the first things we will have to do is draw our forces into a tighter unit.

"I need each of you to spread the word, tonight, for all able-bodied men to group. We need to make repairs to the south wall, and the gates need work, as well. We have supplies enough for about a month of siege, but there are more in the fields and villages surrounding the city. We should be planning and gathering supplies in case the caravan is delayed on the road.

"We need to send men to gather these resources, to bring the women and children safely within the city, and the supplies, and arm the men."

"How many?" A wide ogre of a man called out. "How many do we face?"

Krislan cut in quickly. "We don't know how many, or even if they plan to attack. Our scouts saw thousands, but they didn't witness the entire gathering of the enemy force. It could be much larger. Also, we don't really know who is leading this force. You should prepare for the worst."

"And when is this captain of yours to reach the city?" the woman asked. "This—formidable man?"

Krislan started to answer, but Dharni cut him off. The captain's voice had gone ice cold, but there was a hint of amusement twitching at the corners of his lips.

"He is more than a captain, Padma. He is Exalted. I believe you will find him an adequate addition to our defense."

"We have seen Exalted before," she replied, her voice slightly less confident, but no less haughty. "The Dragon-Blooded have been in and out our gates often enough. In fact, if Thorns had their way, the Dragon-Blooded would have ridden those gates down."

"Solar Exalted," Dharni said softly. "Captain Dace has been touched by the Unconquered Sun."

He turned to take in the entire gathering with his gaze before answering, "I would be thankful for such aid. I would also be a bit more careful about insulting those who offer to help, without full knowledge of whom I was insulting."

The room had fallen silent. Most of those on the council stared at Dharni outright. Only the small, white-haired man seemed unperturbed. He had grown thoughtful.

"Dace, did you say?" he asked. "I knew a Dace. He fought here with the mercenaries at the Battle of Mishaka. Big, powerful man. I probably wouldn't be sitting here if he hadn't swept in out of nowhere.

"I was trying to get back into the city. The siege began..." The little man's eyes grew distant as he remembered. "I know a few tricks of the city, and I thought I could slip back in. I wasn't as clever as I thought. Two of the men of Thorns were ready to remove my head, when he came out of nowhere. He drove one into the wall with his charge, spun, and before that second man could raise his weapon, his own head was flying, courtesy of the swing of a battle axe.

"I remember because I asked his name as I ran, and he called back after me.

"'Dace,' he said. 'Remember me when it comes time to pay, old man,' and he was gone as quickly as he'd appeared, back into the battle. "

"I don't know all of the captain's history," Krislan replied, "but if that mercenary you met was bald, it sounds like him."

The small man nodded and rose. He turned to the others, and they watched him attentively. "All of you go and raise your men. Send messengers to every street and home, send riders to the outlying farms and villages. If we are going to defend this city, we are going to need an army and, from the sounds of things, we have very little time in which to raise it."

The others rose, one or two at first, then in a rush. Most of them did not look convinced, and a couple seemed on the verge of turning back and voicing their concern. In the end they filed toward the doors, whispering among themselves and hurrying their steps. Finally only Krislan, Dharni, and the short man remained.

"I am Byrne," he said, offering Krislan his gnarled hand. The sergeant took it and smiled in return.

"They are not always such a hard group," the little man continued. "They do not want to believe we are in danger. Most of them haven't been on the council long enough to remember a real war, and fewer still have the stomach to fight themselves.

"Add to that the fact your captain is Solar Exalted, and you can see why they hesitate."

Krislan nodded. He knew that most would still fear Dace, if they knew his true nature, but he'd seen no benefit in concealing something that was likely to be revealed if there was a battle. Better to surprise the enemy.

"We have good men, though, and plenty of them. When we

call, they will come," the old man continued.

"It's fine," Krislan replied. "I meant what I said. I'll help in any way possible."

"I'm sure Captain Ashish will know better than I what is the best use for you and your men," Byrne replied. "Go now, and rest. We will meet again in the morning, and I will have a word with the others. You will find them more approachable by the light of day, and after a night's sleep."

Krislan nodded, and the old man turned to leave. Then he turned back.

"If your captain is the Dace I knew," he said softly, "there has never walked a man more worthy of the Solar gift, to my mind. He didn't have to help me that day—and he was never paid for it. If he, and your comrades, aid in the defense of this city, be certain I will make that right."

Then he turned again, and was gone, leaving Krislan and Dharni to stare after him. Dharni was shaking his head in wonder, as if he'd just seen a horse with a man's head walk by and no one else noticed.

As they left the council chamber, the crier sounded midnight. They walked back to the tavern in silence, each lost in thought, as all around them the sound of voices, horses, and the flickers of torchlight filled the night.

Chapter Ten

Dace and Lilith reached the base of the mountains near the range towns of Marukan without incident. They made good time, talking during the few times Lilith took her human form, and studying one another carefully. Lilith was fascinated with the budding strength she saw in Dace. He showed none of Desus's tendency toward madness, but the spark of his Exaltation burned strong and hot. There were things about him that were achingly familiar, and at the same time unique. At times she was certain she caught flashes of Desus in his gestures and his words, but at other times he was as different as sand from the ocean. At those times she wondered if it were Desus he reminded her of, or some other, half-forgotten.

It was difficult for her, after so long in the wild, to travel with a man and, when she needed to, to speak as a woman. It wasn't so much the urge to shift and take off at the call of prey, as the necessity not to that ate at her concentration. She caught herself more than once gazing into the sky, watching the clouds scud across the bright face of the moon and scanning for birds, bats. The wind blew her mane behind her as she trotted easily and comfortably.

It was in those times that Dace, catching her distraction, studied her in turn. He had had only one encounter with a Lunar, and it had not been pleasant. In fact, truth be told, the creature had frightened him nearly to death, and it was difficult to equate that memory with the lithe woman, or the galloping horse, that accompanied him. He also had vague touches of memory from the First Age that nagged at him, but would not come clear. It was both confusing and comforting.

Lilith did not strike him as unusual in the way he'd expected.

She was beautiful, no denying that, and powerful—he knew the power was there. He had seen it when she shifted shapes, and she carried herself with a grace and confidence that could only be gained by age and experience. How much age he could not guess, and found he did not want to know. She fascinated him and, for the first time since Exaltation, he was in the company of one who, while respecting his power, did not fear him. Not as the Bronze Tigers did, or those he served. Even Risa, with whom he was closer than any other, often watched him more carefully than was necessary

He knew a lot of it was his own paranoia, but it did nothing to lessen the impact of traveling with a near equal—or even someone who might prove more than a match for him if it came to pitched battle—for the first time in months. With the first leg of their journey behind them, they were forced to stop and take stock of what would come next. Lilith had studied the mountains and at last had pointed out the peak that was their goal. Dace wasn't sure what landmark she was using to determine this, but she was confident, so he let it pass. He had spent their time on the road looking for signs of the dead army that was gathering and less concerned with her quest, or her secret box. It was true, though, that from the peak he'd have a good view of the area.

The peak was very tall, very steep, and not accessible by horse. They pitched a small camp at the mountain's base and stood, side-by-side, staring up into the clouds that obscured the peaks from sight. It was just after noon, and very warm, but the sunlight cast shadows that obscured the worst of the heat.

"I'll tie my horse here," Dace said, turning away at last. "I can gather enough water to keep him happy, and he can graze in this clearing."

"There will be no need," Lilith replied quietly.

Before Dace could respond, Lilith had moved to his mount and was whispering in its ear softly. As she spoke, he caught her tossing her head, her sleek hair rippling like a mane. He caught flashes of her eyes, the whites too large, and the eyes rolling slightly. The horse was restless at first, but after chuffing and whickering softly, it grew calm.

Dace watched her in silence. For an instant he'd seen the horse within her, and he understood. She was talking with the animal. Maybe she couldn't explain the details of their search to the horse, but she could convey the need to stay still, to graze in this clearing and drink from the nearby stream, but not to stray. Dace felt a pang of jealousy. For all of his power, he knew no other creature so well. He found himself admiring her in other ways, and he turned his gaze aside. This was neither the time, nor the place, for such thoughts.

When Lilith returned to his side, her expression was quizzical. "What is it?" she asked softly. "What are you thinking?"

To avoid a direct answer, Dace asked, "What is it like?"

He turned to meet her gaze before continuing, studying her features in the hope of getting the essence of her answer correct.

"What is it like to—become another living thing? Do you think as yourself, or do you think as the bird, or the horse? Do you feel what they feel, or a mixture of both? What is it like to fly?"

She laughed then, and the sound broke the last thin, brittle layer of ice that still coated their speech.

"That is more than one question. To explain all you have asked might take a lifetime, so I will not try to do it in a day. Still, I can tell you something of it."

With a single fluid motion she was seated on the ground, her legs crossed and her hands clasped lightly. She watched him and waited, and in a few moments Dace settled himself against a tree, not too close to her, but not very far away either. Not far enough to obscure a single subtle secret of her form, or the words she would speak. "I am always Lilith," she said at last.

"At the same time, I see very much through the eyes of whatever creature I inhabit. I have flown with the hawk, the sparrow, the dove, and the owl. I have soared and fluttered, glided and watched with hooded eyes from a treetop as tiny creatures slipped and slid through the grass beneath me, unaware of my sight, or my hunger.

"I have swum the depths of both ocean and lake, as fish and otter, snake and more. I have run with the wolves and hunted with the great cats, and I have cowered, remaining hidden and out of sight in the form of the smaller, more helpless creatures who quiver in their dens and fear for their lives.

"I have been each of these things, lived in different worlds, different minds and different hungers, and I am, throughout it all, Lilith. But some transformations are truer than others. Some call me Owl Woman because that shape is my truest."

Dace's mind reeled. He tried to choose one, to whittle a single creature from her narrative and imagine his mind joined with it. He thought first of the wolf. Strong, cunning, wary. He thought of the eyes of wolves he'd seen watching him on late-night sentry duty. He thought of the slavering jaws and low, rumbling growl of a feeding wolf, standing guard over its prey against all who might plot to take it from him. He thought of rippling muscles, flowing, the ground rushing so much closer beneath him, and it was all too much.

When he glanced up, Lilith had grown silent and was watching him. Her eyes glittered, and—just for a second—he glimpsed the owl, the perception of wisdom and patience, the deeply piercing glare. Then all he saw was the woman smiling at him.

"A little like that, I think," she whispered.

He started to speak, then stopped. There were no words that could have conveyed his thoughts. Dace glanced toward the sky. His vision was filled with treetops, the peak, and its wreath of clouds. He did not try to imagine floating among them, or beating that thin, cold air with the wings of an eagle. He was thinking about the sunrise, and the day to come.

Very suddenly, thoughts of Risa and Krislan and Mishaka flooded through his mind, and he frowned. His place was at the head of his men, guiding them and fighting at their side, yet here he sat, gazing into moonlight with the strangest woman he'd ever met, and dreaming of memories that were only his by an accident of fate. He did not speak, but his thoughts, once again close to the surface, seemed an open book to his companion.

"I need you to show me where you saw the deathknight," he said. "I have to get back with the information as soon as possible."

"We will not be long on the mountain," she said, sliding closer. "If it takes longer than you think it should, we'll go and I'll return on my own."

Dace stiffened at the touch of her fingers, strong and supple, gripping his shoulders. Then he relaxed. It felt good after the long ride, and it felt good to be so close to her. Dace had kept himself aloof and apart from women since his Exaltation, and the notion that she understood him well enough, even after such a short association, to divine his thoughts did not make him uncomfortable.

Dace felt the tickle of memories, and he let them rise to the surface of his mind. They weren't memories from his life with the mercenaries. They were stronger, and older, and he remembered this woman. He didn't know details, but the knowledge— it was knowledge, not just a sensation, he realized—that he had known and trusted Lilith in the past seeped into his consciousness slowly. He wondered if she would know who he had been in the First Age.

"Regardless of what we find," he replied, "I will return to my men. I don't know enough of the force they will face; don't know how they will handle the defense of the city without my guidance. Risa is clever and strong, but they will only follow her lead so far, and I still don't know how those in the city have reacted."

"Only fools refuse help when they are in need," Lilith replied. "They will accept what is offered. Who can say where it will lead when the battle dust has cleared, but your force will be welcomed to the fight, in the end."

He knew she was right, but it did not still impatience he felt to be there—leading and protecting, fighting whatever threat presented itself. It was his rightful place and he knew it, yet she compelled him.

Her fingers worked the tension from his shoulders and he turned, leaning back into her. Old memories of the walls of Mishaka flickered at the periphery of his mind, but she drove them away, pulling him back against her. Her long, silky hair fell over his shoulders, tickled his neck and cheeks, and her fingers moved across his shoulders and down, still seeking knots of tension, but hungrily, drawing the weariness from him and sending tendrils of heat to wind through his senses.

Dace sat up and turned, catching her by her shoulders and drawing her easily into his lap. Lilith snaked to straddle him, arching her back and raising her arms high over her head. Dace ran his palms down her sides, feeling the gentle curve of each rib, the hot tremble of her skin.

They melted together, and, as he slid her moonsilver armor off her—as her body pressed to him, skin to skin, so hot he felt he might burst into flame, she leaned close. She whispered to him as she had whispered to the horse—as he imagined she had whispered to a thousand thousand creatures over the course of her life.

Her words blurred, one to another, sifting in and through the motions of her body as she moved with him. Dace leaned back with a groan, closed his eyes and soared. He felt the earth slip away, heard the voices of birds whispering over his ears and felt the long, pulsing stride of a big cat as she slid over him and down, catching him in a rhythm that was unfamiliar and as smooth as his own breath.

The moon shone down, bright and silver, and his horse grew restive, cropping gently at the grass of the clearing. High in the night sky, birds cried out in defiance. Dace felt it, heard it, breathed it in and joined his voice to hers, synchronizing breath and heartbeat.

Wrapping Lilith tightly in strong arms, Dace gave himself to the sensations and the night. Thoughts of Risa, and Krislan, Mishaka and the dead wavered at the periphery of his mind, but they melted in the sudden, blinding heat of the moment.

The last thing he heard before slipping into deep, untroubled sleep, warmed by the late afternoon sun, her body draped over his like a cloak, protecting him from the world, was her voice.

"This," she whispered, "is what it is like to fly."

The sun had dipped toward the horizon when they untangled themselves, rising slowly and straightening their thoughts and garments. It was a comfortable moment, not as awkward as Dace had feared it might be. Something had passed between them that he could neither define nor deny. As they turned together to stare at the peak above them, it was the first moment he had felt they were doing this thing together, and not as two distinct and separate entities.

"It's a good climb," he said at last. "There is about two hours of daylight left. I think that should be enough."

Lilith followed his gaze and nodded. "We can do it easily in two hours; though coming down in the dark may prove easier for me than for you."

Dace grinned. "I can manage. Shall we?"

He leaped up the first few feet of the mountain to an out-cropping of rock, gripping it easily with his fingertips and flipping up onto the flat surface. Lilith followed, her movements so fluid she appeared to flow up the mountain. Dace watched her for only a moment, and then he turned and began to climb.

They rose up the mountainside in a harmony of motion, gold and white, first one leading the way, then the other. Occasionally Dace would make a particularly dazzling leap, or scale an impossible cliff by sheer strength. Each time, he would look up from the concentration of the effort to find that Lilith had preceded him, slipping into the form of one of a dozen birds and back, watching him from some point higher up the slope than that which he'd reached.

As the sun painted the tops of the hills and lower peaks around them in shades of orange and crimson, they pulled themselves over the final edge and up onto a plateau overlooking the small forest below, a valley to their left and the long road the caravan had followed from Nexus to the right.

The area was not large, maybe fifty feet across. There was a single large stone projection near one edge with a hollowed-out depression at its base. The rest of the ground was relatively flat and unmarked. Dace paced from side to side, glancing down over the side and wishing for a last bit of sunlight in which to memorize the descent. It was a heady sensation, leaning forward slightly at the edge of such a sheer cliff. He closed his eyes, breathed deeply, and meditated for a long moment on the freedom of flight.

Lilith was more restless. She inspected the rocky soil, look-ing for any sign that it had been disturbed by any other before their arrival. She had made it around the perimeter and to the edge of the dish-like depression when Dace turned and joined her.

"Anything?" he asked her, squatting at the far side of the hollow and frowning at it.

She shook her head. "If something is buried here," she replied, "it is buried deep and will require more than a quick glance to uncover. I don't believe Desus would have merely dug a hole and left it—there has to be more."

Dace was still staring at the depression. Something about it did not seem natural. He tried to imagine an act of nature, or the weather, that could hollow out such a space. He could not. There was a definite concave curvature to the spot. Without saying a thing, he turned and sat down inside the small hollow, leaning his back to the stone. It fit the curve of his spine per-fectly, and his head slipped almost out of sight beneath the base of the outgrowth of stone.

He could see Lilith's legs, and he saw them tense. He could not make out her face from where he lay, but he could imagine her eyes flashing in sudden anger as she stared down at him, laid out on the stone for all the world as if he intended to take a nap.

Dace was silent for a moment, then he chuckled. With a quick roll to the side he grabbed her by her legs and, before she could protest or fight him, he slid her down into the stone depression at his side.

He held a finger to her lips to silence her and drew her tightly against his side. Then he glanced up again, and pointed.

The stone just above their eyes was even and unmarked. While the rocky outcrop rising above was rough, the under-side of the base had been carved smooth. There was an inden-tation in the base. Lilith stared at it as Dace slipped to the side and up again. He stood in the basin and reached to the flat sur-face beneath. He inserted his fingers in the slot and felt a latch. With a smile, he started to trip the mechanism and then froze. Something shifted within the stone. He felt it as a tiny vibration, more a sensation that something was wrong than an identifiable sound or motion.

Dace kept his voice very low and made a conscious effort to relax. His words barely whispered across his lips, but she heard. He gave her a hard shove to the side and said, "Move!"

He saw her slide to the opposite side, then he heard the soft flutter of wings and he knew she was up and away. Gritting his teeth, trying to anticipate what would come next, he finished pressing the latch. A section of the stone dropped away and a small rectangular box dropped into his hand, but he barely had time to grasp it. He felt the stone shift beneath him and he leaped backward.

The stone outcrop, which had seemed a little odd to him since he'd seen it, was toppling forward, straight at him. There was no time to think. He had to go off one side or the other, and it was a long way down. If he tried to leap straight back there would be nothing to break his fall and he would crash into the stones below, almost certainly crushing his skull in the process.

Quickly slipping the small box into the waistband of his pants, he leaped to his left. He had stared down that almost sheer cliff, and he knew there were no trees or outcroppings there. Nothing to help. The far side he had not seen at all, and he could not bring himself to chance it. He tucked into a whirling dive, rammed his hands down into the gravel and dirt at the edge of the cliff, gripping, arching his back. Somehow he found his balance and held it as the huge stone crashed into the ground, nearly grazing his chest.

Then, before he could topple over the edge, Dace bunched the huge muscles of his shoulders, flexed his elbows and pushed off. He spun through the air in a quick somersault and landed atop the stone slab that was now balanced precariously on the cliff edge. He stood there for an endless moment, the stone shifting slightly, then more quickly, tipping over the edge nose first. Dace whirled, facing the plateau and braced himself. He began to run lightly up the stone. The friction of his boots on the stone pitched it backward more quickly, and he literally ran up the falling stone toward solid ground. He saw too late that he was not going to make it and lunged forward, trying to leap off the surface of the rapidly falling stone, reaching out toward the cliff's edge desperately.

There was a screeching cry and something hit him from behind, very hard. He felt the flesh of his back tear, felt his balance shift up and forward. He ignored the pain and gripped the stone edge, slipped, then found purchase. He yanked himself up and onto the stone, falling in a heap, his heart hammering wildly.

Then she was there. The fiery pain in his back released, and he realized it had been Lilith. Talons, that was how it felt to be rent by talons, gripped and carried away, though she'd only been able to give him the last, life-saving boost.

She knelt at his side and then slipped down to the ground to lean over him worriedly. He let her hold him for a moment, not ready to test the pain in his back with motion. Finally, he sat up slightly, one hand resting on the stone, and grimaced.

"Some lover you had," he said.

She stared at him, uncertain whether he was joking, serious, or delirious. Then, seeing him grimace and lean over to place his hands on his knees, she stepped closer and gripped him about his back, supporting him.

"How bad is it?" he asked her. She blinked at him again, and then comprehension set in.

"Oh… I didn't mean to…"

She slipped around behind him and he heard her soft gasp. It was answer enough.

"We need to get down and dress the wounds," he said, rising a little shakily. His back hurt, but he'd suffered worse, and wounds not yet seen take longer to register in the conscious mind.

"Can you climb?" she asked.

He turned to her, looked into her eyes, and then laughed. He concentrated, reaching within himself for his center. With a quick step toward the edge of the cliff where they'd climbed up, he spun and dropped out of sight into the shadowy darkness.

He heard her gasp again, then his concentration was on his fingers, slightly weakened by the loss of blood, and the numbness creeping around from his back, and on the toes of his boots, sliding them against stone, pressing in against the earth rather than out, willing himself to climb, dropping more swiftly than was prudent, but each time catching himself, using small outcroppings and gnarled roots to break the speed of his fall. Soon he was on the lower shoulders of the peak and the ground straightened out somewhat. When he could stand, he turned, breathed in the fresh, exhilarating night air, and ran down the mountain.

Lilith was waiting when he reached the clearing and his horse. She sat, legs crossed, in the center of the clearing. She watched him approach, and he saw that she was frowning. Dace smiled.

"You could have killed yourself," she said testily. "You could have waited for me. We could have climbed down together."

"I'm in a hurry," Dace said, shrugging. The motion was a mistake, because it stretched the skin of his back painfully. "I have been away from my men for too long, and I have no more to tell them than I did when we left." She listened to his words, but she also caught the grimace of pain. She arched an eyebrow, but she did not reply.

Dace dropped to the ground beside her with a sigh. "I'm sorry. Once I was moving I just felt it would be best to be down here, one way or the other."

Lilith rose without speaking. She held a small pouch, and from it took a vial that glowed faintly.

"Let me see the wounds," she said, and he did.

Her fingers were not gentle, but they were sure. She rubbed something cool into the cuts, smoothing the torn edges of flesh and packing the ointment into the deep gashes. A few moments later she capped her vial and wrapped a long, silken cloth he believed must have been one of her scarves about his body, forming a makeshift bandage. The ointment had begun to burn, not painfully, but with a deep absorbent tingle that worked through his muscles. Dace relaxed slowly, and when Lilith had returned to sit in front of him, he pulled out the small box and handed it to her.

"Thank you," he said softly.

"For what?" she asked, taking the box reverently from his hand. "I caused the wounds, it was the least I could do."

"For saving my life."

He saw the eager, hungry look she cast upon the box. It sat in the palm of her hand for a long while, the two of them staring at it, as if expecting it to open and reveal its secrets if they concentrated hard enough.

The box was carved on all sides. There was no obvious top or bottom but, as she flipped it in her hand, Dace caught his own caste symbol on one side. Lilith was turning it quickly, so he only caught glimpses of each side. He saw no catch or hasp.

Then, very suddenly, Lilith wrenched her gaze away from it. She rose, placed the box in a pack among the small amount of gear she carried as they traveled. At least he assumed she carried it—it appeared slung across her back when she reverted to her human shape, but vanished when she was an animal.

She returned, holding out her hand. "There will be time to explore it in the morning," she said softly. "You will ride better by day, and you need to rest—to give the medicine time to work. It is very strong."

"I can feel it," Dace replied, rising and moving with her. Without asking, Lilith unwrapped his bedroll. She made a soft nest of it in the shelter of an overhanging tree and drew him down beside her.

Eventually, they slept.

Chapter Eleven

When Dace awoke, he stretched, his mind clearing rapidly. Then he grew very still. Something was not as it should be, but he could not immediately determine what it was. Then the memory of the previous day's activities flooded in, and he slid his arms across his chest, hugging himself and searching his back for the wounds he knew should be there.

He found nothing. His fingers met only smooth skin, and the effort of reaching, which should have dragged the wounds open painfully, brought no discomfort. He glanced around the clearing.

The horse grazed, right where they had left him. Lilith was nowhere to be seen.

He rolled quickly to his feet and paced the perimeter of the small glade. He didn't call out, but he listened. He heard nothing at first, but he continued, walking as softly as he could manage, stopping every few feet. He knew she was probably out getting water or something equally innocent, but it was his nature to lead. With Lilith hidden from his sight, he did not feel in control of this particular moment.

Then there was the small matter of his shoulders, which should be sore and bleeding but felt, if anything, better than they had the previous morning.

And there was the box.

Moving to where Lilith's small bag lay, he studied her gear. He had seen her tuck the box into her bag the night before. At the time it had seemed the natural thing to do, but there were a lot of questions left, and only the box could provide the answers.

He reached for the bag. In that instant there was a great flutter of wings. He spun, face reddening slightly and his eyes blazing at the surprise. Lilith dropped from the trees above, her form shifting as she plummeted toward the earth. Dace stepped back, momentarily confused by the successive images of the owl, the half-owl and the woman. He recovered quickly, but not as quickly as she stepped forward to face him.

She stared for a long moment, and he was certain she must be angry. He had been on the verge of invading her privacy, going through things not his own to question. Then, without warning, she laughed.

It was a bright, brilliant sound, echoing off the hills with the hint of the hawk's cry and the shiver of the owl's voice, the purr of a cat shimmering through each tone. Dace stood, staring at her as though she'd taken leave of her senses.

Dace stepped back, leaned against a tree and watched, waiting for her to regain control. At the last second he reconsidered leaning on the tree, flinching when his shoulders, which should have been wracked with pain, touched the rough bark. Nothing. There was no pain. There wasn't the slightest sensation to indicate he'd been injured.

Then, without warning, he laughed too.

"What have you done to me?" he asked.

"What do you mean?" Her words threatened at each passing breath to slide off into hysterical laughter once again.

"My back," he replied, turning slowly and lifting his tunic.

Lilith stepped forward, running her fingertips lightly over his skin. When he turned back she was nodding slowly and smiling.

"I told you the medicine was strong. You have healed nicely."

Dace reached his arms around her and drew her closer, studying her eyes. Her gaze did not waver.

"Thank you again." he said at last.

Lilith looked as though she might laugh again, but she controlled the urge. "For gouging your back with my talons?" she asked, reaching up to stroke his brow lightly.

"For saving my life," he replied.

"I put your life in danger," she pointed out. "Healing you was the least I could do."

"And I still say thank you," Dace answered gruffly, turning

away. He moved to where they had slept and gathered his things quickly, stowing his bedroll and checking his pack. When everything was to his satisfaction, he turned to her once again.

Lilith still leaned on her mount, watching him.

"Where is the box?" Dace asked. "I think we should find out what we have come so far to locate before we move on."

"I thought there was no *we*," Lilith teased. She reached into her robe and pulled free the small wooden box, which she held out to Dace.

He took it, staring in appreciation. The lighting had been poor the night before and his concentration had been more on his own wounds, and Lilith's eyes. Now that he had a moment to study the thing, he could see that the small box was a thing of great beauty and craftsmanship. He turned it so that his caste sign was up, a perfect match for the orichalcum coin that Lilith had tossed to him the previous day.

He glanced up at Lilith and asked, "Have you opened it?"

"No," she replied. She watched him carefully, as if she were hoping to see some reaction to the box in his hand. Dace glanced at it again.

"I tried," she said softly. "I have come halfway across the world to find this, but now that I have it, it is a very pretty box, but it is locked. Do you find that ironic?"

Dace stared at her for a long moment, and then examined the box more carefully. If it was locked, the mechanism was well hidden. It didn't seem so much a box as it did a rectangle carved from solid wood.

He held the box up and stared at it, trailing his gaze along the intricacies of its design. There was a hair-thin seam along the center of the side. The surface of the thing was smooth. He thought of Lilith's skin, closed his eyes for a second, and then focused again.

"The design is very old," he said. "I recognize some of these designs from First Age carvings I've seen in Nexus."

"I remember when it was new," she replied, a bit sharply. "Or at least," she added, "when it was first hidden."

Dace ignored her. "I recognize some of it. Do you know what the symbols mean?"

"The circle with the rays projecting outward is obviously the sun," she replied immediately. "It has a silver shadow, the moon. In this symbol, there is a bolt of lightning between the two, splitting them apart. I don't know why it's here, but I know I've seen it before—I once had a medallion with that symbol...." Her voice trailed off, and then died away.

Dace turned to her. He caught the emotion in her eyes, and he softened his voice. "Can you read the words?"

Lilith slid down beside him, kneeling in the grass, and took the box almost reverently.

"It is a poem," she said, "or a riddle. Perhaps you can decide."

She read the words again, then handed the box back, met his gaze, and began to speak.

"When Sun Breaks on Stone
The moon also glitters on
The world's dark face."

Lilith fell silent, and Dace dropped his gaze to the ancient box, letting her words echo through his mind and tumble down the lines of the design. He thought of her explanation of the symbol, so quick to her lips—and so complete. He thought of the night just past, the tumbling stone far above, and then again of the words she'd read.

"I wonder if he means the stone above?" he asked. "If so, then part of the puzzle is already solved, and so we should concentrate on the rest of the clue. If not, then..." His brow furrowed, and he grew thoughtful for a moment.

"What?" she asked, catching his tension.

Dace rolled quickly to his feet and turned his back on her, striding straight toward the mountain.

"What?" she asked again, following him, holding out a hand as if to restrain him.

Dace paid no attention. He stepped up to an outcropping of stone on the mountain's side, glanced at the box and flipped it in his hand so that the image of the sun faced outward. With a sudden motion, so swift and hard that nothing could have denied it once he set it in motion, he crashed the box, symbol first, into the stone.

Lilith cried out, leaping too late to grip his arm. She was

strong, and Dace grunted, nearly toppling to the side. She was rippling with essence and Dace spun to face her, stepping back.

"Calm down," he said, turning and holding his hand up to reveal the remnant of the box in his hand. When he opened his fist, bits and pieces of polished wood fell away, splintered. Lilith stared, stepping back, but he followed her, holding his hand steady.

He held a smaller box. This one was of moonsilver that gleamed brightly in the morning sun. It, too, was covered in intricate designs. They were etched into its surface, winding in and around a series of jewels deeply imbedded. It was breathtaking. As Lilith held it, Dace noted a light shimmer along the edges of the metal as she brought it into resonance. Moonsilver was particularly attuned to the Lunars, but Dace had never seen the combination.

Dace leaned closer and handed the box to Lilith without a word. She took it almost reverently, not meeting his eyes. He held on to her fingers for a moment as she grasped the box, and the pressure drew her gaze to his.

"I'm sorry," she said softly. "You could have told me."

Dace said nothing and Lilith turned her attention back to the box, frowning again. She turned it over, then again, staring at the designs and tracing a slender finger across three lines of script thoughtfully.

"More riddles?" Dace asked, glancing over her shoulder. He didn't recognize the language, but it was obvious from her concentration that she did.

The designs surrounding the letters formed a map. Dace recognized several landmarks, including what appeared to be a tiny rendition of the rocky cliff towering above them. The detail was very small and incredibly intricate.

If it was a map, though, the cities didn't look right to him until he thought about it. Then he realized that the map was perfectly accurate. It was time that had shifted. This map had been crafted so many years in the past that the cities and the world Dace knew did not even exist.

Dace remained silent as Lilith studied the box. The set of her brow warned him not to break her concentration.

Finally, she turned back to him and sighed. "I haven't seen anything like this in so long, I believed it could no longer exist," she said. "This is more than just a map. The jewels represent points of power—essence."

Dace examined the map. It was dotted with carefully faceted jade: white, red, green, blue and black. He knew these symbols well, the elemental materials of the Dragon-Blooded. Earth, Fire, Wood, Air, and Water.

"The box," Dace said, "is made of moonsilver."

Lilith almost laughed. "No need to tell me of the moonsilver. This box is afire with her brilliance. It's almost alive when I touch it. One such as I, one older, crafted this box, I would say, though I do not know if they still live. I have no idea where Desus got it."

Her features clouded for a moment, but the wonder of the box in her hand brought her back. She smiled at him.

"Can you read it?" he asked. He knew the answer already, but felt as if she wanted to reveal what she'd found in her own time, and was content to let her do so.

Lilith nodded. "Three lines, just as before. Don't expect it to make sense, though."

Dace held his smile back, waiting.

"All lines point to one;
Circles point to their center;
Lined circles point home."

Dace stared at her, blinking. His smile faded as the words slipped in and teased at his mind. Not as easy as the first verse. In that she was right. But they did make sense, of a sort.

He took the box from her and moved to the large tree they had slept beneath. Sliding down the trunk, he sat at its base and stared at the box, thinking. Lilith slipped in beside him.

"It could be literal," he said at last. "Where was home?"

"It wouldn't be there," Lilith replied at once. "It wasn't a place he was… happy, in the end."

Dace frowned, turned back to the box. "There are lines, and the jade is in the shape of circles. The essence is the 'center' of each element, so that much seems to be literal. The lines, though…" His frown deepened.

"All maps have lines," Lilith joined in. "But which lines?"

Dace nodded, lost in thought. He was remembering something, and the memory stole his concentration. Lilith fell silent, watching him. Then she asked softly, "What is it?"

He remained silent a moment, then spoke. "When I was a child," he said, "I was dragged off by mercenaries. There were a number of other children, and we spent our time following the soldiers, learning, and hoping to survive. It wasn't an easy life, and it was often boring. Sometimes we would create puzzles for one another. Tests of a different sort than those our teachers and parents would pose. One of my friends was very good at it. He used to be able to imagine an image in his head, then, without drawing the outline, or the form, he would create a map of dots on a sheet of parchment. He would space the dots according to a mathematical pattern, and if you discovered the pattern, you could find the direction of the line. The first line and the last line would be joined for you. Then the line followed, one dot to the next, and if you were clever enough to work the problem out in your head, you could figure out which dots should connect next.

"When you were done, the parchment would hold a drawing of something. Maybe a face, maybe a plant, or a dog's face."

"Or a map," Lilith breathed.

Dace nodded. He stared at the spacing of the inlaid jade. There were twenty-five bits of jade in all, placed at what seemed random spots on the map. There did not seem to be any reason behind it. They were scattered like stars.

Lilith was about to turn away, giving up on the puzzle, when Dace smiled again.

"All in all, there are five bits of jade for each element," he said. "But there's a pattern to it. Starting here, there are three red, then one white, two blue, then four black, five greens in a pattern...." Dace leaned closer to the tiny box, concentrating. It was so intricate and delicate that, if he stared at it too long without blinking, the lines blurred and shifted.

Lilith glanced at the box, where Dace was tracing his fingers over the map, then back to his eyes, impatiently.

"What are you talking about?" she asked.

He held up a finger to silence her and counted to himself, sliding the nail of one finger first one way, then the other, concentrating on the box. Very suddenly, he handed her the box and turned, snatching a stick from the ground.

Without a word, he began scratching in the dirt. Lilith held the small box as if it were a serpent, and stared at her companion as though he'd gone mad. She didn't speak. Dace's face was taut with concentration and she didn't want to disturb him, though she'd begun to suspect he was already disturbed, and that she might have made a mistake.

Dace leaned back, sitting on his heels, and grunted with satisfaction. He glanced down at what he'd drawn in the dirt, and she followed his gaze. What she saw was a series of straight lines in an odd, wandering pattern.

"What is it?" she asked.

"The rest of the map," he replied. Working quickly, he sketched in a few details to give her perspective. "The embedded jade on the box forms a mathematical pattern. It's a simple one; one, in fact that I feel I've seen before. We use such ciphers to encode troop movements when forced to send messengers during a battle. If they are captured, the pattern and code may be broken, but they buy time. I've never used this code," he glanced down at the ground, "but I feel as if I know it somehow. I…"

Lilith gasped softly. "You remember," she said, "because you knew Desus. Or, more precisely, the Solar who died at some point in time to be reborn within you—knew Desus. I suspected it might be true, but now…"

"Maybe," Dace said, frowning. "Anyway, this is the message on the outside of the box. It doesn't tell us what is inside the box, but it's a start."

"You mean, we would have to follow the map as it is drawn?" she asked, glancing back at the moonsilver box, perplexed. "But many of the places that were on that map don't even exist. Still others are very dangerous to travel through."

"You're frightened?" Dace teased.

Her eyes flashed. "Not at all," she replied. "It just seems to me that we are missing something. If the first riddle was the key

to opening the outer box, shouldn't this one be the key to opening the second? What difference could our location make to our
ability to do so?"

"It's a thing of power," Dace replied without hesitation. "It is
possible that it will open itself, should we bring it to the proper
source—to whatever lies at the end of that map."

Lilith frowned. She sat cross-legged on the ground and
stared at the box, turning it over and over in her hands. As she
did so, the box began to shine. It wasn't the sunlight reflecting from the moonsilver surface, but something more. The glow
spread to her hands, glittered off her eyes. Her skin, always
alight, seemed translucent, and bold lines of glowing essence—
like tattoos run through with silver fire—stood out on her skin.
Around her, shifting prisms of light and dark purple shadows
brightened and became visible, shifting more and more quickly
until they formed the eerie outline of the great owl. It grew
more distinct with each passing breath.

Dace watched as Lilith stared at the box, a line suddenly
snaked between two of the bits of jade. This was followed by
another, and yet another, following the same simple pattern
that Dace had outlined in the dirt

The lines were combinations of the colors they joined, some
retaining the hue from dot to dot, others blending blue and
green to form yellow. The dots joined more and more quickly,
the lines shooting across the surface of the box toward the final
bit of jade. Black jade. The end of the map.

Something in that pattern clicked in Dace's mind. Something
about it that was familiar, a memory buried very deeply, yet suddenly clear. Without hesitation he lashed out with one booted
foot, catching the box with the tip of one toe and, with a cry,
sent it in a long, shining arc into the sky.

The box continued to glow with the essence Lilith had trans-
ferred to it. She cried out and fell back, supine on the ground,
eyes following the path of the box. Dace fell across her, his back
to the sky, and closed his eyes.

The explosion was deafening. There was a bright, white-hot
flash. Dace couldn't see it with his body covering Lilith, but he
felt her stiffen, felt the expansion of her chest as she screamed,

though it was lost in the sound. When it was over Dace lay still, holding her close and feeling the trembling sobs wracking her frame.

Slowly he rolled to the side. Lilith did not move at first. When she did, she groped about blindly. She turned her face to the sound of Dace moving and her eyes were closed, tears pressing out at the corners and flowing down her cheeks.

"Are you okay?" he asked.

Lilith nodded. "It will pass," she said. "Things are beginning to focus. I..." her words trailed away.

Dace's horse was bucking wildly, tearing at his tether, and Dace rose, moving to soothe the beast. Its eyes were wild, rolled back into its head to leave nothing but wild, white orbs. The stallion was lathered as if after a long run.

As he worked, holding the reins firmly and speaking quietly to them, he froze. A sound like the ringing of a bell or the soft *ping!* of metal off stone had sounded off to his right.

Lilith stumbled to her feet and over to his side.

She took the reins from his hand, muttering softly under her breath, and in seconds she had the horse under control. Dace was already walking toward the sound, watching the perimeter of the clearing carefully. He didn't want to be a stationary target if the sound had come from a weapon of some sort. It was hard to make out just what it had been, with his ears still ringing from the blast.

Lilith had the horse calmed by the time Dace had made a careful circuit of the glade. He wanted to range farther, to scout the area and be certain they were neither observed nor stalked, but Lilith put a hand gently on his shoulder. He turned to her, ready to argue, but she was pointing toward a cleft between two stones near the edge of the clearing.

Dace glanced to where she pointed, and he saw it. Something glinted in the sunlight, gold and gleaming. He turned. Together they walked slowly toward it. Dace moved warily. Twice they had solved riddles, and twice they had come close to death or severe injury, the first time from slab on the peak, and this time from solving the riddle itself. After what had just happened, Dace approached Desus's box warily.

Lilith knelt between the stones and reached for it slowly.

"Be careful," Dace warned. She glanced up at him, then grabbed the golden object from the ground and stood. Nothing exploded, and she didn't cry out in pain. Dace didn't reach to take the object from her hand.

It was small; larger than a coin; round; with waving points jutting out all along its edge. It obviously symbolized the sun—very ornate—but just as obviously the bright tips of each "ray" emanating from the center were razor sharp, honed along their outer edges. As beautiful as it was, it could prove just as deadly. Again, he saw, it was inscribed.

"Another riddle?" he asked.

Lilith glanced at the sun medallion, then back to Dace. She nodded.

He shook his head. "I'm not sure I'm prepared to die for the answer."

Lilith's eyes flashed. "Do you want to hear it, or dream about it for the rest of your life?"

Dace growled low in his throat. "What? What does it say?"

Lilith turned back to the medallion quickly. Dace could not quite tell if a smile had tilted the corners of her lips. He frowned, and then grinned. She had known he would have to see—would have to know. Though it felt like manipulation, a thing that grated on his nerves more easily than any other, still she made him smile.

"Golden rays slice deep;
Remember, brother."

"More personal this time," Dace said thoughtfully. "But who…" Dace's eyes unfocused for a second, and he fell silent. In his mind, he saw a golden disk, flipping through the air. He saw dark, laughing eyes. He heard a voice he didn't recognize, saying…

"What?" Lilith asked, reaching out to touch his shoulder.

Dace shook his head. "Nothing. I thought I remembered… It was nothing."

Lilith didn't look convinced.

"I have to get back to my men," Dace said suddenly. "I need to know where the deathknight has gathered his forces. I have spent too much time here."

"One last thing," she said. "The ruins of his manse are on our way. I will guide you to where you need to go, but I must stop."

"Why?" Dace asked, frowning. "We have solved your riddles."

"Not all of them," she replied. "Why a moonsilver box with a sun star medallion? Who is this 'brother' and what is not to be forgotten? There is more to this story."

"Desus had a daiklave with his Hearthstone set into the hilt. It was a grand thing, though not quite so large as your own. I never thought about it, but, when I last saw him, he carried another—a lesser weapon."

"You didn't notice at the time?" Dace asked, incredulous.

She turned to him, her hair wild about her thin features, her eyes flashing. "We were not close then. Nobody was close to him. I was intent on survival, and Desus seemed bent on the opposite."

"Yet," Dace countered, "he seemed to realize that as well as you. Otherwise," Dace nodded at the medallion, "we would not be standing here, talking about his Hearthstone. He would have carried it to his destruction."

Lilith glanced down again, pretending to study the inscription. Dace saw the tears streaming down her cheeks, and he gave her a moment before reaching out to grip her shoulder gently.

"Where do we go from here?" he asked. "I will be hard pressed to reach my men before they arrive in the city. It is going to be difficult enough to explain my absence thus far."

"They will listen to anything you tell them," Lilith replied softly. "They follow you, not you they. They are mercenaries, but you have their loyalty, and that will count for more than a few days' absence. You may not see it, but it is true. Even the woman, she who serves the Wood Dragon—was more worried about you than about the coming battle."

Dace knew this was likely to be true. Risa was very competent, and she would join Krislan in the city. The two of them, and the force Dace had assembled and sent ahead, should be able to dig in and ready themselves for a stand, but he wanted to be there, giving the orders—where he belonged.

"If I lose a single man because I tarried too long on the road, this time will be tainted." He reached out and lifted her chin, a sudden, unexpected move. He stared at her for a long, silent time, and then added, "I would not like to stain the memory."

Lilith glanced at the medallion. She turned it over and over in her fingers, and then flipped it deftly into the air, catching it by one tip.

"It seems pretty obvious what is meant by the cutting golden rays. The only question is, what do we cut with them, and where?"

Dace grew thoughtful once more. "Was there a place," he asked at last, "that Desus spoke of in particular that you would associate with shadows? Or darkness?"

"I think I was wrong about the manse being where we need to go," she replied. "For Desus, it was not a place of shadows. But there was such a place."

Dace remained silent, so she continued.

"The one thing Desus would never speak of was a time just before his Exaltation. His life was not an easy one. His father was—difficult. I know few details, because if anyone mentioned his past, or his family, he flew into a rage."

"His home was near here?" Dace asked. "I know of no cities closer than Nexus."

"They did not live in a city," she replied. "It is less than a day. I traveled to the place once, just to see it. I stood on the ruins of what had been his home, and I dreamed of him—long years after his death. I think I must have felt some of what he did when he thought of the place, because my heart chilled at the touch of that ground, and though I took the owl form and flew to the top of the highest tree, it reached out with grim fingers to grip my heart."

She turned to him, her eyes fierce with intensity. "I fled. There was nothing there, nothing I could see, or taste, or battle—but I fled. I have never returned."

"Then," Dace said hugging her quickly and turning toward his horse, "let us go and do battle with the past, but quickly. While Desus will not walk again, there are several thousand others who do, and they may be marching on my own men as we waste our time here."

Lilith watched him as he strode to his horse and leaped to the saddle, his movements graceful, arrogant and powerful. Her heart tripped half a beat, and she clutched the sun medallion so tightly it nearly cut her fingers. Then she took off at a run, and within a few steps it was hooves that hit the ground rather than sandaled feet. Dace's horse matched her pace and they galloped, leaving the mountain, the clearing, and the riddles of the past behind.

The sun hung high in the sky, watching dispassionately as they passed in a cloud of rising dust.

Chapter Twelve

The forces raised by the Council of Mishaka were a rag-tag lot. There were a number of veterans of the Battle of Mishaka and a scattering of mercenaries who'd remained behind and settled after that battle at the core, but there were many others whose skills were rusty, at best. They were unorganized, and confused about why they'd been summoned. They milled about in small groups, talked among themselves, some sullen, others curious, and still others outright afraid.

Krislan walked among them slowly. At first dismayed, he came to appreciate that first impressions could be deceiving. There were seasoned warriors in this lot, albeit scattered. While they appeared sullen, their anger was not directed at him. It was directed at whatever had disturbed their lives. It was something they could work with.

The fear was a weapon, as well. Fear of the unknown. The dead warriors weren't unheard of, but neither were they common, and in the numbers expected to attack the city, they were the stuff of nightmares, not reality. Except—now they were.

Every able-bodied man, woman and child in the city had been set to fortifying the walls. Mishaka had withstood attacks in the past, and the walls and perimeters, while in disrepair, were still solid and serviceable. There was little time, but the determined effort Krislan witnessed gave him hope that they would be ready in time.

Still, he'd feel better if Dace would appear. Krislan had taken to winding through the crowds, offering advice, setting his men to help where they could, but circling every hour or so the wall by the gates. He mounted the stairs each time he passed them, standing for longer and longer periods on the ramparts, watching the road that stretched, long and empty, toward Nexus. Though he strained his sight to its limits, he saw no sign of the approaching force.

There was still time. If the original report had been correct, the enemy forces were gathered far too close to the city for comfort. If the deathknight turned his force toward Mishaka and came at a hard march, then Dace and the caravan's arrival would be pushing it. If the attackers reached Mishaka before Dace and his mercenaries arrived to bolster the smaller force within the city walls, it could be bad.

About noon, Krislan saw Captain Ashish approaching. The man looked tired, but his eyes shone, and he was smiling broadly.

"Things are progressing nicely," Dharni observed, turning to scan the streets and what they could see of the wall. "We should finalize repairs on the walls in time to close the gates tightly by sunset. That will give us time to feed the men and give them some rest. I've stationed scouts at vantage points around the city and far enough out to do us some good—an early warning system. We will know when they are on the way, and we will shut this city up as tight as an ale barrel."

Krislan nodded. He turned again, glancing toward the road, and Dharni followed his gaze.

"Your captain will come," Dharni said grimly.

"It's just that I'm nervous before a battle," Krislan replied. "I'll feel better when we have the full force here, gathered as one. It will be much more difficult if the city is already under siege when they arrive."

"I must admit," Dharni laughed, "I'll feel better when your captain arrives myself. I've heard stories of Solars in battle, but have never witnessed it. I saw a Lunar Exalt once—such power. It is an experience I look forward to."

The two grew silent for a moment; then that silence was broken by loud voices. Two of Dharni's men approached with a third man, a dark, swarthy man with a broad, flat face and eyes too close set in his face held between them. The man protested and struggled, but the others held him tightly.

"What is it?" Dharni asked crisply.

"I'm not sure, sir," one of the two guards replied. He inclined his head at their prisoner and went on. "We found this one staggering around near the tavern. He wasn't kicking in to help with the repairs to the walls, and when we questioned him, he started in about dead armies and deathknights and… well, we just thought you might want to talk to him, sir."

Dharni stepped forward and examined the man they held. Krislan watched from a few paces back. It was obvious from the set of the captain's jaw and the furrows in his forehead that he had no idea who the captive might be.

"Where have you come in from?" Dharni asked at last. "I haven't seen you around the city."

The man spat, tugging free of the two who still held his arms, and straightening his tunic. He glared at Dharni for a moment, but when the captain's gaze didn't waver, the man lowered his own.

"I came in yesterday. We were called to help repair damage to the walls. I heard it in the tavern," he said. The man lifted his head, staring at Dharni in defiance, as if daring him to deny the truth in the words. "I heard that they had us by surprise already, so there was no reason to kill ourselves in preparations for an attack. Heard they was led by a deathknight."

"Heard from whom?" Dharni asked coldly. "You said it was at the tavern: when?"

"Last night it was," the man replied. "In the full dark. They would have closed, but for the word that was spreading, to gather together here, inside the walls, and to bring weapons. Every door was open. I had all my belongings in a single sack— all but my axe. I stopped for a glass of wine and to find out what I could."

"Which tavern?" Dharni asked.

"The Crescent, sir," the man replied.

"Whom did you talk to? Who told you these things?"

"They didn't so much tell them *to* me, sir," the man replied, "as near me. I was standing by myself, knowing no one inside the city to speak to. They talked between themselves, and none too quietly. It's not just me that has heard it. I don't know who they were. They were gone before I finished my wine, and I was already discussing what they'd said with some others."

Dharni scowled at the man. If these rumors were wide-spread, it was going to cause a panic.

"If there was such talk in the tavern," Dharni said, his voice low, but carrying powerfully, "it was meant to make weak-minded, ignorant fools afraid of their own shadows, and to undermine the defense of the city. What is your name?"

"Himangshu," the man muttered.

"Himangshu," Dharni repeated. "Didn't it occur to you, Himangshu, to question the men you heard, or to learn more about what they were saying? Did it never cross your feeble mind to point them out to one of the guards, or even to the owner of the tavern, and have them, and their story, checked out?"

The man hung his head.

"Rumors like these," Dharni said, "could undermine every effort I have made in the city's defense. If we get word that the dead are marching on the city, we will let you know."

The man, Himangshu, was trembling now. "I'm only a farmer, sir," he said. "I didn't think to act. What can I do?"

"Go and help with the walls," Dharni replied. "If you hear more rumors of the sort you have mentioned, report them—and tell others you believe them to be lies."

Himangshu nodded, nearly scraping the ground with a nervous bow. Every muscle in the man's body twitched with the desire to be away and out of this trouble.

"Go," Dharni spat.

The man was gone, and the captain turned to Krislan. "This could be bad."

"Do you credit the story?" Krislan asked.

"I don't know," Dharni replied.

Krislan knew the truth of Dharni's words. If a rumor spread that the dead army was actually marching on the city, it would be like a poison. Worse yet was the possibility that someone had been planted inside the city to spread the story.

"I'll send some of my men to do an extra patrol of the walls and the city itself," Krislan said. "We aren't known, as your men are, and there's the possibility someone will talk who shouldn't.

Also, if we find any weakness you haven't already accounted for, they can report that as well. If there is a way into the city large enough to accommodate an army, it shouldn't be impossible to find. If nothing else, they can help calm those who have already heard the rumor."

Dharni nodded. "If it is a rumor," he said. "Most of my own men are on the walls, or gathering the farmers and volunteers into some semblance of an army. I'll assign someone to show you around—it will make things move more quickly. It is possible," he added, "that the enemy sent scouts in ahead to spread the rumors. If so, we'll find them in short order."

Krislan nodded. It already felt better to be doing *something* actively, rather than standing about and waiting for Dace to ride over the horizon. He strode down the street with new purpose toward the quarters where he and his men had been housed. Most of them would be out helping with the training, but he knew he would find at least a few of them awaiting his orders.

When he reached the tavern, and the rooms beyond, he found one of his men, a young soldier named Sandryn, leaning against the frame of the doorway. As Krislan approached, the boy pressed off from the wall, straightening himself as if he'd been caught at something. Krislan grinned.

"At ease, Sandryn," he said gruffly. "I've something for you and a couple of the others to look into. Find two to join you and meet me inside. We should be joined soon by one of Captain Ashish's men."

Sandryn nodded, turning and hurrying off, relieved to not be in trouble.

Krislan entered the tavern and pulled a chair to one of the tables. He gestured to the dark haired woman who stepped from the shadows to bring wine, and held up the fingers of one hand to indicate five glasses. She nodded and returned to the kitchen.

Krislan leaned back in his chair, lost in thought. He almost didn't hear the men approach, and when he glanced around, he found that Sandryn had returned with two others.

Krislan turned to the door of the tavern just in time to see a grizzled, surly veteran guard slip through. Moments later, they were all seated at the table and Krislan outlined the rumor, what it could mean if it were true, and set them their task. Once past his initial ire at being assigned to the outsiders, the guard, Deepak, proved a good source of local intelligence.

A hurried inventory of the grounds within the city walls helped to rule out large sectors, narrowing the field of their search.

"They are dead, yes?" Deepak asked at last.

Krislan nodded.

"Then it makes sense to watch more than just the walls and gates. I have dealt with enemies like these before, and they don't always travel as you and I. There are darker ways and other entrances they might use, if such a foul place exists in the city. It would be a place of death and decay. I don't think we'll find it near the walls."

Krislan thought this over quickly. He had walked the perimeter twice since waking. Nothing in those two circuits had struck him as out of place, certainly nothing that resembled an entrance.

"It could be well concealed," Krislan replied. "I believe you're right, though. I have walked the walls, and if there is anything there to hide an entrance it is purely magical, because there is no structure or natural formation that would lend itself to the glamour."

"There is one who might help," Deepak muttered.

Krislan turned to him. "Who, and in what way?" he asked.

Deepak grew silent and took a gulp of his wine. He turned away, remained silent, took another drink. Then, making his decision at last, he broke the silence.

"There is one among us with the power to seek out the hidden," he said, his voice low. He stared into his wine goblet, not raising his eyes, and his voice was so low he fairly whispered. "He is generally not well thought of in the city; shunned, if you know what I mean. He is descended somehow from an Elemental. He is god-blooded, they say. He finds things."

"Finds things?" Krislan prompted.

"Aye," Deepak snapped his gaze up to meet the sergeant's own. "Things others can't see. He mumbles about them at night, walks the streets and tries to talk to folks just minding their own business. He sits in the square, some days, and tells things from people's lives as they walk past him, hoping they'll stop with a few coins to shut him up."

"He's making it up?" Krislan suggested.

"No sir," Deepak shook his head, and his gaze dropped to his drink once more. "That he isn't. I've walked past him more than once, and the things he sees are truth. If you ask around," the man continued, "you'll hear differently. You'll hear he is filled with lies, that he is mischievous and only seeking the money, but I know the truth. Those you hear this from?" Deepak glanced up again. "They are the ones with the most to hide."

Krislan nodded. "How would we find this man?" he asked.

"That is never the problem," Deepak replied. "M'chwallya has his own spot in one of the gardens of the square. He is always there, or home. He turns up when you forget about him, always saying the thing you'd least like to hear."

"But he'll help us, this M'chwallya?" Krislan asked.

Deepak nodded. "I believe he will. I don't believe he can help but speak as he does. He says what he sees, if you take my meaning. It's not meant to attack, but to enlighten. It's just that there aren't so many folk in Mishaka who seek enlightenment, and fewer still that care to have others enlightened on the subject of their own secrets. M'chwallya will help if we ask."

Krislan nodded and rose. "Good. I will go with you to find him. The rest of you," he turned to Sandryn, "will begin a sweep of the city. Don't concentrate on the walls. As Deepak and I have stated, there is nothing obvious to be found there. Sweep in diagonals across the city, two-man teams. Report to one another, and to myself, if you believe you've found anything suspicious. And as you go, keep your eyes and ears open for those spreading the rumor. If there is anything to find, those are the guides most likely to lead us to it."

They dispersed quickly. Krislan stood a moment, waiting for all but Deepak to clear out, and then he lifted his goblet and drained it in a single gulp. The day was progressing too quickly now that there were tasks to fill the hours.

"Lead me to this M'chwallya," he said quickly. "Time is the

one thing we are running out of very quickly."

He followed Deepak out the door of the tavern and into the streets. They turned toward the center of the city and almost immediately took a second turn, skirting the main thoroughfares and winding their way through a series of alleys. The stench was horrible. They passed behind taverns and eateries, between a stable and a hostelry, where Krislan saw that a variety of animals were being housed and handled, livestock that had been run in from the outskirts of the city in case of a siege. He saw uniformed livery hands side by side with sackcloth-garbed farmers.

Deepak took no notice of any of it. They stepped through a last alley, dodging barrels and bins filled with refuse, and stepped into a market square. Krislan had never seen the place, though he'd walked what seemed miles up and down the twisting streets of the city. It was a busy square, teeming with carts, wagons, tents and more permanent shops. Citizens roamed the aisles hurriedly, taking in provisions—which Krislan was certain would be had only at exorbitant prices, with war imminent—and those citizens were met and greeted, cajoled and cheated by an indescribable variety of merchants and thieves.

Deepak cut a wide swath through the crowd. His guard's uniform set merchants on sudden notice and citizens scurrying out of his path, but again he paid no notice. Once set on a task the man proved of a single mind and purpose. It took no time at all to reach the very center of the place, and there, seated on a stone slab in a small garden beside the road, sat the most enormous black-skinned man that Krislan had ever seen. The man smiled up at them through slitted eyes, appearing half asleep. He caught Krislan's gaze, and the smile widened.

"Worr'd hedon cum." The big man mumbled.

Krislan stared. "What...?"

Deepak gripped Krislan's arm and shook his head, indicating Krislan shouldn't continue.

"He said, 'worried he don't come'," Deepak intoned. "He's reading you. Nothing you can do to stop him, and if we want him to help, we'll have to listen."

Krislan turned to the guard, frowning. "But how did you understand him?"

"He mumbles," Deepak shrugged. "I've been listening to him mumble all my life. I've probably paid him the equivalent of a week's pay this year to stop. If you don't want him to go on, best thing to do is to drop some coins in that bag by his feet."

Krislan's frown deepened. "We don't have time for this," he said. "If he can help us, then we need to get on with it. If not, we are wasting valuable time."

"I'm 'most gwyn," M'chwallya mumbled. "D'f knights. D'd folk."

Krislan reached into the pocket of his tunic and pulled out two small coins, flinging them into the bag. M'chwallya stared at him, then at the bag. He fell silent.

"Maybe you shouldn't have paid so quickly," Deepak grinned. "I think he was talking about deathknights and the dead."

Before Krislan could react, Deepak had leaned in close. Next to the dark man's bulk, he seemed squat, like some great, armed toad. The guard whispered in the giant's ear, and very slowly, the big man reacted. He nodded his head, up, and back, his grin widening yet again. He glanced up and caught Krislan's gaze, and Krislan tumbled in. The world shifted, and suddenly he was gazing at the city's walls. He knew they were Mishaka's walls, because he'd seen them several times during the day and from many angles, having walked the perimeter. Still, the angle was strange to him. He was gazing out through a forest of raised stones and carved monuments. He shook his head, trying to clear the vision, but it would not pass.

He turned. To his left; uniform rows of graves stretched away. There were small groves of trees, shrubs, and flowers. Everything was in order—exactly as it should be. He turned to his right, and gasped a short breath. There was a trail of dead plants and wisping dust leading straight through the heart of the cemetery. It led beside rows of graves that fought vainly against its encroachment, tendrils of vines having leaked onto the trail as if seeking its center, only to die and wither, no green beyond a black line of death that ran on the two sides of the trail and ended at a wrought-iron gate.

Darkly fascinated, cold sweat drenching his form, Krislan turned down that trail and walked toward the gate. It was rusted, and he could see that the gate itself hung askew. The iron was giving way to the weather, and none had painted it in a very long time. Eventually it would crumble to dust, leaving the mausoleum open to whatever it was supposed to have protected it from.

Krislan drew nearer. He gripped the iron of the fence, and cried out sharply. It was ice-cold to the touch. He released the bars, but in those few seconds he held them his palms had burned with deep, black lines. He stared at the squat stone building, concentrated on the stone where the occupant's name had been carved. It was no use. The name had been chipped away, defaced and chiseled to dust. The dead husks of vines clung to the stone, reaching brittle tendrils out to cover the damage, but there was nothing left to hide. Whoever had died and been buried in the tomb was nameless.

A sudden wind whistled through the graves, riffling through the leaves on the trees and whirling the dust at his feet into a dust-devil of choking particles. Krislan took a step back, raising a hand to protect his eyes. His skin stung with the sudden onslaught of grit, and he staggered back a few steps, moving to one side as he did so until he stumbled out of the black, deadened strip of ground he'd been standing on.

He heard the clear, bright sound of metal clinking against ceramic.

He felt hands on his shoulders, shaking him hard.

He heard voices, several voices, one of them loud and deep. That voice, that one, lone voice, boomed like thunder. Krislan's eyes snapped open, and he stared into the massive black man's face. M'chwallya grinned back at him with white, empty eyes, laughing in a deep, resonant voice and rocking up and back, up and back, a dark metronome against the white stone wall at his back.

Krislan's mind cleared a second after his eyes, and he made out Deepak's voice. It was the guard who held him by the shoulder. Pulling away roughly, Krislan turned.

"What happened?" Deepak asked, concerned.

"I don't know," Krislan replied, "but I think I know how the dead intend to invade the city. Where is the graveyard?"

Deepak stared at him for a moment, and then turned, pointing down an alley to their left.

"How far?" Krislan asked.

"Four, maybe five blocks to the outer edge," Deepak replied.

"There is little time," Krislan said. "Take me there, but first send someone back to Captain Ashish. Tell him that they will enter through a grave, a dark grave with a trail of dead plants leading up to its gate. Tell him we have to find a way to prevent them from using that shadowland to enter from the Underworld."

Krislan turned toward the graveyard, and then turned back. "One more thing," he said. "Tell him to make it fast."

Deepak turned, grabbed a young man who was trying unsuccessfully to make his way past the hulking form of M'chwallya on the side of the road without having his secrets cried to the world. Deepak spoke quickly and only had to shake the boy once before, wide-eyed, the lad turned and sped back the way they'd come.

"Come," Deepak said, his lips spread in a grim smile, "let's go and see if we can slam the door on someone already dead."

Krislan, equally grim, fell in at the shorter man's side and followed. Behind them M'chwallya was mumbling again, calling out to another unfortunate enough to walk too near. Krislan's vision wavered, just for a second, and he broke into a trot.

Someone was crying out something from the walls in the distance, but he couldn't make out the words. With a shrug, he followed Deepak into the shadows.

Chapter Thirteen

When Risa and the main body of the caravan and its escort set out the morning after the encounter with the bone lion, Daedalus rode with them. Risa kept him near the front, where she could keep an eye on him. His weapons had been taken, and he had been given a new mount.

The man was an enigma. Risa knew that she could take him out. He was Dragon-Blooded but, without his weapons, he could not stand against her. Certainly not when some of her troops were Dragon-Touched as well. Although not true Exalts, they were formidable in their own way.

Daedalus, for his own part, seemed content to ride in brooding silence. He glanced often to the west of Mishaka, to where the enemy gathered. His face might have been chiseled from stone for all the emotion it revealed. His eyes were deep and dark, and Risa kept sliding her gaze to them, hoping to catch him in an open moment, or to see some sign of where the man's thoughts might lie.

At the same time she was doing some road scanning of her own. Dace should have joined them the night before, and there was still no sign of him. Daedalus and his wild story validated the small intelligence they'd gathered, and gave them at least a partial answer, as well, to the question of Tarsus's disappearance. Risa had never seen anything like the skeletal lion, but she'd been in and out of enough cities and battles to remember tidbits from old campfire stories. None of the stories had lived up to the reality

And yet, in a clearing in a forest grove miles behind them, the dust of that creature still smoldered, buried with the coals from the fires. Its target rode almost at Risa's side, and none of her questions had an adequate answer. She ground her teeth.

It was not like Dace to shirk his responsibility. They were riding into a situation that was, on the surface, not beyond their ability to handle, and beneath the surface as rotten as fruit left too long in the sun. Nothing seemed 'right'. The numbers of dead warriors were uncertain. Krislan was in the city, waiting for her, but if he'd found anything new he hadn't sent word back yet, so she had to assume he knew no more than she.

One thing was certain: There was something or someone powerful and twisted enough to send the bone lion in search of one of his own men. And, if Daedalus himself were to be believed, a second force would attack from within the city walls—one they would be hard-pressed to defend against, even if they arrived in time.

Dace's absence was inexcusable. In a situation with so much potential for danger, he should be leading them. He should be there to lend the courage of his strength to his men, and to direct things if and when if they got out of hand. If Dace waited much longer she would have to ride into the city without him, after Krislan had reported that he would come and that he was in charge. She would have to deal with both the disappointment of his absence, and the inevitable problems of asserting herself as his second-in-command while they waited for his little adventure to draw to a close.

She decided that she couldn't wait for Dace. With a quick shake of her reins, she brought herself alongside Daedalus and matched strides.

"I think it's about time you told me what we're up against," she said.

Daedalus turned to her, his eyes never losing the deep, calm expression they'd taken on since the defeat of the bone lion. He regarded her in silence for a few moments, and then turned back to the road ahead.

"There are thousands," he said at last. "The reports you have from your scouts aren't far off, if the situation is still what it was when I—departed."

"Then we will have to be ready for them," Risa spat, still angry at Dace and at the situation. "There will be no dead straddling the walls of Mishaka if I can help it. And Dace should be there before we are, or join us on the road."

"So you have said," Daedalus replied. "You may be right. I have never met your captain. I have met the Drinker of Seeping Poison, however. I have met him, served under his command, killed for him, scouted the city of Mishaka... and been hunted like an animal for his sake. You may win the day, but do not believe you will walk in and out as if to a summer festival. The darkness you feel all around you—the drums you hear late in the night, pounding so hard and deep the earth shakes? That is war. Make no mistake: It will be a war."

"You believe they have another way into the city, as well?" she asked.

Daedalus nodded. "They will come through the Underworld and exit through a tomb in the city. It will be a hand-picked force of nemissaries, and possibly the Drinker of Seeping Poison himself," he said, keeping his voice low and divorcing it from emotion. "The way is shorter than that taken by the main force. It is dangerous, but what is danger to those already dead?"

Risa frowned. She had considered holding back slightly, to make her way to the city at a speed that would give Dace every opportunity to reach them before they entered the walls. The thought of the dead warriors had spurred her on, and now even the progress they'd made grated at her nerves. Waiting for Dace would be foolish, and she knew it.

"Mara! Vok!" Risa barked the two names as commands, and the two broke from the command and rode at her side in the space of a breath.

"You had better be telling me the truth," she said, turning back to Daedalus. "If Dace doesn't arrive before I reach that city, they are going to have to trust me. I would not want to introduce myself by telling tall tales about unclean graves."

"Believe as you will," Daedalus shrugged. "I have no reason to lie to you, but in your place I wouldn't believe me either. If you hadn't come along, I would as likely as not be dust, or still running for my life. I owe nothing to my former master—nothing pleasant, in any case. Let's hope he doesn't decide to lead the army himself."

Risa turned back to the road so he wouldn't catch the concern in her eyes. She knew that she was no match for a deathknight in one-on-one combat. Not even with the entire caravan escort at her back. If that was what they faced, then it was going to be one hell of a fight if Dace didn't come in time.

"Why do they call him the Drinker of Seeping Poison?" she asked, not turning to her companion.

He glanced at her, as if to see if she were serious. "He is a necromancer," Daedalus replied. "He has many curses at his disposal, and is very fond of various poisons. He tests them on himself."

Risa closed her eyes for a long moment, then kicked her mount to a gallop, crying out to those riding beside the caravan to move more swiftly. They were actually making good progress for such a large, ponderous force but, with thoughts of the deathknight filling her mind, they seemed to crawl.

The road rolled beneath them, and they flew toward the walls of Mishaka as though a horde of demons rode at their tail.

Chapter Fourteen

Krislan sat at a table in the small tavern, surrounded by three of his own men, Deepak, and Captain Ashish. The sun had dipped beneath the city walls and candles flickered in all corners of the room, their flames battling with the darkness. A soft pool of light leaked over the features of all those present from the brighter flame of a lamp that had been placed in the center of the table.

"So, now we have a good idea of the city's defenses and possible weaknesses," Dharni said, watching Krislan carefully. "There are questions remaining to be answered, and time grows short.

"First," he held up his index finger, still watching Krislan, "there is the question of this grave and the danger it presents. How do we defend against an enemy who arrives from the Underworld through a tomb, and that tomb within the confines of our own walls? There was a Dragon-Blood here a month ago who hailed from Lookshy. I believe he knew the proper wards, but I have no experience or craft for a task like this."

"The doorway is small." Deepak spoke up, meeting his captain's eyes. "They cannot exit as one. It may be possible to defend that gate, depending on who or what comes through. They won't be able to bring a large force through such a small opening."

Captain Ashish nodded.

"Then," he continued, "there is the matter of the deathknight. My scouts have returned and we have more information, though it's incomplete. He is called the Drinker of Seeping Poison. We must assume he has been sent to gather his army by the Mask of Winters, though this raises other questions we have little time to consider. Will he lead the army, or will he send them to our gates and remain behind, content to wait and to watch? *Can* he lead them through the Underworld without crossing the shadowland himself?"

No one spoke, so he continued to his third question, raising a third finger as he did so, and turning full on to face Krislan, who met his gaze levelly.

"The third question that faces us," he said, "is the location of your captain. You have offered us your support, and for that we are grateful. You have forces arriving at our gates soon with your lieutenant, Risa, who is Dragon-Blooded, and will be a great asset. This is very good news.

"But," he continued, "my scouts also bring word of one who matches your captain's description. He was seen in the company of one other far from the road or the caravan. I have to assume he has chosen to scout the deathknight himself, but we don't know whether he has returned to the caravan or if he intends to meet them here. We have to form some defense against this deathknight that we can depend on if the promised support doesn't arrive in time.

"The Council will want that answer," he said with finality. "Our strategy might have been very different had we not counted on that support. We might have taken our women and children to the mountains, evacuated the city and planned from safety. Now we are faced with an impossible battle, and the answers to the impossible will be expected of you."

Krislan had remained silent through this tirade, not wanting Dharni to interrupt once he started to speak. His anger had grown throughout the speech, his face reddening and his fists clenched. More than once he'd had to force his hand from the pommel of his sword, sweat breaking out on his brow at the effort. He had been insulted, albeit indirectly, and called a liar. His captain had been insulted by one who did not know him, and had no right to speak as he did. Topping this off was the fact that, to all appearances, both he and Dace were guilty on all counts. There was no answer to provide on the question of Dace's absence, because he knew nothing about it. All they had was the word of scouts he'd not spoken with. Risa would know something more, but would it be enough?

For the moment there was nothing to be done on the question of Dace, so Krislan forced his mind to the matter of the grave.

"My men and I," he stated slowly, controlling his voice with an effort, "will guard the shadowland in the graveyard. When Dace and Risa arrive, or just Risa, as the case may be, if she and I can find a way, we will ward that tomb. A thing that can be opened can be closed, and even a deathknight cannot cover the distance from where that army gathered to here in time to turn the day if his access is denied."

Krislan rose, turning to all in the room with eyes darkened and brow furrowed. "You did not even know that there would *be* an attack until we warned you at our arrival and you sent out your scouts," he continued. "There is no way you could have learned of the attack in time to withdraw safely from the city. Such a party could not travel as swiftly as an untiring army of the dead, and they would win the city uncontested.

"We may not be the support you were counting on," he turned to Dharni and his voice grew colder, "but we are all the help you have, at this point, and it is offered freely.

"I'll end this by saying," Krislan drew himself up and bunched his shoulders, his anger spilling through the widening cracks in what remained of his calm, "that if my captain is not leading that caravan, there is a reason. It will be a good reason, and it will not be for me, or any of you, to question. It is a cowardly thing, I think, to hinge the defense of your home on the promise that some all-powerful warrior will come and defeat your enemies. Better to stand and fight for what is your own. Better to lose on those terms, than to whine about what might have been."

He was shaking, and he stopped before he could say anything truly insulting. Dharni was regarding him with a calm, even stare, not smiling, but not angry, either.

"Impressive speech, sergeant."

The voice came from the doorway behind them, and Krislan spun, startled. In the doorway stood the councilwoman named Padma. She studied him with emotionless, hooded eyes. He hadn't even noticed her entrance.

The white of her robe stood out in the elongated shadows of the room, and her eyes flashed with borrowed candlelight. A wide leather belt had replaced the simple one that had cinched the robes in the council chambers. From this hung a long slender blade on one side, and on the other a dagger with an ornate, jeweled hilt. It should have looked ornamental and foolish, but for some reason, the way it rode her hip and matched its jewels against the glitter of her eyes gave it the sinister aspect of an insect's stinger, poisonous and powerful.

"I will join you at the grave site," she said. "I know somewhat of desecration, and of consecration. There are things we can do, spells we can try, that might make that shadowland impassable. At the very least," she actually smiled for the first time since Krislan had first seen her, "I will be defending my home and not whining about the lack of heroic Exalted heroes who may or may not ever come to my aid."

Captain Ashish stepped forward.

"It will be very dangerous, lady," he said softly. "I would be remiss in my duty if I did not warn against such participation on your part."

"And I would be remiss in my leadership if I were to sit back and wait to be devoured by the warriors of the dead, or made the slave of a deathknight," Padma replied. "My mind is set on this, captain. You will find I'm no stranger to battle."

They all regarded her and then, slowly, Krislan stepped forward and took her hand, meeting her gaze firmly. "I would be honored to fight at your side, lady," he said. "My own lieutenant, Risa, is one of the most formidable warriors I have witnessed in battle, and she has taught me two things about women, and war. The first is that one can never trust the first impression of any of his five senses when judging any warrior."

"What is the second?" Padma asked, her eyes twinkling brightly.

"That it would be easier to chip a mountain to gravel with a dagger than to change a woman's mind, and it's best just to get on with the matter at hand and let fate speak for its own."

"She must be quite a woman," Padma replied. "I won't comment on your outlook on women at present, Sergeant. I think there is room for improvement."

"Risa is quite a warrior," Krislan corrected, ignoring the second part of Padma's reply. "She is Dragon-Blooded, drawing her power from wood. She is…"

"Here," another voice spoke up from just outside the doorway.

Padma spun, and Krislan stepped forward again, saluting as Risa stepped through the door. A tall, dark Dragon-Blooded warrior that Krislan had never seen, and a small contingent of Dharni's guards accompanied her.

Suddenly, the small tavern was very full. The two Dragon-Blooded overpowered the moment. Their presence was palpable with their confidence and strength, but something was odd. The man was unarmed and Risa, though focused on those gathered, and on Krislan in particular, kept glancing at him. Her expression was anything but friendly.

"So," Dharni spoke first, "you are the Lieutenant Risa we've heard so much about. I have to say that, barring your captain's arrival, your presence has inspired more confidence than any of our own defenses."

Risa smiled thinly. She was used to compliments, and she detected the underlying questions and challenges in Dharni's words.

"We have ridden long and hard," she replied. "What little our scouts have been able to gather is that the main force of the dead are on the move. They are definitely coming here, though I'm uncertain in what number. They could reach your gates by late tomorrow, probably attacking by night. Daedalus," she turned to her companion and watched him with a frown creasing her otherwise ethereally attractive features, "seems to think this deathknight will use a shadowland within the city to lead a second force. Just so we're up front, Daedalus is formerly a lieutenant of the Drinker of Seeping Poison."

All gathered looked at Daedalus with sudden distrust, and he met their collective gaze levelly. "There is always more than meets the eye in any situation," he said at last. "You'll have either to kill me or trust me at this point, because there isn't time to do otherwise."

Krislan, who obviously preferred the latter choice concerning Daedalus, ignored him and spoke to Risa before he could consider the effect his words might have on the moment. "Dace?" he asked. "Is he near?"

Risa's expression darkened further. Krislan saw a flicker of worry cross her features, quickly replaced by anger. He hoped the insight was due to familiarity and that the others would only catch the anger.

"He went to scout the deathknight's camp. He was to join us on the road," Risa stated flatly. "There has been no sign of him, and he has sent no word. I have never known the captain to shirk his duties, or his command. I can only assume that something vital or pressing has delayed him, and that he will join us as soon as he can manage. In the meantime," she swept her gaze over the room, taking in each face, reading each expression, "we would be best served by assuming that we might not have his assistance, and planning around that. Then, when he arrives, it will be all that much more welcome."

"Well spoken," Padma cut in. She stepped forward, not at all cowed by Risa's weapons or her manner. "I am Padma, one of the City Council of Mishaka. I am pleased to meet you, and thank you for your assistance." She took Risa's hand for just a moment, meeting her eyes. "We were just planning how to arrange our defenses."

Captain Ashish spoke up. "What about this Daedalus?" he asked. "Is it wise to have such a powerful warrior who has so recently been in the employ of our enemy here within our walls?"

"No one need speak for me," Daedalus replied, before Risa could speak. "There is little time for it now, my friend, or I would tell you the story of how I came to be here tonight. I would tell you of the service I gave, and to whom, and where it got me. I stand here because this warrior," he nodded to Risa, "saw fit to aid me when there was no reason she should do so. Now we're all waiting together for an attack from the very man who would have had my soul ripped from my flesh and dragged down and cast into the Abyss. If there is one strong arm you can count on in what is to come," he held up one gloved fist, "it is this one, whether you believe it or not. Granted my weapons or not, I will fight."

Dharni returned Daedalus's gaze, studying the warrior carefully. They held that stare for a moment; then Dharni nodded and looked away.

"These are odd times," he said, "and they make for odd alliances. On a day when the forces of Mishaka join with a company of mercenaries out of Nexus for the first time since the Battle of Mishaka, I suppose I'll have to live with the fact we need to welcome one of our enemy's own into the fold. Where would you stand?"

"I will stand with those at the graveyard," Daedalus replied without hesitation. "They will need a warrior of my strength, I believe, and..." He grew silent for a moment, lost in his own thoughts. Then he raised his eyes once more and smiled grimly. "And if the Drinker of Seeping Poison decides to pay us a visit," he concluded, "that is the doorway he will use. I would like to be there to show him his pet has failed, and to do what I can to prevent his exiting the shadowland."

There were questions remaining. The line about the death-knight's pet, for one thing, but they all had heard enough of the story, with the exception of Padma, to have at least an idea of what Risa had helped Daedalus to defeat.

Padma turned to the Dragon-Blood and gazed at him levelly. "I have seen battle," she told him softly. "I have stood by the side of many brave men and women, seen some fall, and seen others make—poor decisions. If you make such a decision within my sight..."

Padma's voice trailed off, but her hand rested on the jeweled hilt of her dagger, and Daedalus glanced down at it. Something flashed across his gaze, then was gone like mist in sunlight. It was there, and then it was not. He nodded.

"You will find no reason to plant your blade in my back, lady, rest assured. I may die defending your city, which I admittedly have no concern for, but if so, at least I will have died on my own terms. This fight is for your land, your homes, and your families.

"Myself?" he continued softly. "Revenge will be enough."

Nothing was said for a long moment, and then Risa spoke again. "I think it is time we got back to the planning, don't you, Captain?" She gazed at Dharni, and he nodded. Daedalus stepped up behind Risa, to the side; close to Krislan, who kept a wary eye on him, internally weighing the benefits of having a second Dragon-Blooded warrior among them against the possibility that he was a traitor and might turn on them at any moment.

As the man had said, they could trust him, or kill him. A Dragon-Blooded would not be easy to incarcerate and would require tending and guarding that they had no time for. They would fight with all they had, and they would win or die. Dace would come, or he would not. Already the blood pounded through Krislan's veins, and his mind drifted toward the coming dawn and the day that would follow.

Dharni's voice droned in the background, outlining where each lieutenant would make his stand, who would be kept in relief and where they would be staged, which walls were weakest, and which of those among his men could be best trusted to fortify those weaknesses.

Padma proved a shrewd ally in the planning, gaining more than one appreciative nod from both Dharni and Risa. Krislan already knew what part he was to play, so he let his thoughts and his eyes wander.

His eyes found the councilwoman, Padma. His mind found Dace. Dace won.

Where was he? After years and years of blood and sweat, battle and drunken nights staggering down darkened city streets together, it was hard to reconcile Dace's absence. Krislan ached with the need to get Risa alone and question her, but he knew it was not the time. There might never *be* a time for it. There was little enough time for anything, and eventually they would have to set a guard and rest, as much as they could.

Krislan would not sleep. He'd had no wine or ale since midday, drinking water during the heat of the afternoon and strong tea after dusk. His mind was clear and his muscles quivered with the anticipation. There was no hope of sleep, but he could rest, and, if he closed his eyes tightly enough, he might be fortunate enough to dream.

Dreams were powerful, he knew. They could show you the future or the past. They could help you sort out answers you already knew to the questions that haunted you. He wondered, as Dharni dismissed the group and they dispersed into the shadowed streets of Mishaka, whether he'd dream of Dace, or if this night—possibly the last of his long life—would belong to the woman Padma.

As they exited the tavern and made their way to their various quarters, he smiled at the councilwoman and winked. She favored him with an enigmatic, searching smile of her own, and nodded.

It was enough to answer at least one of his questions. As the streets bustled with last-minute preparations and the still steady influx of men, women, children and livestock from the lands surrounding the city, he made his way to his room, closed the door and lay back with a heavy sigh.

All through the city, rooms were overflowing. Barns and sheds housed families, and livestock was tied in the streets. The inns and taverns ran dry with regularity; men and women scurried about, some storing what they might need against a coming siege, and others carting what they could to be sold among the newcomers and the soldiers.

Krislan saw the moon, high in the sky and bright like a silver sun, shining down on the walls of the city in the distance. He closed his eyes. Morning could not come too soon.

Chapter Fifteen

Dace let Lilith led the way and, within a few hours, they reached the edge of a forested area he'd never passed through. It was on the fringe of the Marukan range, skirting back toward Mishaka, but still a ways off from the road where they'd started. It stretched off into the distance, deep and shadowed, and Lilith, back in horse form, paced from the road and in toward the center of that forest without hesitation.

Dace followed.

Dace had begun, with the lull in activity, to worry over Mishaka and his men. He wondered what Risa and Krislan must be thinking. He wondered what *he* was thinking. What he was doing.

He watched Lilith as he rode, matching his own mount as closely as he could to the symmetry of her motion. He closed his eyes and heard her voice, first as woman; then as bird, crying out sharply; then as lover, sharing the deep, pulsing strangeness that was other forms and other voices, other minds and hungers.

She was old, so much older than he that his grandparents would not have been children when she wedded her Desus. She was of his world, but she was of others, as well: Worlds that had changed and crumbled, fallen and tumbled into dust and sand and rot. He wondered briefly if she would even recognize what she passed, had she the time to stop and share a walk through Nexus. He wondered, on top of all his other thoughts, why he would think of her walking those streets at his side. Dace was not in the market for a companion—not other than that of battle, and the company of Risa and his men.

There was a path, once they'd entered the line of trees. It

wasn't clear. No one had traveled it in long years, and the forest stretched root talons and vine fingers to reclaim it from those fallen to dust. Only the faint remnant of a dirt track remained, winding between the trees, and a vaguely defined swath cut through the greenery defined their route.

As they wound deeper into the woods, Dace felt an odd shift. The world he was familiar with faded bit by bit. It was hard to imagine how many years it must have been since any other had come the way they now traveled. He wondered when it had been that Lilith last came, and then pushed the thought from his mind. The gap in their ages, the inconceivable number of years she'd walked the earth, was beginning to unnerve him.

There was another part of him, however, that awakened a bit more each time the years peeled back and showed themselves in his companion's eyes. This deeply buried part of him burned to know, to remember everything, every passing year of both past and present lives. Dace wanted to know if he had been close to Lilith's lover, Desus, or if he'd known him at all. He wanted to know with whom he'd spent his time, doing what.

Thoughts caromed about in his mind as the shadows of the tall trees grew longer and darker. He tried to concentrate, to memorize the twists and turns they made, but it slipped away. By the time Lilith slowed and shifted back to her own form to wait for him, he was as thoroughly lost as he could ever remember being.

Lilith stared at the next curve in the trail. She showed no sign that she wanted to continue. Dace saw that every muscle in her neck and shoulders was tense and her knuckles were white. He shook the cobwebs of centuries of memories from his mind and rode to her side, laying a hand on her shoulder.

"What is it?" he asked.

"We're nearly there," she said. "It's just that it's been a long time. It's strange—the years stack up like the grains of sand on a beach, but when I think of this place, when I remember his face, his laugh—his anger—it doesn't seem long ago. It seems like yesterday, or last week. It is hard to explain what so many years can do to your mind."

She turned to him, smiled thinly. "I'm afraid I'm making little sense."

"Not at all," he replied. "The difference is, the memories I have are mine, and yet they aren't. I have only bits and pieces, and they fit together poorly. You have too many pieces, and they overlap. We have more in common than I would have thought."

They turned together toward the trail and the trees. Lilith reached into the folds of her robes and pulled out the sharp-edged amulet. Dace saw it glitter as they passed between the trees, the light catching on the gold surface, and then shaded with each passing tree. The effect was mesmerizing, and the ruins were upon them before Dace had noticed them slipping into view.

Lilith stopped, stowed the amulet, and stood in silence, staring at the ruins of a large, impressive villa. The walls stretched out into the trees on either side, tapering down as if they'd been beaten from their foundation by huge hammers. The doors, or what had been the doors, were crumbled stone, broken and dangling from rusted iron hinges. Vines grew in and out of the windows, down the wall and on toward the woods to either side of the walk.

A stretch was clear from the road to the ruins of the doorway. Between the two, nothing grew. Even the dust and dirt of the crumbling home and the encroaching years had not covered that ground.

"Has someone been here before us?" Dace asked.

Lilith shook her head. "It was the same the last time I came. There is more—you will see it all. I believe I know what we are meant to see, where we are meant to go. What remains is to understand what we are meant to do."

"Whatever we do," Dace said, "we have to do it quickly. There is something itching at me, something about Mishaka, about the coming battle. I have never failed to be where I said I would be, when I said I would be, and now I have broken both of those streaks in a single day—in the face of an unknown enemy."

Lilith nodded. "I understand. Come."

She walked to what had been the front door of the ruined

building and through, turning to the right and disappearing from Dace's line of vision. Hurriedly he followed, kicking his mount's sides lightly. The door frame was large enough to accommodate his mounted height easily.

The interior of the building was nearly as wide open as the clearing beyond the door. The rear wall was gone completely. The wall to his left stretched back a ways, then crumbled to broken stone and disappeared into the overgrowth of the woods beyond.

To his right, the building had survived a bit better. He followed Lilith, not able to see her, but knowing she'd turned right, and rounded a corner. He rode into what must have been an interior garden or a courtyard. Lilith was still moving, off to the right, down what would have been a main hall. There was little left of the building itself. Dace could make out enough to tell the layout of the building, but it was difficult to get more of a feel for the place. Its sheer breadth gave the impression it might have been the base for many stories, but there was no evidence of it. Not even the remnant of a stair.

They moved down the hall, through several smaller rooms and what looked as if it might have been the kitchen, a deep, sooty-black patch in the earth denoting the base of a long-crumbled stove. Dace followed as Lilith slid quickly through a rear exit and down a short, sloping lawn. The grass was overgrown, but again, like the walk in front, when you got a few yards down the grass the weeds and brush faded and died. Lilith walked down a barren trail. Nothing grew there. As Dace's mount passed the rear exit of the building, Dace saw the first of the gravestones.

He slowed his mount to a walk and came up behind Lilith. She stood quietly beside his horse, and the two of them stared out over a lightly sloping clearing peppered with moss-covered gravestones. Some had fallen. Others were so overgrown with grass and vines that they were visible only by a glimpse of light-colored stone or a break in the greenery. Except for one.

One grave stood out. It was marked by a building of carved stone with twin doors that swung to the sides. They were open, as though pushed from the inside out. Dace stared through that gateway to the world of the dead and felt ice rushing through the blood in his veins, catching every few inches to dig into his heart and send shivers up the over-tense tendons of his arms and into the small of his back.

"A shadowland," he whispered.

No vine touched the stone of those walls. No grass stuck out at odd angles from the base of the stone. Nothing, in fact, moved at all within the small clearing that held the mausoleum. No birds rested on the stone; no insects crawled over the moss-free stone. Alone in the corruption, decay, and overall dissolution of the ancient home, the grave site stood as stark and strong as it had in the days of its construction.

Lilith walked into he graveyard and stopped at a marker a few yards from the mausoleum. Dace slipped easily from the saddle, dropping his reins and leaving the horse to graze as he stepped through the gate and made for Lilith's side. The gravestone at her feet read *Lina, Beloved of Alve..* There were dates etched into the faded, crumbling stone. They were not clear. The erosion of time and wind had done their part to conceal the age.

"Who is it?" Dace asked.

"Desus' mother," Lilith said. "Age is not a factor when you are dead. She is the same as when I was last here—dust. When she lived, near the end, she mourned the loss of her son, and at the same time she was so proud—so fiercely proud—that he was chosen."

"It is a great honor," Dace replied softly. "Some view it as a gift, others as curse. I consider it a responsibility."

"That sounds like something Desus might have said," Lilith replied, "but he wouldn't have meant it. By the time of his death, he was convinced that he was above the rest of the world—far above. Perhaps it is the ability to look at the world from that perspective that causes one to be chosen."

"I don't know," Dace said softly. "Nothing was ever explained."

Lilith nodded.

"You didn't bring me here to show me this grave," he continued.

Lilith tore her gaze from the tombstone.

"No," she agreed. "It was something else entirely."

She turned from the mother's grave and stepped closer to the large twin-doored tomb.

"Alve," Dace said. "His father."

"Yes," Lilith replied simply. "Desus always told me stories of his childhood that made my heart ache and the hairs at the base of my neck stand on end. I thought he told me because the stories would make him seem stronger, would help to put me further under his control. I had good reason for this belief. Everything else in my relationship with Desus was a matter of control—why should this be different?

"It was different. He told me because I was too close to fool with his veneer of calm, and he believed that anything he did or said with me was safe. He controlled me, and if he didn't want me to tell a thing or show a thing to others, I would not. That was how he saw it, and it was not so far from the truth. So—he showed me this."

Dace still stared at what had once been a simple graveyard. He had heard of such a thing, but he had never directly witnessed it. He knew that there were rituals attendant to the dead, and that they must be acknowledged and adhered to. He had seen the priests worrying over the rites of the dead, had heard them drone on about proper burial and final resolution. There were equally stringent rituals for those who wandered the Underworld. Dace had seen shadowlands before.

The doors to the mausoleum stood open wide, as if beckoning to them. They gazed in silence, staring into that void and feeling the icy tendrils of its influence stretching out to them. Neither was in any particular danger, but the effect of the place and the draw of it were very real.

"His father did not die well," Dace commented.

Lilith shook her head. "He died as he lived. Desus warned me away from this place, but I was desperate. I needed to know him, to know why he acted the way he did—at times—and how he thought. I believed that if I knew what life had been like for him as a young man, I could find a way to change him—or to understand him, and change myself to fit the mold. This is all I found."

"There was not much more of the home than stands now. Something, or someone, cut the home down to size. I believe this was after his family had left. I believe that after—this," she gestured at the tomb before them, "the family was none too anxious to remain. Desus was gone, Exalted and beyond their influence, and Desus's father was—evil. I can't think of another word that describes it fully. If it had not been for the Exaltation, Desus would never have survived to adulthood. His father would have killed him for one offense or another. They were on a collision course from the moment Desus was born."

"What happened to the father?" Dace asked.

"He was killed by his son," Lilith responded. "He was killed, but it wasn't enough. He lingered, in the thoughts and dreams of his son, in the memory of his enemies. He was buried, but he was never put to rest. I don't know all of the details."

Lilith grew silent and Dace drew his mount close by her side. He curled her into his arms and held her, waiting.

"Desus told me a great deal, but not everything. There were things about his father that he wouldn't talk about at all. He wouldn't come here to see what had happened. I'm not certain that he knew the truth of what happened, because it was many years after his death before I came here myself. He had no desire to know what happened to his family, even if what happened had a negative effect on the world as a whole."

"So here we stand," Dace commented.

Lilith nodded. "Here we stand. I don't know what shadow we are supposed to cut with the blades of the amulet, but I know we were meant to come to this place. I should have talked to him about it. I should have made him talk, made him listen. His father was a monster, but that didn't mean he had to follow in those footsteps. He could have been great—was great—before he lost focus. If only he had listened to me, things could have been so different."

"You weren't responsible for him," Dace replied. "Only for yourself."

"You think so?" she asked, turning to him, her eyes flashing. "Then why do you gaze longingly at the trees and the road beyond? Why is it that, though you are here with me, your mind is with the one you call Risa, and with your men? Are you responsible for them? If they all die, who will be to blame, the enemy, or...?"

Dace regarded her silently for a moment, and then spoke. His voice was measured and clipped, emotion held in check by great force of will.

"Desus did not follow you. He may have loved you, but he did not count on you to lead him through or out of trouble. He did not take his orders from you, and when he lost his focus, as you put it, it was not because he went where you told him to go. There is your difference, Owl Woman. You are responsible for your own actions, I am responsible for mine, and for those of any who choose to follow me. At this moment, I'm wondering if I've chosen wisely."

Lilith fingered the golden star again. She glanced up at him. "I haven't shown you all that I know of this place," she whispered. "I wasn't certain it would be important, but now—now I think that it may be the focus of why I was drawn to you—why we have come to this place together, at this time. I thought this quest of mine was about me—my past and my present, possibly my future. I thought it would lead me to Desus. Instead..."

She glanced away and stared back into the tomb.

"Why did you bring me here?" Dace asked.

"I did not bring you here," she replied. "You followed me here. There is a difference. The grave is not consecrated. The ground upon which it rests is tainted. I know you can feel it. I can taste it, sense it, almost hear the voices of those trapped beyond. This shadowland is old, but there is still a trace of the death and evil that created it."

"Why did you bring me here?" he asked again, more forcefully. Dace grabbed her shoulder and spun her around to face him. Her eyes were bright, and her lips were pulled back in an expression lost somewhere between terror and a smile.

"It can take us to Mishaka," she replied. "If you aren't afraid—and if I can find the way. I know you wanted to gather more knowledge of the deathknight, but I've kept you longer than we intended. I can get you back to your men and to the caravan, if you let me."

Dace spun, staring into the darkness of the pit, his nerves on fire with the sense of imminent danger. He turned back to Lilith and studied her face. Then, softly, he said:

"Show me."

Chapter Sixteen

Dace sat beneath a withered tree and emptied his mind of thought. Lilith had emptied the contents of a small pouch she carried onto the stones near the doorway of the tomb, and there was nothing he could do to aid her in whatever it was she planned. Dace feared that he knew the answer well enough, and the fear itself was an odd sensation. It had been a long time since he'd felt anything akin to real fear. As he grew into his power, met each challenge one after another without failure or even serious challenge, the temper on the edge of his emotions had evened. Now he felt like a raw recruit facing his first campaign, and he knew he could not face what was to come in that state.

He had brought the candles with him, and they were situated before him in the proper pattern, their flames guttering in the wind. His thoughts wound down an inward spiral, drawing the fears and shadows into a deep, inner pool where they slipped beneath the surface and disappeared. He let the fear of what might be happening to his men, to Risa, and to Krislan, fall into that pool as well. As his thoughts stilled, images surfaced, rising like slow-moving bubbles from that same surface.

The images were disjointed. If he concentrated on one, he knew the entire pattern would fail and slough away like river water over moss-coated rocks. He did not know if these images were meant as messages, or if they were tangentially based on the thoughts he suppressed.

He saw Mishaka. It was not the Mishaka of here and now, but Mishaka as he'd known the city in the time of the Battle of Thorns. The walls rose, strong and silent. Wind blew the banners of the city, flapping them loudly, great wings that threatened to tear the tops from the buildings.

He saw green fields with long-nailed, ice-pale arms stretching through from beneath, filthy-faced ghouls dragging themselves back from death, bound to a master stronger than death by half-seen tendrils of essence. They dripped putrid flesh and loamy soil, and they rose in an endless procession as the bubble-like image spun in constant circles.

He saw the great home that he had just ridden through, but the walls were whole. The windows were alight with lamp flames and horses were tethered in front. Shadows moved beyond the windows, and voices carried on the wind, but he could not make out their words.

Then even the images were gone, and he floated. It was here that he felt his strength, the essence that surrounded him, stronger in one place than in the next, but always present. Much of it, he knew, he held within himself.

Dace had no idea how long he'd meditated when he heard Lilith step away from the tomb. He was alert and on his feet in a single fluid moment, so quick that he startled her as she reached to touch his shoulder. She pulled back in alarm; then, seeing that there was no anger in his eyes, she smiled ruefully.

"I should have expected that," she said softly. "I was never able to slip up on Desus. He could sleep as soundly as a stone, but if something moved that was out of the ordinary, or if a sound was out of place, he was ready to face it in seconds. It's kind of eerie."

Dace laughed softly. "I'm not really used to it myself," he admitted. "I have always slept lightly. In war, it's best not to rest too soundly. Now..." His words trailed off.

"Are you ready?" She glanced back toward the entrance to the tomb.

"You haven't told me exactly what I'm supposed to be ready for," he replied, stepping up beside her and following her gaze.

"You have come with me this far," she said, "and I will follow you now, until this partnership is through. I don't have all my answers, but time is against us now. It's my turn to do as I have promised.

"I know only one way to the city that is faster than any horse can carry you," she continued. "I walked this road once before, long ago. Things are not always constant in the Underworld, but there are ways to navigate it. I did a favor for—someone. He led me through safely at a time when death stalked me through the night and haunted me by day. It was a long time ago, but it isn't something I could have forgotten.

"There are creatures in that other place, creatures like none you'll see here in the daylight, and yet—they are alike. Death creeps through their veins. Some crawl, some hunt—some fly. They can be killed, it seems, and I did so. It was a huge hawk, its wingspan twice my height. Its breast was bright red, and its eyes…" She shuddered and fell silent, just for a moment, then continued. "It nearly killed me as well, and when I tore out its throat and ate the heart," her gaze darted up to his face, watching for his reaction, for signs of revulsion or loathing. Dace was as unmoved as a chunk of granite, his eyes cool and attentive.

"I was able to steal its form. I retched for two days, and when he led me from the Underworld, for that is what it is called, I nearly died. The flesh was poison to me and the blood that flowed through the thing's veins burned like fire. I crawled into a hole beneath a tree, wrapped in the fur of a badger, and I slept as if dead. It is a wonder that no other found me during that time. Even an animal might have killed me. I was weak, and I could barely bring myself to breathe because the air rushing down my throat brought back the stench of its flesh.

"It did not seem as loathsome in there," she nodded at the tomb once again. "Everything there was difficult for me, the battle nearly more than I could handle. My guide was little help, as he knew the ways of that world but was no warrior. While I walked that road, I was unable to connect with the essence here. I couldn't regain lost strength. My guide had a map, and I copied it before I ever allowed myself to be led into those depths, because I would not be trapped there if he was destroyed. I have that map still."

She reached under her moonsilver armor and drew forth a bit of cloth. Kneeling, she spread it across a large stone and Dace dropped to one knee beside her, glancing at the spidery lines scrawled across the surface. It was strange. He thought it was possible that he recognized a few landmarks, but the map made no sense to him. Bodies of water were missing, mountains did not rise where they ought, and strange names and designs dotted the page.

"What place is this?" he asked.

"It is a map of this same area. I entered the lands of the dead through this very shadowland with my guide. My map shows the road back to Mishaka, but in the Underworld," Lilith replied. "It is the world inhabited by those more comfortable with darkness and the dead than with your sun, or even the pale reflection in my moon. There are roads through that country as surely as there are through ours, if you know how to reach them—and more importantly, how to make your way back. I saw the death-knight gazing into a tomb such as this. It is likely he will use such a road himself, if he moves on Mishaka. If we travel this road, and if I'm right about the Drinker of Seeping Poison, then, if he is moving on your men, we'll find him along this darker road."

Dace stared at the map. He could see Mishaka marked clearly, but then, the landmarks were all off. "Are the distances accurate?" he asked. "It should be well over a day's ride to Mishaka from here, no matter what world we move through." He gestured at the cloth map

"The map is more than a simple record or locations. It can help speed us on our way," Lilith replied. "But you must understand that things are not the same in the Underworld as they are here,". "There is essence, but it is tainted. You will not be able to renew any that you use until we exit at the far end of our journey, assuming this map is still accurate, and that there is an exit at Mishaka. I can't guarantee what we will find on the way, or that the roads run as they once did. We won't have the guide that I had. If we meet one of great power within, we may never return to the surface—or worse yet we might lose the desire to return at all."

Dace stared past her into the mouth of the tomb. The temperature of the air around them seemed to have dropped several degrees as Lilith spoke. On a stone before the entrance, she had arrayed a small sequence of items. There was a long, thin blade; the gold, bladed talisman; a small mound of dirt the size of a man's thumb; and a candle.

"What is that?" he asked.

"The map is attuned to the dead," she replied. "For it to grant us any benefit, it requires sacrifice."

She rose, rolling the map and tucking it away once more, and made her way to the stone and the objects she'd laid out. "This is grave dirt," she explained. "I scraped it from within the tomb." Lilith produced a flint and managed to start a small flame, enough to light the candle, which she sat beside the mound of dirt. It was a small candle of an odd, yellowish color, and the scent that wafted up from the small flame was sickly sweet.

"It is made from the fat boiled from the corpse of one long dead," she whispered. "Don't ask me where I got it, or how. It is necessary. I am no necromancer, but I have learned things."

Dace nodded, but she wasn't watching him. She took the long, slender blade in her hand and held her finger over the pile of soil. With a quick flip of her wrist, she sliced a small gash in her flesh and held it over the soil. Blood dripped—one, two, three drops—and she pulled back.

"Give me your hand," she said softly. When Dace hesitated, she glanced up at him, her eyes bleak and harried. "Quickly. We have only materials for the one attempt."

Steeling himself, Dace knelt beside her and held out his hand. Without hesitation she sliced a thin line across his fingertip and held it over the mound of grave dirt. One, two, three drops, then away. The candle flame had gained strength. Lilith leaned close, breathed a word across the flame, and they both watched as the fire shifted.

Eerily, it bent to the side where the mound of earth waited. The candle had built up a reservoir of wax at its top, but now the wall was breached. The flames leaned and danced, reaching toward the soil and the blood, as if hungry to envelop them in its hot embrace. Before the onslaught of heat, the side wall of the candle collapsed and the wax spilled over the side, rolling onto the stone and making its way in slow, rolling waves toward the dirt.

Dace's pulse had quickened. He felt each slamming beat of his heart, and there was a heat. He felt it reaching for him, licking at his sides and teasing up the sides of his face, flashing across the skin of his chest and constricting his breath. He wanted to reach out and brush it all off the stone, to stomp the flame out of existence and leap to his horse, riding for the walls of Mishaka with every ounce of speed the beast could offer, but he held himself in check.

The images he had so easily suppressed as he meditated slammed back into sudden focus, warped and painful. Risa's face, drawn back in a rictus of pain and shock. Dead vermin swarming over the walls of the city. Krislan crying out to him, arms raised and the dark, death-black blade of a shadowed figure sliding through him from behind and ripping upward to silence his screams. There was no time.

The flames licked and sputtered. Wind brushed over them and flattened the red-orange heat into a layer of deep-fired energy, leaking the wax into the base of the grave-dirt mound. Dace saw the blood, impossibly, rising to the surface of the soil and sliding into the flame. The wax washed over it all, and around, surrounding the pile.

Neither of them breathed, and then, as suddenly as the flame had leaped to life, it died. Snuffed. The air, which had cooled as they talked and as Lilith worked, had dropped to the temperature of ice. On the stone before them a perfect circle of wax rested, hardening in the chill. Lilith leaned close once more, whispered a single word into the mixture and pressed her thumb into the surface of it. Then she lifted it carefully by the sides and turned to Dace.

"Quickly," she whispered.

Intuiting what she expected, Dace pressed his own thumb into the opposite side of the disk from hers. In that moment, the growing darkness shifted. Where there had been only shadows, other forms shimmered to life. Corrupted forms. Twisted and bent, hideous and dead. The map glowed with a greenish light that had not been present before.

Lilith turned and grabbed up the bag and the other items she had laid out. "Quickly," she hissed. "We must enter now, at sunset." Dace leaped to his mount and grabbed his own bags, releasing the beast from its bridle in a quick jerk.

Lilith called out something to his horse. It was not in any language that Dace recognized. It was not in any tongue meant to pass human lips. The beast perked its ears, shying away from the glowing tomb entrance and whinnying loudly. Then it turned and rushed off through the trees.

"He will find his way home," Lilith said, gripping Dace by the arm. "We must find our own way." Then, not releasing her hold on him, she turned and stepped toward the entrance to the Underworld. Glancing back only once to see his horse disappearing through the shadows, Dace turned and followed her.

The mouth of the tomb swallowed them whole.

Chapter Seventeen

Dawn broke on the morning after Risa's arrival in Mishaka, and there was no sign of Dace. No messengers had been received, and though scouts had been sent in all directions, not just toward Thorns, there had been no sign of him. Despite the trust Risa, Krislan, and the others placed in their captain's judgment and integrity, it was a grim awakening.

Captain Ashish was civil. He continued preparations, working the troops Risa had brought into the planning and formation, taking advantage of seasoned leaders to bolster the lack of experience in his own men. They were a formidable force, and the walls of the city had been fortified as well as could be expected. They had been standing for hundreds of years, and though there were signs of that age in places, they would hold yet a few years more with enough stout hearts and strong backs to defend them.

That was the question, of course. How many would they need? How long a siege could the dead maintain? How strong was the necromancy that empowered them, and how dear would be the cost of the defense? Though the soldiers Dace had sent were a force they would not have had on their own, it still felt like a betrayal to the people and leaders of Mishaka that that Solar who had been announced as part of their defense had not appeared. Secretly, there were many who were relieved at this, fearing the madness of those touched by the Unconquered Sun almost as much as armies of dead warriors. They watched Risa and Krislan with hooded eyes, muttered behind their backs and, when they were not busy at this, they stared off toward the walls, the gates, and the road beyond in nervous fear.

Risa didn't blame them, nor did she acknowledge their

words or their frowns. She had been sent to do a job and, with
or without Dace, she aimed to complete it. Captain Ashish was
focused on the outer walls. After his initial cool reception, he
had proven a sharp strategist and able leader. He had left the
tomb and the possible secondary attack front to Risa. Krislan
had taken his men to the cemetery and dug in. He'd laid traps,
put up hurried barricades, even brought in lumber and barrels, a few wagons, and pressed them into use to barricade the
wrought-iron fence of the graveyard itself.

A watch had been set, at least three men on site and several others watching from vantage points that allowed a view
of the entire gravesite. Sleeping and eating had been delegated
to shifts, and those who could were catching what might be the
last fitful moments of sleep for days—or even their lifetime. No
one rested easily.

There was a restless energy shifting through the streets. The
market had closed, and even M'chwallya, the giant, dark-skinned
seer, had removed himself from those streets. Provisions had
been carted in from as far as fifty miles out, families pressing
what pack animals they had into service, loading wagons and
stripping their homes of everything that might be used to fight
or fortify. Establishments that normally sold food, beer, wine
and entertainment had been staked out by the guards, opened
as temporary kitchens. Barns and courtyards, temples and fine
houses were surrounded by small camps of refugees and volunteers, or filled with sleeping children.

It was late afternoon, and the sun had begun its journey
from the center of the sky to the plains in the distance when
the first scouts began returning. At first they straggled, one,
then another reporting movement at a distance of several miles.
Then the trickle became a flood, and the city came to life.

One group moved in slowly, a horse led between them. A
rider was tied in place, leaning forward on his mount and rocking slowly. Those around him watched carefully, keeping him
mounted as they wound slowly into the city.

Their leader dismounted immediately, and Dharni met him.

"We found him on the road, sir," the man reported. "He was
half dead, ready to fall from his saddle. He hasn't spoken too

clearly, but he mentioned the deathknight, and dead soldiers. If we'd left him, he wouldn't have made it another day."

Dharni nodded and directed them to untie the man, dragging him down as gently as possible. He could barely stand, but Dharni, with no time to waste, lifted the man's head by a grip in his hair.

"Who are you?" he asked.

Tarsus stared at him, dazed. He mumbled his name, then reeled to the side, losing his balance despite the two scouts who held him upright and the screaming pain of pulled hair.

Dharni stared down at him.

"Get him to Krislan's quarters, and quickly. He may know something. He is one of the mercenaries."

The scouts snapped quick salutes and half led, half carried Tarsus into the streets and away, turning down the alley toward the tavern where Krislan, Risa, and their men were housed.

Tarsus was barely coherent when Risa and Krislan met to question him. Risa was relentless, but they got little of use from the battered scout. He was emaciated and weak. His skin was slick with fevered sweat, and his eyes were glazed.

"It doesn't matter," Krislan said at last. "There's little he could tell us that your friend Daedalus hasn't already reported. You saw the way he reacted when that one walked in."

Risa nodded. Tarsus had sat up very suddenly, his eyes wide, first with fear, then with recognition. He hadn't said anything coherent, but it had been obvious that he was genuinely trying to convey something to Daedalus. Daedalus himself stood silent through it all. He showed no particular compassion for the scout's illness, but he didn't flinch from an opportunity where, had he been lying to them, he could easily have been tripped up.

In the end, they left Tarsus in the care of two of the local women, the proprietress of the tavern where they were staying, and her daughter. Risa told the women to send for her if his condition changed or if he started to speak more clearly, and they dispersed to the duties they'd been about at his arrival.

All of Dharni's scouts were accounted for, and the gates swung closed. Huge iron bars were slid into place to bar them against attack and battering rams. The walls swarmed with guards, some shouting directions, others questions, all hurrying to their appointed places.

You could stand in the center of the square, Risa thought, close your eyes, and hear the heartbeat of Mishaka speeding. She stood, leaning on one of the pillars supporting the balcony of the rear of a tavern that looked out over the cemetery. She watched the gate, which was the only part easily visible through the fortifications, in silence.

Without having heard a thing, she sensed a presence at her side. The hairs on her arm rippled and she glanced over to where Daedalus stood, one hand on his hip, the other on the hilt of his blade.

"Soon," he said softly. "If his plans have not changed, it won't be long before the dead come into view."

Risa nodded. "If what you knew when you—parted ways—with them, hasn't been changed to make what you know useless," she replied. "I hope they had little faith in you."

Daedalus turned to her, the frown barely flickering over his face before laughter swept it away. "You hope they consider me lion food, then," he said. "For all our sakes, I hope you are right."

"Will he come?" Risa asked. She didn't name her fear, but she knew he would know of whom she spoke.

"I don't know," he replied. "I really don't know. He told me he didn't need to pass through the shadowland himself to send the dead ones through, and I believe that. I have seen him work dark miracles that would freeze your spine; such a thing seems almost trivial. It would be different if it were a living army, or a force less familiar with the Underworld, but the dead do not fear those roads. A journey through the lands of their own would pose no obstacle to them. If he comes, it will be because he fears things are going badly, or because he feels the victory in his grasp and cannot resist the urge to gloat."

"He won't get a chance to gloat if he sends nothing stronger through that black hole than some dead slaves," Risa said softly.

Daedalus looked her up and down, and then caressed the lash at his hip. He smiled. "That is true," he said, almost

brightly. "The dead are hardly more than a diversion in battle unless they fight in great numbers. I believe your Sergeant
Krislan has done an admirable job of shoring up the defenses
at the graveyard. The iron fence has been supplemented with
wagons and other things to slow the progress of attackers, and
the very fact of the size of this tiny shadowland is in our favor.
I wouldn't think more than one or two at a time could squeeze
through the door of that mausoleum, and I don't believe their
second lives will be long ones."

"Then," Risa smiled, gripping her dire lance tightly, "he will
have to come because he fears things are going badly. I would
say that will make him angry."

Daedalus's grin widened. "You haven't said a thing that was
more true since I've known you," he said.

"It's never a good day to die, and if we are now seriously
contemplating the arrival of a deathknight intent on having
both our heads on separate platters, we'd better start planning
on how we will deal with that."

There were quiet footsteps behind them, and both turned.
The councilwoman, Padma, was making her way to their side
from within the tavern. She carried a leather bag. The long, thin,
jeweled blade still rode her hip, glittering hungrily.

"I believe that I can help," she said, smiling. "I may not be
able to destroy the shadowland, but I believe I can ward it for a
while. It may not be enough to stem the tide, but it will buy us
time."

"Any and all help is welcome here, Lady Padma," Risa
smiled. "Though the main force of the enemy will fall on the
outer wall, it is here that the real danger lies. We can't allow the
dead to swarm within the city walls, and if their leader comes
to their aid, it will be through here."

"Then," Padma replied, striding toward the graveyard
gracefully, "I had better get started."

Risa and Daedalus watched her for a moment, then turned
to one another and shrugged. They stepped from the wooden
porch and followed in the woman's wake, wondering just what
she might have in her bag, and how powerful it might be in the
face of what was to come. The city was full of surprises.

While Risa and Daedalus were following the councilwoman into the graveyard, Krislan was wandering restlessly among his men. He had them in squads surrounding the cemetery. If their first lines of defense failed, he wanted to be able to work a containment operation on the perimeter of the fence. There were too many women and children in the city relying on them: Though they might hunt and kill every one of the enemy who escaped into the streets, they would do so at a cost, both to the integrity of their defense and the safety of those in their charge.

Krislan stopped and talked for a few moments with each second he'd placed. Their questions were all the same: Where was Dace? Would they be enough without him? What was going to come through that tomb?

Krislan fielded each question as well as he could. He had no real answers to give them, but he'd been in a thousand situations like this. Krislan was as at home in a battle as he was in the barracks, or a tavern, or even his own rooms. The men sensed it. Though Dace was not there to lead them, Krislan's words were spoken easily and confidently. He knew them. He knew their lives, their loves, their families, and what they hoped to do when the campaign was over.

He stared off at the walls and wondered if he had held too many men back for the cemetery. The main force would hit the walls within the hour, and he knew that many of the men Dharni had drawn to his command were green and untested. If they broke, all was lost. The walls had to hold, because, while it would be simple enough at first, if failure at the graveyard drew the attention of the deathknight, it was almost certainly *not* going to hold. If the battle reached the streets of the city on both fronts, it was as good as over.

Krislan shook his head and turned from the walls with a final shrug. It had been Dharni's call, and Krislan had to admit, grudgingly, that the captain knew what he was doing.

Risa, the deathknight, the Dragon-Blooded Daedalus and

the councilwoman had just turned in through the gates of the cemetery, and Krislan headed in their direction. If they were working some magic, or some plan for the defense of those gates, he needed to know what it was. Besides, it would give him an outlet for the nervous energy threatening to eat him from the inside out.

"The key is consecration," Padma explained. "It isn't enough that you, or I, should believe the grave sanctified. There are rituals that must be performed, and the power invoked must be greater than that which created this shadowland in the first place."

"Who was buried here?" Krislan asked.

"That," Padma answered, without looking up to meet his gaze, "is a good question. A better one is when was the shadowland created. You can sense that this place is tainted, but it has been well hidden, and isolated to this small portion of the graveyard where none visit. The name here has been cut away, though I don't know why."

"A curse?" Risa asked. "Where is the ghost?"

"There are many dangers here," Padma replied, almost serene. "The ghost is likely to prove the least of our worries. I believe it to be trapped, which is partially how this deathknight has managed to disguise the purpose of this place. The grave is desecrated. It is a common form of protection to claim a curse lies on the grave, or the ground surrounding it. It prevents those of more specific beliefs from breaking the stones, or removing the remains, once buried. I believe there may have been a spell placed on this mausoleum, so that while we noted it as distasteful, we didn't note the true danger of it."

"So," Daedalus cut in, "the spell is broken?"

"Not fully. You don't see through to the Underworld, do you?" Padma replied, frowning at him. "Of all those present, I'd expect the fewest questions from you."

Daedalus colored and fell silent.

Padma emptied the contents of her bag onto a flat flagstone

and was spreading them out carefully. There was a small mortar and pestle, two clusters of some sort of root, a tiny vial of greenish powder, and a small metal bowl.

Without looking up, she grabbed the roots, crushing them with the mortar and pestle to a fine paste. When she was satisfied, she turned to Krislan.

"Do you have your canteen?" she asked.

Krislan handed it over and she unstoppered it, dripping a few drops of water onto the paste. Returning the canteen, she picked up the vial of powder and opened it carefully. Her breath seemed to come more slowly and something in her manner— the reverence with which she handled the vial, once it had been opened—affected those who stood around her. Every breath was held as she tipped the glass.

Three grains. The powder was not too fine, but still, though both Risa and Daedalus's senses were fine enough to detect the finesse behind the motion, the grace of the measured addition to the mortar was exceptional. Without hesitation Padma reached for and found the small stopper, closing off the green powder and setting it aside.

"Jade," Daedalus whispered.

Padma did not look up, but she nodded. "Not just jade. This is from a relic handed down by my father's father. It was crushed when a temple collapsed, and he collected it, grain by grain. It was a small figurine, green jade. It was a talisman of protection."

"How will you use it?" Daedalus asked.

She glanced up at him, saw the understanding in his gaze, gauged it, and answered.

"I will try to create a ward," she replied. "I cannot hope to consecrate the grave in the time we have remaining. The root I have is from a tree growing on the hills of the Marukan range. The roots of this tree had grown sixty feet into almost solid stone. They are very strong."

Daedalus nodded thoughtfully.

"It will slow him," he said at last. "I do not believe it can hold, but it will cause unexpected difficulty, and it will slow them all."

Padma turned away without responding, grinding the green powder into the root carefully, and Daedalus fell silent. He fingered the handle of the lash at his side, and ran his gaze carefully over the graves. Risa watched him, then followed his gaze. It wasn't a bad place for an ambush, if the ward that Padma labored over failed.

"If he can't send them through easily," she asked, "what will he do?"

"I can't speak for the Drinker of Seeping Poison," Daedalus smiled at her, "but as one of his former lieutenants, I would expect him to burst through with a show of strength, damning whatever force denied him."

"So," Risa continued thoughtfully, "he might come through recklessly?"

Daedalus answered carefully. "I cannot say that for certain. If he suspects that there is anything of danger on this end of the trail, he might not come at all. But... if he forces his way through, I think he will do so in a show of strength. I don't think he'll be expecting more resistance than the ward presents. He will believe it's our last stand, and that he has defeated us."

Risa glanced around the graveyard again.

"Not a bad place for an ambush," she repeated aloud.

Daedalus nodded. "Not bad at all. It has... possibilities."

Padma ignored them. She was whispering over her mixture of root and powder, which had been blended beyond separation into a sort of paste. She rose, finally, and drew the jeweled dagger from her hip. Very carefully, she scraped the greenish compound she'd mixed onto the blade and, starting on the left side of the tomb's entrance, she began etching a line into the stone. Every inch or so she added more of the mixture to the blade, until she'd drawn a semi-circle, sealing the half-open tomb door symbolically.

Then she drew forth another small pouch. From this she poured white granular powder into her open palm, and repeated her semi-circular pattern, creating a second line behind the first.

"Salt?" Krislan asked. He'd seen the salt line used against ghosts before.

Padma nodded. "No sense taking chances on that ghost I said wouldn't be any trouble," she said. "Also, I believe it may help with the walking dead, as well."

Then, very suddenly, she drew the dagger up and down, putting all her slight weight behind the stroke. The blade sliced cleanly into the stone, dead center on the half-moon-shaped line she'd drawn. As she released it the blade quivered, shivering back and forth. Krislan took a step back. He couldn't be certain what he'd seen, but the way the stone had opened, almost like a gut wound, made his stomach churn.

Either the blade had danced, its tip imbedded deeply in the stone, shivering like a living thing—or the stone had rolled, pitching at the intrusion of the knife and writhing in pain at the sudden slice. It was not possible, of course. Metal could break stone, but it did not slice. It did not slide in, as if into the skin of an enemy, and hang, quivering—as he had just witnessed. Krislan's tongue was raw from the sudden clamp of his teeth.

But as Padma stepped away and back, he caught her.

It was a reflex. He hadn't meant to touch her at all, but she'd seemed to stagger, and he moved without thought, breaking what might have been a nasty fall. They stood, still as the stone beneath their feet, watching the blade.

"It is done," Padma whispered.

Krislan didn't release her. Not immediately. Instead, he asked her:

"Will it hold?"

She glanced at Daedalus, who was still scanning the nearby graves for the perfect spot to plan his own ambush. She caught Risa's gaze, just for a second, then turned fully, not removing herself from Krislan's arms.

"It will," she said softly, "or it will not. I have done what I can. We are not without our strengths here in Mishaka. You may find yourself surprised, before all is said and done."

"I have been constantly surprised," Krislan replied, "since my arrival. Why should now be any different?"

In the distance, in the direction of the main gates, cries broke the silence. Voices called out in all directions and, very suddenly, the attack that had lived in their minds and their nightmares crashed against the strength of their walls.

The sun, which already hung low in the sky, seemed to dim.

Chapter Eighteen

The guards on the walls near the gates stared off across the fields toward the forests beyond. Something was moving on the horizon, but it was impossible to make it out. It seemed to be a line, a dark fog seeping out along the base of the trees and into the plain. It moved slowly but steadily, and as it spread from the forest the darkness flowed in its wake.

Men turned to one another, confused, staring first into the field, then up and down the line of sentries, who stared back at them in equal confusion. Word was sent for Captain Ashish, who hastened to the main tower to the left of the gate.

Captain Ashish stood for a long time, gazing out over the parapets. He shielded his eyes from the dim remnant of the afternoon's light. His shoulders stiffened after a moment, and he cursed, very low.

"They are coming," he said softly. "By the Five Elemental Dragons, they are coming like the tide."

The word spread up and down the line. The sound of weapons being checked a final time, sliding in and out of their scabbards, was accompanied by harsh whispers and louder cries, echoing through the streets. Then the horns followed.

Dharni stood and let them echo out around him and into the fields beyond the walls. He watched as the enemy slid closer, resembling nothing more than ants swarming out of a hole in the ground, or rats bunched over the carcass of something unfortunate enough to die too close to their lair.

It was difficult to make out individual forms, but as they drew nearer they separated somewhat, and he could see that their numbers were huge. Rank upon rank stretched away toward the horizon. The ranks were rag-tag and chaotic. They stumbled over one another, and there were few men mounted. There was the glitter of weapons, but not every one of the oncoming horde seemed to wield a weapon. Dharni breathed deeply, closed his eyes, and calmed his thoughts. Such a force would break on the walls. If they had nothing more to offer, then the real threat lay from within. But there were so many.

There were larger shapes deeper in—siege engines? Catapults? Too soon to tell. The first of them would reach the walls within the hour. He was about to turn from the wall when he caught sight of two mounted warriors skirting the edge of the horde. They moved with authority, herding the dead like cattle, or so it seemed from a distance. Dharni stared a moment longer. If there was a weakness in the oncoming force, other than its general disarray, it was these men. Such a force without leadership would crumble and fall. It was a key, and in a situation like this, when every door seemed locked, any key was worth its weight in gold. Eyes gleaming, he turned and descended to the courtyard below, moving swiftly.

The forces of Mishaka were mustered below, stretching into the streets in all directions, waiting for his orders. Captain Ashish stopped about ten yards in front of the foremost rank and stood, sweeping the length of them with a stern, thoughtful gaze.

"The time has come," he cried at last, "for us to defend what is ours. The enemy is within sight of our gates, but the walls are strong. *We* are strong. We have allies with courage and valor. I can't tell you that we will all return to our homes unbroken. I can't even tell you that your homes will be yours when all is said and done, but I can tell you this."

He stopped for a moment, paced up and down the front rank of guards, civilians, and outlanders, all with their gazes fixed on him and their eyes blazing. Then he stopped, staring at a point somewhere in the center of the ranks.

"If we stand together, we can hold these walls. This city has a history of war. Great battles have waged across the borders of Mishaka, and great enemies have been turned aside. Today, we join those who defended these same walls less than a decade ago. Let them stand beside you. Feel their strength. Feel the power of the city seep through your boots and into your sword arms. This is our city, and our day."

He turned his back on them, raised one arm, then brought it down. At that same moment, he cried out:

"Posts!"

There was a great shuffling of boots, clanging of metal and din of voices, as the defenders of Mishaka took to the city walls, manned what weapons remained, and prepared for the oncoming horde.

Captain Ashish watched them for a moment, hoping it was enough, that his words could spur them beyond their experience and lend them the courage they did not have on their own. They had come to this city as straggling bands of strangers, but they took to the walls as a single force.

Then, shaking his head to clear his thoughts, he turned away. He had a man to find and very little time to find him. With a few quick steps he entered the first alley on his right and disappeared into the growing shadows of the cities streets.

Dharni moved quickly. He knew his lieutenants could handle the initial preparations, the positioning of the men and the final checks of the walls, but he would need to be there when the first wave hit. They would need him, standing at their sides, calling out orders and drawing their courage to bear with the strength of his will. He knew the price of leadership, and he was born to it.

Still, that last sight of the human warriors riding at the side of the dead had given him the beginnings of a plan, and he was ready to grasp at any straw that might pull them free of the morass of dead warriors running and stumbling toward the city walls. There were still lights in some of the taverns and other business establishments, but the men had gone—either to the walls, or the graveyard. Dharni broke into a trot and entered the nearest tavern.

Behind the bar he saw two women huddled, one old and gray, the other a darker, mirrored image, minus the wrinkles. Both sets of eyes regarded him fearfully, and he held up a placating hand.

"M'chwallya," he said softly. "Do you know where he has

gone?"

The younger woman started to shake her head, but the old woman spoke up.

"Aye," she replied. "I seen him a bit earlier. He sleeps in the back room of the Thorn Tavern."

"I know the place," Dharni replied. "He is there now?"

The woman shrugged. "He is not on the street, and the only times I've known him in all my years, he has been in one or the other of those places."

The horde had drawn closer to the walls, close enough that more detail could be made out; the ragged flapping of what clothing still clung to them, the glint of their weapons. They still seemed a single mass at this distance, but that mass was separating, spreading as it came.

Up and down the wall Dharni's lieutenants busied themselves preparing their men. The captain has given only quick warning that he was leaving, promising to return before they knew it. But now, the enemy was almost within range—was so close, in fact, that the wind brought their stench and the whispered abomination of wind whistling through ruined skin and bone that sounded damnation and death in a thousand dead tongues.

The horde broke against the wall, and there was still no sign of Captain Ashish. Lieutenants up and down the wall barked orders. With a cry, the warriors of Mishaka rose to the challenge. Up and down the wall stones were dropped, and that first intimidating line of zombie warriors fell back slightly, regrouping.

Near the rear of their ranks and rolling forward, huge, bulky shapes came into view. Siege engines, catapults, moving more slowly than the dead themselves, but coming inexorably closer. Long, snake-like forms worked their way up through the dead ranks, low to the ground and crawling like morbid centipedes, until they broke through the front lines and faced the wall in a long row. Behind and beside them, the dead warriors gathered in groups.

Those on the walls who had faced the dead before began crying out, sending the word up and down the lines:

"Spine chains! They have spine chains!"

As if on cue, the long, serpentine formations of bones wormed forward, rushing the wall on taloned bone hands. They were formed of skeletons chopped off at the waist, the head of each wound around by the rib cage of that above it. They were fused into one entity, the head at the end controlling the direction and motion, and they scuttled like giant insects to the base of the wall, curling upward and clutching at the stone, gripping without regard to the remnants of fleshless fingers.

The lieutenants along the wall directed stones and pitch dropped where the hideous creatures made contact with stone. Where it was pitch, burning torches were dropped to light the things, sending dead warriors scurrying in all directions.

Pain was not a factor, and the spine chains continued their assault even as they burned, one or two actually beginning to get purchase on the wall. One of the things ran back through the ranks of its own army, which spread slowly and clumsily to allow it to pass. At first it seemed a random act, but then its goal became obvious. A large catapult had been dragged closer on huge rollers. As the chains dragged the weapon taut, the spine chain crawled up and over the frame, curling itself like a coiled, burning snake.

Almost too late the defenders realized what was about to happen, and as the huge siege engine was released, sending the spine chain in a looping, fiery arc toward the walls, men followed that arc and were on it in seconds, as it crashed into the stone, shattering at the impact and sending burning pitch in all directions.

Along the wall signals were cried, and the cauldrons of pitch were dumped, rolled along the wall, soaking the oncoming horde. Higher up, in the watch towers, flaming arrows were loosed, and the skeletal wall burst into flames that licked against the city walls and boiled down through the massed zombies.

Among the attackers, horsemen rode back and forth. They appeared to be men, but the veterans on the wall passed a word down the ranks. *Nemissaries.* There might be some men there as well, but the lieutenants of this dead army would be nemissaries, animated zombies with ghosts appropriating their flesh. They screamed taunts at the wall and herded the masses of the dead forward, layer upon layer near the wall.

Then the rear of the horde parted, and something larger rolled forward. Screams and cries of terror rippled up and down the walls. Huge wheels ground ponderously toward the wall, dragged and pushed by hundreds of the dead, ropes stretching out into the swarm, and the creatures clung to them, dragging the thing closer. It was a tower, ladders rising from the back and sides, and it would reach within a very few feet of the top of the city's walls.

Even as it rolled closer, the army of animated corpses crawled up and around and over it, brandishing swords and diving down again into the mass of decay swelling closer and higher, unrelenting and silent. The only voices were those of the defenders, and those of the captains of the dead, riding their circles in the distance and directing the attack.

The dead army moved in surreal pseudo-silence. Their weapons clanged, and in the distance there were the cries of their leaders. The siege towers creaked. Marching steps creaked and groaned as old bone was brought back into action. Their voices were dragging legs, clashing blades, and the ominous clicking and scraping of long-dead sinew and bone, grinding itself into action at their master's bidding.

Those on the walls fought valiantly. Regular ladders joined the spine chains along the wall, more and more of them, forcing the defenders to defend at more points along the wall, spreading them thin. The fallen dead were piled at the base of the wall, mound after mound as the creatures used their comrades for support and climbed, only to be crushed under by the next wave, until the entire wall was alive with handholds of bone and crushed skulls gripped by the bones of feet bereft of flesh and pressing upward. The defense of the walls held, but it was only a matter of time.

From within the walls a clamor arose. Those atop the wall spun, just for a moment, to see that those mustered in the street, waiting to surge up the ladders and stairs in support of the first

line should they fall, were parting. Captain Ashish hurried
toward the wall, or, rather, hurried as much as the lumbering
gait of his companion would allow.

At the captain's side walked M'chwallya. His huge, staring
blind eyes gazed straight ahead at the wall, and he walked with
the captain's hand on his biceps, leading him toward the stairs.
Those at the base of the wall parted. Those atop the wall began
to cry out to their captain, passing on reports from up and
down the wall. Dharni listened, but only with half his attention.
He was intent on getting the blind giant up the stairs and onto
the tower to the right of the gate.

When he had managed this, seating the giant beside him, he
gazed down and out over the enemy. Their leering, death-mask
faces had risen to only a dozen yards below the wall now, and
they climbed steadily, scrabbling at the stone like giant, fleshless rodents. M'chwallya seemed oblivious to it all. He was talking in a low voice, whispering about Dharni's private thoughts.
The captain was tempted to remove his head with a swift back-
stroke of his blade and give his plan up as foolish.

Dharni stared out over the field of dead attackers. His archers
were doing their best to pick off the nemissaries—as Dharni
had ordered them to—but to little effect. Every time one was
struck down, the ghost inside would simply possess a nearby
shambling corpse, remount its skeletal steed and resume giving orders. Sometimes they even paused to take the helm and
weapons off their previous body.

He watched as one nemissary fell under a volley. The mass
of dead around him seemed to lose some of their drive, but only
for a moment. Soon enough one of their corpses had been appro-
priated and they returned to the march on Mishaka's walls.

Dharni turned to M'chwallya. The blind giant seemed to
regard him in return, but when Dharni moved, M'chwallya's
eyes did not. They continued to stare at the wall where Dharni
had stood. Dharni glanced about him to be certain none were
listening to the words. He reached into a pouch at his side, drew
forth a silver piece, and pressed it into the giant's hand.

"Listen to me," he hissed to the giant. "They say a god's
blood runs in your veins. I believe it, because you've laid bare

my secrets before. You know who I wanted to see without her tunic two nights past, and you know that I wish I had stayed at home, caring for my mother, but could not bear another day in that house. You've told me these things, and more, more than I care to hear, more than I care for you or any man to know.

"Our city is about to fall, overrun by the army of a deathknight. We are fighting, but we are just men. Look at this army of dead. Look with your blind eyes and tell me *their* secrets as you tell me mine."

"D'night c'ms," the hulking, god-blooded seers said. "Th'u the g'ave."

Dharni snarled in frustration. "I know, I know! But if these walls don't hold, the deathknight's rear attack won't make a difference."

A roar rose to the right. Dharni spun. The dead had managed to arrange two of the spine chains and a huge ladder together on the wall, the hands of the strange creatures gripping the poles of the ladder and binding the mass into a clinging net of wood and bone. Zombie warriors clambered up en masse, and there were too few at that point to defend.

Then another cry rose. A group of soldiers stormed up the stairs inside the walls. It was the mercenaries who had accompanied the caravan: Dace's men. They hit the wall running, blades drawn, and cried out to one another as they came. They hit the wall at the same time the dead warriors topped the wall and there was a crash of blades, harsh cries as weapons bit deep. The ladder in the center was gripped and heaved up—forced back to the wall—lifted again and with a long, creaking groan it toppled back. Dead warriors stared at the walls, unblinking—without thought—as they crashed backwards into their own troops and sent them into disarray.

A curse rose to Dharni's lips, but he bit it back. The giant at his side was mumbling again.

"D'ed're h'ngry," he said. "Feed th'm."

"Yes, yes, the hungry dead," Dharni snapped, "but what does that mean..."

The captain's voice trailed off as he looked again at the massed forces of the dead, especially about the fallen spine chains. The nemissaries were whipping their unthinking forces back into some semblance of formation, but it was slower work this time, and Dharni saw why. Not all those at his walls were dead—in among the force were slaves and wretched but living souls. They seemed to be tending the siege engines and serving as support units, but in the chaos of the fallen spine chains several of them were falling to the claws of the walking dead. The zombies seemed to take great pleasure in sinking their rotted teeth into living flesh.

Dharni shuddered at the thought of those hungry corpses finding feasting on the men and women of his city, but his mind quickly moved to tactics. Another siege engine was approaching the wall, pulled forward by rows of living slaves. "Runner!"

A boy made it to Dharni's side and was gone a moment later, carrying his message to the archers arrayed at high points on the city's walls. Dharni held his breath as the fighting continued below him, and the rows of living slaves pulled the next massive siege engine toward him. The nemissaries pulled the zombies back to allow the slaves through. *Now*, Dharni thought. *Now!*

A volley of arrows shot from the walls and rained down among the unarmored slaves. Red gore ran on the battlefield as they fell and died under the rain of wood and iron. The nearby walking dead, some pierced with arrows but still ambulatory, seemed to react to the scent of blood.

The archers fired again, but this time concentrating on the few nemissaries among the bloodied mass, driving them off or destroying their corpses. The walking dead, devoid of command, set about feeding on the wounded slaves among them. Chaos spread around the siege engine, as nemissaries tried to reassume command but found that the walking dead's hunger for life made them less willing to take orders.

Dharni could see that this chaos wouldn't last long, but it had slowed the onslaught. Maybe it would buy them enough time.

Chapter Nineteen

The Drinker of Seeping Poison closed his eyes, savored the chill, stagnant air of the Underworld. He took in the sound and scent of death, the crackle of essence and energy where the worlds of day and eternal death clashed. He felt the weight of the talisman in his palm and the burn of the soulsteel of his blade, its hilt hot and cold all at once in his grip.

They were not far behind from the Underworld equivalent of the walls of the city, and he could imagine his army wrecking havoc in the land of the living.

Behind him, a smaller, hand-picked group made up of his two closest lieutenants and a handful of nemissaries marched in tight ranks. There wouldn't be much room for them to exit at the far end. It would have done him no good to bring larger numbers, so he'd gone with the best he had. If Daedalus hadn't proven to be a traitor, he would have been there.

The Drinker of Seeping Poison had been afforded the time to think on that betrayal. It had made little sense at the time, and it made—if possible—even less as he continued to consider it. Daedalus was the perfect lieutenant, and the deathknight had had no reason to expect anything less than perfect obedience.

What made sense was that someone had wanted the attack on the city to be announced. There was no way at this point to know if the man, Tarsus, had gotten through or not, and it no longer mattered. The question that did matter, and one that would have to be addressed at some point in the future, was who had wanted the man freed. Who had pulled Daedalus's strings?

The Drinker of Seeping Poison had hand-picked the Dragon-Blooded warrior for this mission. If that choice cost him the city, the Walker in Darkness was not going to be pleased, particularly not since they had managed to raise their force and launch it at Mishaka without bringing the Mask of Winters down on their heads. No one would believe the Walker was behind it. That part of the plan had gone flawlessly.

With these thoughts itching at him, he concentrated on the army above and the road in front of him as they rode on toward Mishaka through the darker landscape of the underworld. There wasn't much farther to go.

Dace and Lilith hurried down a twisted trail. The way was lined with stone formations and the bent, gnarled trunks of trees without leaf or bud. The road beneath their feet was cold and repulsive to the touch. There was a hum in the air, the sound of thousands of voices crying out for succor, screaming in pain as they passed over, pressing their weight to the pavement.

"What is it?" Dace asked at last, trying to cover his ears with his hands and finding that it did nothing to lessen the sound. "What is that sound?"

Lilith glanced at him, then down at the road beneath their feet. She did not answer. As he followed her gaze, Dace realized no answer was needed.

Their way was lighted, but not by any source he could pinpoint. There was no sun, nor any moon shining overhead. There were mists and odd pockets of shadow lining the road, but for the most part the landscape was bathed in a sort of greenish, liquid glow. It seeped through the pores of Dace's skin and gave it a crawling sensation.

Nothing moved on the road and, after a quick consultation, they turned to their right and moved toward Mishaka. It was difficult to judge distances on the map because they knew little of the landmarks of the Underworld. They also didn't want to expend any unnecessary essence while moving through this cold land.

"It isn't far," Lilith whispered. Or maybe she'd spoken aloud and the dense, chilled air had swallowed the sound.

Dace nodded grimly. He would not show weakness, but he felt it. The air, the ground beneath them, even the dank, clingy illumination drew his concentration from him in long, stretching strands. He could sense how this might change him, how that warped essence could grant him strength if he let it. How he might rot from within and become a part of it all.

Up until the time of his Exaltation, despite good health and the strength he'd been born to, he had felt himself aging. Decaying. It had grown worse later in life, and he could still feel the faint breath of it on the back of his neck, though the Exaltation—the essence—had almost halted it.

The Underworld strengthened that faint breath to a breeze, then to a chill wind. It sank through the pores of his skin and leaked back out, but not without attaching itself to him. Each time his boots struck the sickly pale stone of the road he felt something deep inside, but he ignored it.

Dace was strong. He could fight if he had to—to live and get back to the light of the sun in the world above. He felt the mortality he'd all but left behind, though; the weakness of a life he had thought once was strong.

Gritting his teeth, he sped his pace slightly. Lilith managed to remain at his side, but he knew she must be fighting a similar battle. She was old—so old, and so wise in her own way—that if he dwelled on it too long the distance between ages—literal ages, not just those of human life—might drive him insane. She bore it all with stoic calm, but he could see in her stride and in the set of her shoulders that she was struggling, possibly harder than he. She had been here before and had known what to expect, but that was only a feeble advantage. The place was death, and it was closer than Dace wanted to come to it.

"We are here," Lilith said, stopping before a dark cave mouth in a rock wall near the side of the cold road they traveled.

"This is Mishaka?" Dace felt a renewed sense of dread as a cold wind seemed to blow from the cave mouth.

"No," Lilith said, "but it is a passage toward the city. Through the Labyrinth."

Dace said nothing. He knew little about the ways of the Underworld. "It will get us there in time?"

"This is what the map is for. It will help us navigate the Labyrinth, but only once."

"Let's go then," said Dace and stepped into the mouth of the cave.

Dace and Lilith pushed their way through the tight walls of a strange catacomb. She held the map's parchment, which now glowed a putrid green, and seemed to be redrawing itself with their every step. The map was not alone in that, it seemed, for every time Dace glanced back over his shoulder the path behind them failed to match his memories of what they had just traversed. Immediately after rounding a tight corner, he looked back to see a featureless straight corridor stretching toward infinity.

If they hadn't had Lilith's map, dace was quite certain they would be hopelessly lost in this maze. He found himself longing for the relative sanity of the simple Undreworld.

The catacombs and passageways grew in size as they progressed, until it seemed to dace they were on the roads of some mad underground city. A city with inhabitants.

They rounded a corner and ahead of them on the road, traveling the same direction as they were, was a small party, one mounted and two on foot. There was something *off* about the group. The horse, if horse it was, had an odd stride. It wasn't so much a limp as a stumble, as if the bindings between bones wasn't sound. But that wasn't it, really. There was nothing clumsy in that gait, just—off.

Dace slowed, drawing Lilith to the side of the road and holding her close as he whispered.

"What should we do?" he asked.

"If they don't see us, nothing," she replied, her voice very low. "If we are discovered, and they turn to see us here? We kill them. The masters of the Labyrinth do not take kindly to the living using their passageways. These are servants, but we do not wish to meet those they serve."

Dace stared into her eyes for a moment as if looking for

some other answer, but whatever he sought, it was not there. He nodded. They held back, though every second Dace felt himself becoming more disoriented. The other party was moving at a slow but steady pace, but they never seemed to get any further from Dace and Lilith. It was as if the Labyrinth itself was keeping them close.

The madness of it chaffed at Dace's mind and chipped away at his strength. He needed to be through this, to be with Risa and Krislan, standing tall to defend Mishaka. Instead he was walking through the darkest, most dangerous hours of his life at the side of a beautiful Exalt whom he barely knew, carrying secrets from one so long dead that his dust was only a vague memory to the wind, and hoping against all reason that he would arrive in time to make a difference.

"Enough of this," he said, forcing himself out of his reverie. "Another group could arrive at any moment. We have to get moving again."

"I agree," Lilith said. "The enchantment of the map will not last forever. We must deal with these three, and quickly."

Dace and Lilith moved forward at the same slow, casual pace. If they caught the party's interest too deeply, the others would send a messenger before Dace and Lilith were close enough to stop them. What was required was stealth, and a great deal of luck.

Not turning his head, Dace spoke to Lilith softly through the corner of his mouth. "Move as if you belong here. Pay them no attention at all. If we speed our pace only slightly, we'll eventually catch them."

Lilith nodded very slightly. Her eyes flashed, just for an instant, and Dace felt her desire to deal with those ahead directly. He was pleased that she deferred to his decision.

They walked on, and it was obvious moments later that the party ahead was milling about, slowing their pace and doing whatever they could to allow the two behind to catch up. Dace cursed softly under his breath. Lilith gave no sign she had noticed, but Dace sensed her tension, and he hoped she could hold it in check until they were close enough. They might get only one chance to take these others out, and it would be good to get an idea of who and what they faced before launching that attack. They wanted to get through this with the least expenditure of essence possible. For once in his adult life, Dace did not relish the idea of battle. Not here.

Lilith, on the other hand, was having trouble holding herself in check. Dace noted moments where her form wavered, where images of other forms and times and strengths passed over the space her image occupied, only to be lost in the dim, clouded light.

The distance between where they walked side by side and where the others waited diminished quickly. Dace had sped his pace again, not wanting to put off the inevitable, particularly if it included a battle. He wanted to reach them and make short work of them. If they had to kill these men, then it would have to be quick and complete. There was no time or margin for error. Lilith began to speak as they drew nearer to the other party, her lips barely moving. Dace heard her clearly and kept his eyes on the road ahead, betraying nothing.

"I will take the two on foot," she said softly. "you take the mounted one and the mount as well. If it arrives wherever they are headed with no rider, that is as clear a message as if one of these," she nodded ahead down the road, "rode in themselves to announce our presence."

Dace nodded. He allowed himself a single, searching glance up the road. The two that she would be responsible for were squat and powerful, each easily twice the width of a normal man.

As Dace and Lilith drew nearer, the mounted stranger rode forward out of his group, holding his reins arrogantly in what they could clearly see at the closer distance was a gloved hand, leading to an arm and torso covered in shimmering metal links.

"Where are you headed?" the man asked, easing his mount closer. He rode easily, but the odd, disjointed gait of the horse beneath him gave a false impression of clumsiness. Neither Dace nor Lilith was fooled.

"Not far," Dace replied. He wasn't certain what would set them off. He had no experience of this netherworld, and Lilith was keeping her eyes downcast, as though fully subservient.

"How odd," the man observed. "*Not far* is exactly where we, ourselves, were headed."

"We wouldn't like to trouble you," Dace replied. He met the man's gaze but kept his mind focused on the periphery of his sight. The man, or soldier—which is what he seemed to be, though in what army Dace couldn't tell—communicated to his mount with short tugs of the reins and subtle pressure from his legs. Dace did not doubt that the other two who held back, watching to see what their leader would do or say, were catching these messages as well.

"No trouble at all," the man replied. His hand had been sliding back along his thigh all the while, as though casually, toward the hilt of a large sword that hung from his belt. It shone with a sickly, pale light, reflecting the greenish glow that suffused the place as if it were drinking that tainted light in and spitting it forth, revived.

"Surely," Dace continued, "you would be better able to reach your own goal unencumbered. We travel slowly."

"You have traveled," the man said, allowing his hand the final slip to the hilt of his weapon, "as far as you are likely to travel, without the leave of my master. He would consider me remiss if I did not insist on your accepting my invitation to meet him and come to terms."

"Then," Dace replied, standing up straighter and letting his hand drop to his own weapon, "I believe we have somewhat of an impasse. My companion and I are quite used to keeping our own company, and I'm afraid your master will have to come and seek me out if he wishes to pass the time."

The mounted soldier sat, transfixed by the unexpected opposition to his will and beginning to experience the first pangs of doubt. He continued to return Dace's stare; then something seemed to snap into place in his mind. Dace wasn't sure if it was his own weapon or something in his expression, but whatever had caught the knight's attention, all pretense was gone.

"Kill them!" the mounted soldier snarled. His weapon was up and over his head with startling speed, causing Dace to wonder for a second if the man were of Dragon-Blooded descent. Then there was no time to think.

Dace drew his huge daiklave and swung it up over his head, barely managing to catch the first strike as the warrior bore down on him, driving his mount forward in the hope of catching Dace by surprise. The clang of metal on metal rang out loudly and Dace cursed, wishing only for silence. Their first order was to kill these would-be marauders, but it was also important not to attract more unwanted attention.

And he felt the stroke. It caught him by surprise and very nearly cost him his head. The weapons crashed together, and Dace reached within himself as he snapped his daiklave up to block that first blow. There was a numbing sensation of pain and shock as they struck. In that moment he knew the danger he faced.

In this place, he had only so much to draw upon. He could not afford prolonged combat.

Dace growled and whirled the daiklave in an impossibly swift arc. He did not aim for the rider, but swung instead at the legs of the oddly disjointed horse. Even as fast as he struck, he caught the beast only a glancing blow. All of what had seemed clumsy in the beast's stride fell into a strange symmetry as it moved in defense of its rider.

The thing reared, drawing its legs tight, and whirling, catching only the tip of Dace's blade on its flank. The rider struck again, and Dace fell into the rhythm of the battle. He slipped to the side, feeling the blade slide so close along his flesh that it might have shaved hair, then he lunged up and back. He hooked his arm over the dull back of his attacker's blade and, as the man tried to draw it back upward, Dace twisted his body and dragged the rider from his saddle.

Dace leaped then as the man fell, twisting and cursing and bringing his blade up in a sweeping arc. The man screamed, whirling his blade up to block Dace's attack. Dace paid him no mind. The beast the man had ridden had spun, lifting its hooves in the air. It lunged for Dace, who managed to sidestep the attack and swing his weapon at the horse's flashing hooves.

He caught a glimpse of wild, rolled-back-in-the-head eyes as the animal screamed. His blade had shorn off both front legs cleanly and it was falling. But even in that motion it lunged again, teeth snapping at his shoulder. Dace slammed his fist into the beast's face, dropping it off to the side, and he leaped again, letting his legs flip into the air as the momentum of his slash at the horse drove him up.

His attacker's blade sliced where he had stood, striking nothing but air. With a quick grunt, Dace suppressed a cry of victory and rage. He dropped, driving his blade beneath him in a clean slice that removed the Underworld warrior's head from his shoulders and sent it rolling down the road.

A cry rose behind him. As Dace dropped toward the ground, he arched his back and whipped his legs around and down like twin pistons, driving them into the road and planting. He glanced to where Lilith had faced off against the other two, ready for whatever might come.

Almost.

One of the men lay on the road, rent and torn horribly. The second had spun and sprinted down the road, away from the fight. Lilith chased after him and in step or two she had taken the shape of a great strix, a great owl. Her wingspan was such that she seemed to fill the wide road and she sailed with the silence of all nocturnal hunters.

Her prey turned just before she hit him, his scream cut off as Lilith's great talons cut into his flesh and her bulk knocked him to the ground. Her head descended lighting quick, plunging her sharp beak into the man's flesh and tearing out wet chunks.

Dace turned from the carnage. Near him, the crazed horse writhed, bloody ichor seeping from the stumps of its legs. There was a dark intelligence in its dying eyes, watching them as they started down the road. When it screamed, Dace turned and, with one swift stroke of his blade, severed its head from its writhing body. Everything fell silent.

When he looked back, Lilith had resumed the shape of a woman and was approaching him. Clad in her moonsilver armor, the blood of her victim dripped down her throat.

"The blood of the dead is sour," she said, and spat.

"We have to get out of here," he choked. "We have to move."

Lilith nodded, and drew out the map anew. "This way."

They headed off down a passage that Dace knew had not been there a moment before.

Chapter Twenty

The march was steady and monotonous. The Drinker of Seeping Poison held back, letting the others range before him and scout the way. He kept to the course of the road. In the living world, he knew, his forces would be storming the walls of the city. His walking dead were automated by his necromancy, but the nemissaries would direct them.

The troops with him now, approaching the shadowland at the heart of Mishaka from the Underworld, were under much closer command. They would strike with precision and fury, and with the Drinker at their head. He pressed his force on relentlessly. There was only so much speed possible, but he strove to make use of it all. As concerned as he had been earlier over giving his main force time to breach the walls of Mishaka, he was equally concerned, or more so, that he not arrive too late to be involved in the slaughter.

There was also the question of aid from beyond the city; mercenaries, a renewal of ties with Lookshy that he wasn't aware of, or any number of equally irritating possibilities. He didn't know if they would send mercenaries, but he was fairly certain they would send something, or someone. The only question that remained to him was how many, in what form, and had they arrived ahead of his own army.

A lot more questions remained than the Drinker of Seeping Poison would have preferred. He knew his plan was sound, but he knew, as well, that the soundest plans sometimes went awry. As good as it felt to be walking the roads of the Underworld with his silent lieutenants marching beside him, he still had a care for what might lie ahead. It would not do to step into something he was unprepared for—not after taking such pains to prepare for everything.

As he strode through the dismal, dreary landscape, he entertained himself with thoughts of the city in ruins. He thought of the woman he'd seen in the graveyard, and wondered if she'd gone into the city with stories of how he had "haunted" the dark tomb. More likely, he thought, she had run to her hovel of a home, cowered in a shadowed corner and refused to say a word.

It was in his favor that the tomb was desecrated and well shielded. Local legend kept those few away who would have drawn near, those who were aware of the stories of the man buried there, and his ghost. That ghost had been incarcerated in the Underworld as part of keeping the shadowland hidden. It was a haunted place with no "haunt" as far as the world beyond could see.

There were undoubtedly those in the city with knowledge enough of the dark arts to realize what the place was if they had reason to investigate, and it was true that the army of dead warriors at their gates presented such a reason, but he was counting on their neglecting to remember it under fire, or, barring that, on their inability to do anything to stop him, even if they suspected his approach.

Mishaka was a very old city. He knew that it had withstood greater forces by far than those he brought to bear, and not so far in the past. He knew, as well, that the inner strength of the place, the core of the city, had rotted since then—that the citizens had grown complacent in their illusion of safety. The locals would remember the conflicts of old, but they would not be prepared to repeat them. The very walls of the city were not what they had once been, though he knew they could still withstand a great deal. The Drinker of Seeping Poison counted on the inevitability of decay and the total sovereignty of entropy.

His own army seemed to defy this mindset, but in truth, they exemplified it. Among those raised to his cause were warriors, farmers, the fallen of every state of life, and in the end, they had come to bits and pieces of a single whole. Only his own thoughts betrayed sentience in the horde, and for them he spared as little as was possible to keep them moving steadily toward the city.

By dawn, when the shadowland was more attuned to the land of the living, the Drinker and his forces would be ready to emerge and take Mishaka once and for all.

The Drinker of Seeping Poison felt himself drawing near to the shadowland. He began to reach out with his senses, tasting the very air for the sensation of that place, the dark, decadent flavor of the desecrated ground, the tangy scent of blood and battle that could not fail to waft from there as the walls were assaulted and the battle raged.

He stopped. His lieutenants, sensing his tension, stopped as well and gathered about him, staring into the distance in all directions, up and back down the road and out into the expanse of the Underworld.

Something was wrong.

There was a tang of salt on the air. He faced a ward of some sort. The gateway was still present—nothing had changed that—but there was a barrier.

The Drinker of Seeping Poison frowned. He'd expected that there might be some slight form of resistance among those of the city. He'd even anticipated the possibility that someone might discover the tomb in the graveyard and work some peasant's ward. This felt like neither. It was strong, but the strength was born of objects, not personal essence. It was artfully conceived, but it was not backed by any store of power. It was a barrier, pure and simple. If it held, it held, and if it broke, it broke. The power was in the spell, not the creator of the spell, so it was not an Exalt that had created it. Still, it was irritating. It would take little essence to remove it, but it meant there were defenders on the far side, or at least one.

The Drinker of Seeping Poison reached out and drew his small troop to a slow halt. He strode purposefully up through the center. Soon, the tomb at the center of this small but ancient shadowland stood a few yards away, as he had seen it last in his vision. There was a difference. Nothing physical barred the way, but there was no movement beyond the stone doorway.

There was no light, or motion of wind and shriveled plants to catch his attention. The tomb's doorway was a void of shadow, and it led nowhere.

The Drinker of Seeping Poison stepped nearer. On close examination, there was a greenish haze covering the opening like a fine mesh of the rolled leaves of trees, or a fiber spun from the grass itself. It crossed and re-crossed the tomb's mouth, obscuring all sight of the far side and blocking the way. It looked very fragile, as though he could brush it aside with no more effort than he might need to clear a spider's web from a window. He stood for a long moment, gazing at this intrusion on his plans. Then, with great care, he stretched out his arms, the fingers of each hand spread wide, and he gripped the green strands tightly.

There was a faint spark where his skin touched the green fabric, or mist, or whatever exactly it was, but there was no pain. He smiled. Not so difficult. He closed his eyes, bunched the muscles in both forearms and yanked outward with a quick burst of strength. His fingers stretched the fabric just a bit, and then sprung back toward the center. The glowing, greenish tint of the stuff flared for a moment, but there was no tear. The Drinker of Seeping Poison frowned and stepped back. The ward was going to give, he knew, but it would not be quiet. It was going down with a bang.

Lilith leaned on Dace's shoulder as he peered carefully around a rocky outcropping. The way to Mishaka was just ahead, but there was no way to reach it. If they stepped a foot from where they were hidden, they would be in clear site of the deathknight and his followers, and at least one of the nemissaries was staring in their direction with its unwavering gaze. They posed no real threat, but their leader did, and Dace didn't want to take on the Abyssal in his own land.

They had emerged from the Labyrinth not a mile from here, emerging from what seemed to be an abandoned well. The map that had guided them through the twisting maze beneath the

Underworld faded and crumbled as soon as they set foot on the cold, but solid ground. It had not been difficult to follow the Abyssal's force from there.

The shadowland seemed to be warded. Dace had seen the deathknight repelled by some unknown barrier, and he doubted if a quick charge on their part would get Lilith or him through either. If one attuned and accustomed to these roads couldn't exit the thing, it wasn't likely that Dace or Lilith would be more successful.

Dace leaned carefully around the stone to watch as the deathknight faced off with the ward. Dace knew what the group they had come upon meant: His men were to be attacked from the rear, pinned between the deathknight and his chosen crew of hand-picked warriors and the horde outside the city walls. He hadn't expected things to be so far advanced, and this was a situation he never should have allowed. He'd followed his own desires and abandoned those who depended on him, but there was no time for self-castigation.

If the deathknight was able to win through the ward, he would lead his force into Mishaka, and Dace would follow. Despite the drain this journey had put on them, Dace and Lilith would match their might against the deathknight's. But here in the Underworld, with their reserves already drained, Dace was less certain.

Lilith reached under her armor and retrieved the gold, sun-shaped medallion. Without a word, she pressed it into his hand. Dace was going to protest, to tell her now was not the time to worry over it, and that they could face it together when the task at hand was complete, but before he could speak she had stretched up, placing her lips very close to his ear.

"Take it," she whispered. "It was his, and it's orichalcum. I can't wield it but you can, and if it has a secret still to tell us, you may decipher it in the end."

Dace felt the skin of his hand warm where the metal touched him, and a tiny focus of essence built between him and the small stylized sun. At that moment, anything that might increase his strength was a gift of the gods, and he could tell from her expression it had not had a similar effect on her. If

anything, she seemed relieved to deliver it into his hand.
Gripping the star, Dace leaned heavily into the stone.
He hoped there would not be long to wait.

Chapter Twenty-One

Risa had placed herself atop the desecrated mausoleum. Since Padma had laid her spell, the illusion that had hidden the shadowland was fading. She remained there, balanced on one knee, as they waited. Daedalus had chosen a similar vantage point, waiting atop the sloped roof of a nearby tomb, resting on the tip of his sword, but poised in such a manner that Risa was reminded of a snake about to strike. She shook the image from her mind.

They had all heard and felt the disturbance earlier. Someone, or something, had tried to break the ward that Padma had erected over the tomb. Whoever it was had failed for the moment, but there was no way to anticipate when they might try again with more power and more success.

The only question that remained was whether they would face a flood of dead warriors or one more powerful than the entire horde when that ward finally fell. Risa glanced at Daedalus once again. She remembered the fight with the bone lion very clearly. He was quick, strong, and clever. Still, she didn't fool herself. There was very little hope of the two of them defeating a deathknight in battle. Their one hope lay in surprising the enemy and, failing that, they could only try to draw back slowly, losing as few of their own as was possible and trying to reach the main force in the city. She still had faith that Dace would come, though the edges of that faith were fraying like those of a worn tapestry. For the moment, she knew she could not depend on him in what was to come. They would have to do what they could on their own.

The plan they'd devised gave them a chance, poor as it might be, and Risa intended to give her entire focus to its execution.

She only hoped that her faith in Daedalus wasn't misplaced. If he was still loyal to the Drinker of Seeping Poison, lying to her to make it back to the one he truly served with his weapons and his life, which half her men believed, then it would be over before it had even started. Something in the way he'd looked at her when she'd explained her plan had made her believe. She hoped there wasn't some subtlety she'd missed. He was a powerful ally, but he could be her last enemy. It was a gamble.

The graveyard had fallen silent with the first assault on the ward. Padma had removed herself to the safety of the first line of buildings. Risa had instructed her how to deploy the troops that would serve as the backup if she and Daedalus failed. The plan was to cover the tomb for as long as possible, but if things went wrong—if the two Dragon-Blooded warriors fell—to draw back as slowly as possible toward the center of the city while sending messengers ahead to warn Captain Ashish and Sergeant Krislan. There was little they could do, even if they knew, but Risa did not intend to allow a deathknight to come at them from the rear without warning. They deserved at the least to meet their fates head-on.

From where she stood atop the tomb's roof, Risa felt it first. It was a tremble in the stone, a disturbance in the essence. Not her own, just something she could vaguely sense. She glanced over at Daedalus and, in that same moment, when their eyes locked in understanding, he knew as well. She saw on some level of thought that his hand tightened on the hilt of his sword, so tight that the tendons in his wrist and forearm bunched, and the knuckles of his hand grew white from the effort. There was no deception in his gaze.

If it had not been for her intercession, he would be dead these days past, lying somewhere in the woods where the bone lion found him. Now he might die here instead, but if so, it would not be because he was hunted like a dog.

Then the tomb exploded outward, shearing the stone from the framework of the door, and a figure strode through with shadows gathered about him like a cloak. What had been Padma's ward, the webwork of green, melted to deep, dank gray and settled over the figure, melting into his form—the essence withered and absorbed. Without a sound to mark her motion, Risa drew her spear overhead and leaped, bringing it down with all the speed and force at her command. At that same moment, Daedalus let out a low scream of rage, catching the figure beneath Risa by surprise and drawing his attention— almost long enough.

The Drinker of Seeping Poison crashed through the ward. She saw him, a dark form against the backdrop of shadowed earth and looming graves, as she dropped through the air. As she moved, she accelerated the tip of her spear, driving it down toward the back of his neck. He stumbled just for an instant as the backlash of the broken ward on the tomb rippled around and through him. Then he moved.

He moved so quickly that she would not have credited the motion at all if the tip of her spear had not glanced off his shoulder, shearing through his cloak with little effect and driving on toward the earth. No thought, motion only, as she drove down on that tip and then flipped up and away, narrowly avoiding the arm that whipped in a quicksilver arc through the air where she'd been. Risa landed on her hands, flipped herself up and farther back and landed with a snarl, staring into the deathknight's visage.

She wanted desperately to glance to where Daedalus waited, crouched low, but she knew to do so was the end for them both. She met the deathknight's stare, drew the long slim blade from her hip and slipped cat-like into a battle stance. All sound and motion stopped in that moment. The Drinker of Seeping Poison stood, staring at her, a foot from her own quivering spear, driven deep into the earth and abandoned for the moment. He did not seem to be able to decide what to make of the threat. In that moment, knowing it was suicidal but unable to distract him in any other way, she launched herself, whipping the blade in a lightning slash toward the folds of cloak protecting his face from view.

He simply was not there. The blade bit nothing, drawing her arm almost painfully around as the expected resistance failed her, and though she slashed it back the opposite way, leaping forward again, she might as well have attacked a ghost.

Something crashed into her side and she tumbled away, moving as much as possible with the unexpected blow. He was after her before she'd truly begun to flee, slashing out again, arrogantly ignoring his own weapons and using his hands alone, driving them at her again and again. The first blow had struck solidly. Each successive strike glanced off her constantly moving form. Risa retreated, drawing him after her in an arc. With a cry she launched herself backward and toward the tomb where Daedalus waited. She came up, back against the stone, and saw the deathknight closing in. His gaze was fixed on hers and his hands were raised as though he would drive them through her and the stone beyond her, crumbling both to dust.

The blow did not fall. There was another cry, and Daedalus had launched from the stone over the Drinker of Seeping Poisons' head. The surprise was greater this time, because the deathknight was focused on his kill and Daedalus did not leap up or out, but straight at the deathknight's face. His blade slashed and there was a scream of anger and pain. The Drinker of Seeping Poison dropped back a pace, and Daedalus was on the ground. He did not hesitate. He drew a dagger from his belt and, with all the strength of his broad shoulder, flung it at his ex-master's face.

The dodge was nothing but a blur. The Drinker of Seeping Poison was moving again within seconds, but it was enough. Rather than attacking, Daedalus leaped beyond his foe and gripped Risa's spear tightly. He yanked it from the earth, staggering as the great dire spear, attuned to Risa's hand, sent him off balance. Then, with great concentration, he flung it at her butt-first. With a cry, Daedalus lunged and gripped the deathknight tightly. The essence glowed from him as he exerted everything into that one moment. Just for a second, the Abyssal was immobile.

Risa staggered back, grabbing her dire lance from the air. With a grunt she swung it up and down, driving the butt into the ground and using that motion to launch herself up and forward, the lance tilting as she moved, the sharp tip leaning toward her target.

The Drinker of Seeping Poison snarled. He tore loose from

Daedalus's grip and batted at Risa, nearly catching her again. Still upright, Daedalus sprang forward, and the deathknight was forced to swing back, drawing a long, fork-bladed weapon from his belt and slashing out toward Daedalus's blade. He caught the blade in the tines of the forked weapon and would have snapped it like a twig, but he had to spin, yet again, to block the spear whistling toward his skull. In those precious seconds Daedalus wrenched his blade free and drove desperately back to the attack.

Then the nemissaries burst through the door of the tomb, and behind them the deathknight's lieutenants. The Drinker of Seeping Poison drew back slightly. Both Risa and Daedalus were forced to leap upward once again, taking positions on two of the tombs to fend off the scratching, clambering, dead-eyed corpses that flowed from the mouth of the desecrated tomb like a river of rot.

The Drinker of Seeping Poison moved through the mass of them, keeping an eye on both opponents, but smiling now. He moved toward Risa first, but he spoke to Daedalus.

"So, you survived after all," he said. His voice was tainted by hatred, but at the same time he seemed on the verge of laughter. "You have no idea how I regretted sending you to your death. That is, I regretted it until I realized why you did what you did. You really are a very good actor. Your master must be proud."

Risa turned, just for a second, to stare at Daedalus, who watched the Abyssal with hatred in his eyes.

The talk was idle, meant to soothe and distract. Risa did not know this, but with the deathknight bearing down on her slowly and the small circle of dark, very capable-looking warriors fanning out behind him, she had no time to worry over the words. Daedalus watched his former master with dead, cold eyes.

"You may come to regret not killing me when you had the chance," Daedalus replied.

"Oh, that's not a problem," the deathknight replied, still moving slowly in a circle away from the mausoleum, slipping closer to Risa with each step. His movements were subtle and it was obvious that he had no intention of hurrying the moment.

He had the aspect of a snake: ready to strike, but working for the opening. "No one that would understand what has happened here will ever see you alive. You must know you can't harm me. Not if there were ten or twenty of you. Not if there were a hundred—and there are only two."

"If there was only myself," Daedalus replied, cutting his way easily through the deathknight's guards, who were falling back to protect their leader, though he hardly needed the support. Daedalus drove his blade right, then left, blocking each attack easily and smoothly and dancing between the blades of warriors and nemissaries alike, "You would still have something to worry about," he continued. You underestimated me once, and it was a mistake. You won't get a second chance."

The Drinker of Seeping Poison drew his head back, and he laughed. He turned to keep Risa in his gaze, drawing his long wicked blade and keeping the forked blade in his opposite hand. The laughter was still on his lips when Daedalus leaped. He drove straight through the scattering guards and relentlessly toward the deathknight. He cried out and drew his blade back for a final, death-dealing blow.

In that second, the Drinker of Seeping Poison's laughter died. His blade whipped up and around, driving through the air to meet Daedalus's own thrust. Risa took advantage of the moment. She dove toward the Abyssal's back from her own perch on the tomb with a cry of her own. The deathknight shifted even as the wicked jade tip of her dire lance whipped through the air toward his throat. The blow glanced off and Risa fell, rolled to her feet and spun back with a snarl.

At that moment, a voice cut through the din of battle and everything seemed to slow. The deathknight's men drew back once more, this time moving away from the tomb and toward the gates of the cemetery in confusion.

A cry arose from the city then, and Padma burst from the line of buildings beyond the fence with her troop of guards and several of the mercenaries. The deathknight snarled at his men to meet the charge and turned back to his own battle.

The voice did not belong to any of the three. Risa spun to the sound. The Drinker of Seeping Poison grew very still, poised with both blades held loosely and easily.

They all turned and, in the mouth of the tomb, his daiklave drawn and essence burning around his body like golden fire, stood Dace.

"If you are so eager for a fight, filth," Dace called out, "you'd better turn this way."

The Drinker of Seeping Poison stared. The Abyssal's chest tightened and he took a single step back. But that was all.

Still, Dace gave Risa renewed courage. She cried out fiercely and turned back to the deathknight with a snarl.

With a leap, she was at her captain's side. The deathknight still stood, watching mutely, the corners of his lips turning up in a grim smile. He saw what she saw, knew what he faced, and there was no fear in him—only a deadly calm and the assurance of his power.

The guard that had accompanied him was gone, out of the gates and headed on into the waiting force beyond. The nemissaries animated one corpse, then another as each fell, and the clash of weapons rang through the graveyard. Padma and Krislan met the threat, and the graveyard became a smaller battleground now.

From behind Dace emerged a woman in silver-hued armor. Or at least she was a woman for an instant. As soon as Risa had taken note of her, and recognized her for the woman who had come into camp on their way to Mishaka, Lilith melted into the form of an owl and soared into he sky. Risa had no time to think on this. There were immediate threats to deal with.

The Drinker of Seeping Poison did not move. Risa caught sight of Daedalus in motion beyond his former master, keeping tombstones between himself and the Abyssal's peripheral vision. The deathknight had no attention to spare him or Risa. He was focused on Dace.. Energy crackled between the two combatants, and Dace's features were rigid with concentration. The Drinker sheathed first one sword, then the other and gave a small, mocking bow to Dace.

Risa thought fast. She could drive in, attack from the flank and hope that Daedalus would catch the motion and attack from the far side, causing the deathknight to split his attention between the two of them and give Dace a chance to attack, but it was too uncertain. The two were faster than human warriors, or even Dragon-Blooded. Both her attack and that of Daedalus might miss the mark entirely. They might distract Dace, instead of their common enemy. They might be the diversion that would cause her captain's death.

She'd seen Dace drive a blade through solid stone to cleave an enemy, and she took heart in that. But the deathknight was no simple opponent. He could match Dace blow for blow and Dragons only know what the captain had gone through to get here from within that cursed tomb.

So she waited, crouched and ready, keeping herself in motion so she would not be an easy target; what move she did make would have the element of some surprise behind it. She kept her eyes on the deathknight. Dace would be doing the same, she knew, and it would do no good for her to follow her captain's movements. The one they needed to take out—the one that mattered most in all of this—was the Drinker of Seeping Poison. That one had to die.

Suddenly, the Drinker of Seeping Poison lunged at Dace, arms outstretched. Dace countered, raising his blade, but as he did so, the deathknight seemed to fade, dematerializing. Only the sound of boot on gravel alerted Dace as the attack came from the rear. The Drinker of Seeping Poison had shifted and re-materialized.

With a growl, Dace drove forward and spun. The deathknight was on him. The Drinker of Seeping Poison's form had stiffened, and he held his hands before him, rigid like claws. The air had grown colder, and there was a bright blue fire burning from the tips of his fingers, dancing and singing about him as he struck.

Dace countered with the hilt of his daiklave, barely turning the blow, and where the deathknight's skin struck the hilt, the weapon iced over. Dace cringed from that cold and backed up a step, but it was a feint. He drove the blade forward in a lightning arc toward the deathknight's throat.

His opponent was quick and side-stepped this attack, returning by drawing his own blade, at last. It was long and dark, forged of soulsteel and winking in the dim light, seeming more to steal the illumination from the air than to reflect it. The Abyssal began to whirl the blade hypnotically and, as he did so, trails of black shadow streamed from whirling of the blade, making the blade hard to follow. "Dace," Risa cried out, "be careful!"

It was a pointless warning. There was nothing she could do without putting him at risk. If the deathknight swung on her, Dace might open himself to attack trying to prevent it.

Then she saw Daedalus, skirting the cursed tomb that held the shadowland and moving around behind Dace. She frowned: What could he be up to? Why would he be flanking Dace, instead of watching his former master, unless...

She sprang. There was no time for thought. If Daedalus intended to attack Dace from behind, it could be all over. Dace moved well enough, for the moment, but his opponent was fresh, strong, and deadly. Any additional burden might signal the end.

Risa skirted the tombs, paying no more attention to Dace and the Drinker of Seeping Poison for the moment. She leaped to the roof of another squat tomb and down the other side in time to see Daedalus kneel on the ground and law down his sword.

With a frown, she dropped beside him.

"What are you doing?" she asked. "We have to watch them—find a way to help Dace."

"I can help," Daedalus replied. He fished about in a pouch on his belt, and Risa watched anxiously. Behind them, the sound of clashing blades rose. She turned back.

The deathknight's second attack was furious. His blade danced and whirled. The shadows seemed to clutch at it, then echo its motion in opposite directions, or hang in place where the blade had been, confusing its motion.

Dace was bathed in sweat. He had countered every blow, but seemed to be slowing. Risa noted with a grim expression that he seemed barely able to defend himself, let alone mount a counterattack.

Just then, Dace whipped his huge blade in a glittering arc,

low to the ground near the Abyssal's legs, nearly catching the dark warrior by surprise. Nearly. The Drinker of Seeping Poison flipped up and back with a quick cry, avoiding the stroke of the blade and renewing his own attack the second his feet touched ground.

"Whatever you're trying to do," Risa whispered harshly, "you'd better hurry up and do it, or there will be no point."

Daedalus ignored her and brought forth a small chain of black iron from around his neck. He drew it over his head and lay it in his left palm. He then closed his left hand and drew the chain out by yanking it with his right. As he did so he whispered in some dark tongue Risa did not know.

Daedalus opened his left palm, revealing where the chain's sharp links had cut deep gashes. Red blood welled up from there, but so did some inky blackness. Soon that ichor defied gravity and rose into the air, transforming first into shadowy smoke and then into the shape of some hungry spirit.

"Necromancy," Risa whispered.

"Not quite," Daedalus answered. "A bound ghost released." The spirit sailed from over Daedalus and into the night sky.

"Whatever it is, is leaving," Risa hissed. "Come, we have to do what we can."

She was turning back, her spear held tightly in both hands, when Daedalus stopped her, one hand on her shoulder. Risa whirled, ready to strike him if he detained her again, but when she spun, she found him staring into the sky intently.

The spirit was dropping now, not slowly, but with dizzying speed. It dove straight at the battling Exalts and, as it drew near, released a rage-filled cry. The sound reverberated through the cemetery, caromed off the graves and soaked into the stone. The Drinker of Seeping Poison spun as if to defend against the new intrusion.

Dace moved as well, but not in defense. He side-stepped and slid his hand to his belt. He dropped to one knee in a squat. Suddenly he rose, flicking his arm out like a whip.

Risa saw something glitter, heard the cry of the ghost rise again, and saw the deathknight whip his blade up towards the oncoming attack with a cry of his own. Just as it seemed he would cleave the moaning spirit into two halves, he faltered, stepping back as though confused. Dace moved in, slashing up and out with a booted foot to drive it into the Drinker of Seeping Poison's throat.

Just before that impact, Risa saw it. Something gold and gleaming protruded from the deathknight's throat. The spirit fell on the deathknight then and inhaled, pulling black essence from his very eyes and mouth.

Dace struck again then, his daiklave flashing into the Abyssal and through the hungry ghost. The orichalcum blade planted itself in the deathknight's chest and in the ground beneath it. When Dace pulled it free, his enemy was dead and gone.

Daedalus didn't pause at the Solar's side, but went directly to the fallen deathknight. He whipped his blade up and began to hack, wildly at first, then methodically. He severed one arm, then the next; moved to the legs, kicking each bit and piece of flesh away from the still-quivering, writhing form on the ground before him.

He leaned close then, catching the Drinker of Seeping Poison by the hair, and lifted him so the two were face to face in that final instant. He'd planned many things he would say if this moment ever came; a thousand lines had run through his mind. All of them failed him in that instant.

With a growl, he released his grip on the hair and, with a final mighty stroke, lopped the head from the deathknight's body. As it rolled free, he stepped in quickly. "We'll need to burn the corpse," he said. "To be done with him."

Risa went to get a torch.

Chapter Twenty-Two

Krislan and his men fell back slowly, using the narrow streets to their advantage as the deathknight's guard rushed after them. They were few in number, but they were strong, and the nemissaries lent an added power to their attack. Their intent was to overwhelm and overrun any opposition between themselves and the front gate, to try and win through the inner defenses and force a breach in the wall for the army beyond.

Krislan wanted to break and run for that graveyard. He knew he'd be next to no use against the deathknight, but he feared for Risa. Krislan had not come to trust the other Dragon-Blooded, Daedalus, despite the man's apparent honesty, and the sergeant didn't like leaving his lieutenant alone with only that one for aid when the enemy was so powerful.

Too powerful, in fact. In his heart, Krislan knew that without Dace they had little hope of standing against such an enemy. Risa was strong in her own way, and Krislan had heard the story of Daedalus and the bone lion enough times to understand that, at least in his ability to fight, the man was a good one to have at your side. Still, a bone lion was not a deathknight, and even such a pair of Dragon-Blooded as the two he'd left in the cemetery had little hope of doing more than slowing the Drinker of Seeping Poison. If Dace didn't arrive soon, the only hope was to meet up with Dharni and his forces and organize some form of retreat from the city.

Krislan leaped from the alley where he'd stood secreted among the shadowed forms of a half-dozen of his men, and lopped the head from a howling nemissary. The thing toppled, the dead body crashing to the earth then rising slowly. Krislan cursed and, as the thing's comrades turned toward him, his own surged up at his side, driving into their flank. The fighting was quick, furious, and final. The small group of the enemy was quickly driven back, but they had the advantage of the narrow street as well. With Krislan advancing, it wasn't difficult to hold him in check. The nemissaries, corpses animated by disembodied ghosts, did not tire as easily as the mercenaries, and the battle raged one direction, then the other. Krislan was bathed in sweat and already his sword arm was weary.

They were drawing near to the main street. The gates would come into sight soon. Krislan barked to one of his men, sending the soldier rushing off toward the city's main gate in search of Dharni.

"Tell him we will hold them off his back as long as we can," Krislan cried. "Tell him to turn some of his forces to our aid, or we will not hold."

The man was gone without a response, but Krislan knew he'd deliver the message. All of those under his command were well aware of the situation and there would be no time or energy spared in carrying out his order. Krislan didn't know what support Dharni could offer, but his men were tiring. Those that the councilwoman, Padma, led off to his right were in worse shape yet. Most of them had never been in a battle, and a number had fallen to the overwhelming numbers of their attackers.

Krislan had seen Padma herself wielding a long, thin blade and driving a grinning warrior from the back of one of her followers, then dragging the man back into the shadows. There was more to the councilwoman, he decided, than met the eye. But that was a thing that could only be pursued if they won their way through the current battle and the horror to come when the deathknight fell on them.

With a dark cry, the Abyssal's small force drove down the center of the street, making a sudden break for the far end and the gates. Krislan growled at those behind him and stepped further toward the center of the street. His men circled in behind him, and he saw that Padma and what remained of her force slid from the shadows on the far side of the street to join them.

"We have to stop them," Krislan grunted, nodding at the approaching attackers. "We strike them down, but the nemissaries take the bodies of their companions and come at us again. Or the bodies of our own" His gaze darkened. "I don't know how long we can hold. I can't see the end of the damn things."

"They died once," Padma replied.

There was no fear in her voice, Krislan noted. She stood steadily at his side, ready for whatever was to come. She was a strong woman, and with some surprising skills for a city council member.

"Something is happening," she said softly. "Something we can't see. Don't you hear it?"

Krislan turned to her. "What do you mean? Is it the deathknight? Is he coming?"

"I don't believe so," she said, lowering her weapon.

Krislan was about to warn her to remain on her guard but, as he turned back to the attacking horde, he saw that they faltered. The foremost among them, those farthest from the graveyard, wobbled on their feet and seemed uncertain whether to continue down the road.

Krislan growled and leaped forward. His men, and Padma's as well, surged around him. They caught the hesitating warriors in the center of the street and overran them. The first onslaught caught them slightly off-balance. Some mercenaries were injured and fell aside, but others leaped in to fill the holes. By sheer force of numbers they pressed the Abyssal's followers back toward their master and the graveyard, and within moments, Krislan's blade parted the last of their heads from dead shoulders. The human warriors broke and ran back toward the graveyard, but again they stopped, and Krislan was on them. Then the battle was over. The sound of approaching footsteps from the road behind them echoed off the walls.

There were loud cries, and Krislan spun toward the gates. A troop of guards was hurrying toward them, weapons raised. Krislan strode to meet them, holding his hands up to slow their progress.

"There is no more threat here," he said. "I don't know how, but the deathknight must have fallen. The dead still stumble at the walls, but they are like puppets whose strings have been released."

"To the walls!" the sergeant in charge of the small troop cried. "If there is still fighting to be done, it is there."

Krislan nodded. He was about to turn and order his men in behind the others, when he saw someone moving near the end of the road. Three familiar figures came into view.

Krislan sheathed his sword and turned, running toward the small group with all the energy and strength still his to command. The sergeant of the guards called out behind him for him to follow, but he hardly heard the man.

"Dace!" he cried.

His captain strode forward, essence burning from his brow. Risa and Daedalus were at his side.

"What happened?" Krislan asked.

The three continued walking and he fell into step beside Risa.

"The deathknight has fallen," she replied, when the others remained silent. "We need to make it to the walls."

Krislan nodded. He led the way, joined moments later by Councilwoman Padma.

"Dharni still holds the walls," he said as they walked.

Risa nodded. I don't believe you'll find much fight left in them," she replied, "but I imagine he'll welcome the reinforcements."

"When this is all over," Krislan growled, "one of you is going to have to tell me what the hell happened back there."

"Gladly," Daedalus grinned, tossing a quick mock salute. "It was a good fight. The better man won—that is the short of it. The long will have to wait for evening, wine, and an end to this fight."

"I'll take you up on that," he said, taking off toward the main gate at a trot.

Daedalus fell in easily at his side. They rounded the corner back onto the main street and headed for the gates of Mishaka.

They found Captain Ashish standing on the rampart, just above and to the right of the main gate. Krislan was shocked to see the giant M'chwallya in the guard shack.

Dharni turned to them, a sardonic grin on his face. The captain had his hands clasped easily behind his back, and he was staring out over the field. What Krislan saw when he followed that gaze with his own stopped him in his tracks. The plain was littered with bones. They were stacked against the city walls, crumbled in piles and heaps. There was some movement, riders and others moving across the battlefield. Krislan gasped as a giant strix swept from the sky and tore one of the riders from his mount, only to drop him a few seconds later from a prodigious height.

"Ha!" Dace said. "Has she been at them long?"

"She drove back two waves of them before the dead all fell," the Mishakan captain answered. "She's been picking off the nemissaries ever since."

"So," Krislan said at last. "When the dark one fell, they all fell."

"So it would seem," Dharni replied, "though not immediately. They continued to attack after they lost direction, but without real purpose. The beast woman made short work of them then, and the rest eventually just collapsed."

"So I see," Dace said. "Risa, let's help finish those last few. Krislan, stay with the captain and make sure we don't have nay left inside the walls. You as well," he said, indicating Daedalus.

Dharni watched Dace and Risa leave to join the beatwoman on the battlefield. He was glad to see them go, and glad not to follow. He wanted very little to do with the creature he's seen lay waste to an army of the dead.

Dharni took M'chwallya by the arm, helping him to rise and leading him gently down the stairs. The big man was uncharacteristically silent and tractable. He glanced at Krislan and at Daedalus, but he said nothing of their lives, their secrets, past or future. He allowed himself to be led down the stairs. Krislan saw that, as they passed, others filed into the guard house and hefted the great bow, bearing it reverently after their captain.

With a shrug, Krislan followed, Daedalus close by his side. They walked a few paces behind Dharni until they'd rounded the corner and begun the trek back toward the center of the city. Guards fell in behind them, whispering among themselves, but Krislan could make out none of what they said.

They moved through the alleys until they came to the central square where Krislan had first met the dark giant. With almost reverent compassion, Dharni led the big man to his constant seat near the square, waiting to release the huge arm until M'chwallya was settled, staring placidly out at the taverns and alleys, oblivious to the carnage littering the roads.

"Thank you, my friend," Captain Ashish said. He turned away and shouted at the tavern across the street, "Bring food and wine. Lots of it. Mishaka has a new hero—see that he is comfortable."

Tentative heads poked out of windows and doors, staring at Dharni in wonder, but moments later men and women scurried to do as he'd bid. The captain turned back.

M'chwallya did not return his gaze, nor did he acknowledge the thanks. He stared off across the street, straight through the stone walls of the bar across the street. Captain Ashish watched him in silence a few moments more, then turned, giving Krislan a shrug, and stepped away.

As they all turned, the deep voice of the dark giant floated across the empty space between them and drew them to a halt, just for a second.

"He c'm afer all," M'chwallya said. "He c'm an D'f died."

Dharni turned back. He stared into that huge, indifferent face, and then he broke into a smile. "That he did," Dharni replied. "He came, and Death died."

Once they had set patrols to find the last of the dead in the city, Krislan left Dharni and returned to the graveyard. He found the makeshift pyre Risa an Daedalus had built still smoldering, and Padma near it.

"The shadowland is still here," she said when he approached, "but this one will not return. At least for a time."

"Did you see the beast woman out there," he asked.

"Yes," she said. "A daughter of the Moon as your Dace is a child of the Sun."

Krislan stared at her for a moment longer. "This is a mad time."

"Perhaps," Padma said, taking him gently by the arm. "But leave it for the morning. Leave it all."

She drew him closer by that touch, and thoughts of Anathema, Exalts and the dead seemed to fade into the background. She led him from the cursed graveyard and where his skin met hers, an energy tingled; something brighter than the adrenaline that had powered the preceding days and nights.

They passed the central square on their way from shadow to shadow, and Krislan heard a deep voice floating in the air behind him.

"Very hot," M'chwallya whispered. "Might m'lt."

The darkness swallowed Mishaka, and all was silent but the soft pacing of the guards making their rounds and the whisper of the wind through empty streets.

Chapter Twenty-Three

Morning broke at last. The sun worked its way into the corners of the city, banishing shadows and poking through curtains and windows to coax the citizens of Mishaka, warriors, merchants, guards and mercenaries, into wakefulness. The streets were alive with activity. There was a great effort underway to clean the remains of the enemy from the streets. Dust had been caught in the grip of the wind and tossed about, coating everything in a thin, pale film.

Krislan rose groggily to find that Padma had gone on ahead of him. There was fruit and a dark, heady tea waiting for him on the table beside the bed. Dressing quickly and doing what he could to make himself presentable, he devoured the food and washed it down with the tea, finding that the drink worked miracles on his head and senses. By the time it was gone, he was alert and felt ready for almost anything.

He stepped into the street and asked the nearest person, a young lad with tousled hair and a broom half again as tall as himself, where Padma had gone.

"There is to be a meeting," the boy replied, slightly wide-eyed at coming face to face with a man of the sergeant's size and war-like appearance without warning. Krislan saw the boy glance more than once at the doorway where he'd exited Padma's quarters, but the lad made no comment.

"The Council is to meet, and the others," the boy continued.

"Where will they meet?" Krislan asked. "In the Council chamber?"

"No," the boy said, pointing up the street. "They will meet at the Broken Arrow Inn. One of the others, pardon my calling them so, you being one of them, and all…" The boy blushed and lost his tongue for a moment. "One of the others is still weak, and they thought better than to move him, sir."

Krislan patted the boy on the shoulder and turned in the direction indicated. The Broken Arrow was the place he'd left Dace and Risa. He had vague memories of the walk that had brought him to Padma's quarters, and he quickly began to retrace his steps. As he passed through the square, he was happy to note that M'chwallya was not yet in his customary seat. The sergeant had no desire to know what the big man would say that morning.

A few more moments travel, and he came to the doorway of the inn. There were a number of armed men milling about outside, and he saw that two of them were in conversation with Captain Ashish. Krislan stepped closer and waited for the captain to be finished.

"Good morning," Dharni said, turning with a wicked smile creasing his weathered face.

Krislan blushed slightly, then laughed and held out a hand, which Dharni clasped in a powerful grip.

"Any morning after a battle that you are still alive to see is a good one," the sergeant replied. "Very good, in fact."

"The others are inside," Dharni said, turning and moving toward the door to the Broken Arrow. "Your captain is in much better spirits today, but Risa has insisted that he continue to rest, so here he remains. I think I'd avoid getting in her way when her mind was set, myself."

Krislan laughed. "And it would be a wise decision," he replied. "I've known Risa for a while now, and she is not one to take insubordination lightly, even from our captain."

They entered together. Krislan saw that all of the members of the council he'd seen a few nights before had gathered. They had drawn several tables together in a facsimile of their council room, and had arranged themselves much as they had been arranged when he first came before them. Padma had taken her place at one end, and Krislan saw the short, dwarfish man, and the others. Dace sat, propped on a long couch that had been drawn up beside the table. Risa stood behind him, one hand on his shoulder. Off in a darker corner, also behind, a woman with the flowing white hair, silver armorand the eyes as old as the moon stood. Krislan shivered and made his way around to stand back a little behind Risa.

"I think we are all here now," Padma said softly. "We all know Sergeant Krislan, and most of us have had the pleasure of working with Lieutenant Risa," she nodded at those she mentioned, still smiling. "Before we continue, though, perhaps we could be introduced to our newest arrivals so that we may properly thank the pair of them for our salvation."

Dace reached up and pushed Risa's hand away gently. He stood slowly, rising to his full height, his weathered, well-mus-cled skin gleaming in the soft sunlight pouring in through open windows. He addressed them carefully, turning and meeting each set of eyes as he spoke.

"I am Dace," he began. "My companion is Lilith.. I have been remiss in my duty. I have made promises I did not prop-erly keep."

He hesitated for a moment, and then continued. "I beg your forgiveness for not arriving with my men and making short work of the threat. I did not know of the shadowland inside Mishaka's walls, or of the second force attacking through the Underworld.

"The resourcefulness of your own forces, particularly the leadership of Captain Ashish, has been exemplary. I am not even certain, had it not been for the deathknight, this Drinker of Seeping Poison, that we would have been necessary at all."

Captain Ashish nodded slightly, acknowledging the praise in silence.

Dace stepped back and seated himself once more. Padma waited to be certain that he was finished speaking. Then she continued.

"We have spoken among ourselves in the early hours of the morning," she said. "While you are right in saying that you did not arrive when it was promised, the fact is—you did arrive. When things were as dark as they were likely to get, you were there. Though you had little strength left to you, you spent it in our service, and for this we thank you. If the city had contracted your services in our defense I would feel differently, but the aid you did bring was of your own accord. The caravan arrived safely. That was your only charge.

"Your Sergeant Krislan will tell you it was not an easy thing for us to trust aid from Nexus. We were determined *not* to trust you, as a matter of fact. When the sergeant spoke of you in such glowing terms, a Solar Exalted riding to the rescue of our city, the thought that first came to mind, and stuck, was 'what do they want?' Though Sergeant Krislan assured us that you only came to our aid, we had no proof of it and, though trade is brisk, we have little communication with the leaders of Nexus."

Dace nodded. "I was afraid you'd feel that way, but I trusted in Risa and Krislan to make good on my promises, and through those promises to prove my word."

"As they did," Padma replied, smiling. "Better, I believe, than you might have anticipated."

Risa stepped forward, tapped Dace on the shoulder, and whispered in his ear quietly. Then, at a nod from Dace, she stepped back.

"Risa has reminded me," he said, "that our victory owes a debt to one other—an ally from a very unlikely quarter."

Dace turned, nodding at Daedalus, who had kept himself back and out of the way. "Daedalus was the first to warn us of the shadowland inside Mishaka. If it had not been for his aid, the deathknight might have wrought much greater damage on the city. He fought valiantly, and I'm tempted to think he's redeemed his earlier actions."

Daedalus nodded, his expression giving away nothing

"It has been a time of strange alliances," Padma said. "I hope that you will carry our good will back to those who sent you to us, as you have carried their good will to the walls of Mishaka."

"I will, and gladly," Dace replied. "It may be that this is just a beginning. There are enough dangers in the world to make allies valuable. I am at your service if you find yourself in need of a mercenary captain, and I believe you can count on Nexus as an ally if you are in need."

"We will keep that in mind," Padma replied. "And we will be more attentive to our own defenses. This attack has shown us the folly in entropy. We will be finalizing the repairs of the city walls, and we will be revitalizing the guards. Captain Ashish will be supervising that effort for us, and a better man could not be found, I think, for such a task."

Dace nodded gravely.

"I thank you for that," Dharni cut in. "I believe that I am well suited to the task of guarding this city, and very pleased to hear that the lessons learned over the past few days have not gone unheeded."

After a few moments of silence, the gathered members of the council began whispering among themselves, and Padma stepped forward once again.

"The final wish of the council," she said in closing, "is that you and your men will accept the hospitality of Mishaka for a day or so to replenish your strength and allow us to renew your supplies before you return to your homes."

Dace smiled. "We'll happily accept your offer," he replied. "Another day of rest will serve us well."

Padma bowed slightly and turned, making her way from the room. Krislan waited a few moments as the rest of the council filed out, then followed. She was waiting for him outside.

"I have much to do today," she said softly, "but I would be pleased if you would accept my personal hospitality for the remainder of your stay in the city."

Krislan grinned. "I was hoping you would say that," he replied. "I'm sure there will be plenty for all of us to do before the sun is set, but I will return to you then."

Padma nodded and turned away. Krislan watched her go, then re-entered the Broken Arrow.

Risa was off to one side in deep conversation with Daedalus. Dace had retired to the darker corner, where Lilith had remained throughout the morning's activities.

Dace noted Krislan's return and beckoned to him. The sergeant hurried to his captain's side.

"We need to go back to the cemetery," Dace said. "I need to try to locate something. Can you lead us there?"

Krislan nodded. "Easily. I'll be seeing that place in my dreams for a long time to come."

Dace nodded. He stood, waited for Lilith to step up beside

him, and then followed Krislan out of the inn. They moved down the street, slipping through the alleys that Captain Ashish had shown Krislan on his first trip through the city, and passing through the square. M'chwallya was there but, seeing Dace, he held his silence, tracing their progress with his pale, blind eyes. Krislan shivered, turning from the giant and moving more quickly than before, hurrying down the last alley and on through to the graveyard.

As they approached, they noted that the one area was almost free of the debris left by the crumbling army. Once the deathknight's men had left the cemetery, they had not returned. The place was eerie, shadowed and still.

They trooped in, Dace in the lead with Lilith at his side, Risa, Krislan, and Padma bringing up the rear. No words were spoken.

Dace glanced about the pathway and at the tombs, the toppled stones and the dead, lifeless ground near to the entrance of the tomb. The ash pile that had been the Drinker of Seeping Poison lay not far from there.

He used a stick to rout about in the ash to find what he was looking for, and soon enough caught sight of a golden gleam. He reached down and picked up the star-shaped amulet. It used his tunic to polish it, wiping away ash and caked blood.

This complete, he held out the amulet to Lilith, who took it solemnly.

"We will bury the ash far from here," Padma said, breaking the silence. "And then begin the process of warding this cursed place for good."

As they left the graveyard, Dace and Lilith fell back.

"Well," Dace said, you have what you sought, lady. Was it worth the journey?"

Lilith turned the amulet over and over in her hands, as if waiting for it to reveal some hidden truth or secret. Nothing was forthcoming, so she raised her eyes and answered.

"I have more questions than answers, " she said at last. "I have faced things that have haunted me longer than you have lived, and I owe those things to you. Without you, I might never have solved the puzzles, or survived the attempt at solving them. I'm no closer to the one I seek, but I have found signs of his passing. I have found signs of what has been and, interpreting them, I can see that—for whatever purpose we might meet in the future, I was still in Desus's thoughts near the end of his time.

"And so," she concluded, nodding gravely, "it was well worth the journey." She raised her gaze to meet his steadily. "For many reasons, well worth it."

Dace held that gaze for a moment, then reached out to touch her cheek, stroking it gently, and pulling back again. He nodded and smiled. "I have likely learned more than you, lady," he said. "I have made what may have been bad decisions, but they were mine to make, right or wrong, and the consequences have given me experience and strength. I'll have to live with the consequences of my poor judgment, but the better part of that memory will be you."

Lilith lowered her eyes, but smiled enigmatically. "It seems I'm a bad influence, and for that I apologize. If I had foreseen how this might all end, though, I would still have done as I did. I will return to where we found this," she held up the golden star, "and from there I will begin my search anew. I'm certain there are still answers to be found there."

"We will meet again," Dace said. It wasn't a question. Lilith nodded. She didn't raise her eyes again, but her smile widened.

"I am sure that is true," she replied.

Just then, Daedalus called to them, and Lilith turned away, using the disturbance to break the spell of the moment.

"I wanted to introduce myself formally," Daedalus said, stepping up to where Dace stood and bowing slightly. "I wish that I came before you with a brighter history, or less reason for you to kill me on the spot, but I am what I am, and what I am at this moment is happy to be alive."

Dace measured the Dragon-Blooded warrior with a long glance, then nodded. "I have heard all that you have done in service of Mishaka since that one," Dace nodded back toward the ash pile, "turned his eye from you. But I have also heard of the ghost you summoned."

"One that helped you defeat the Drinker," Daedalus said.

"But what I did was as much for my own peace of mind as in defense of Mishaka. I will return now to the service I have left, and hope that you will continue to count me as a friend."

Dace frowned at this and Daedalus plowed on, maintaining eye contact with the Solar. "I never truly served the Drinker of Seeping Poison. I was placed among his ranks as the eyes and ears of another, and it was in the interests of that other that I released your scout, Tarsus, hoping he would warn the city in time. I know that you believe the deathknight served the Mask of Winters, but you are wrong.

"There is another dark force, and it was his intention that you believe this attack came from Thorns. The Walker in Darkness sent the deathknight and the dead. In the name of the one I serve, I wanted that truth to be known, and that the warning came to you from the Mask of Winters through me."

"You serve Thorns?" Dace growled. His hand dropped to the daiklave at his side instinctively, but Daedalus held up a hand.

"I am not your enemy, Dace," he said softly. "The ghost I unleashed was one bound into me by my master, and I freed it to help you, just as he wanted me to. But I understand distrust.. I will take my leave immediately."

"Your kind was never meant to serve the Deathlords," Dace said. "You shame yourself."

Daedalus continued to meet his gaze, then turned and strode away, not looking back. "Take my message to those you serve," the Dragon-Blooded warrior called over his shoulder. "Make sure they understand who was the enemy here."

Dace watched him go. For a moment he considered stopping the man, either killing him, or taking him prisoner on the spot, but something in the words spoken rang true. There had been no reports of movement out of Thorns, despite the growing force of the dead.

Dace felt he had somehow just made a bargain with a devil.

Epilogue

Dace and Lilith stood on the walls of Mishaka, side by side, staring off into the afternoon sunlight. They had walked through most of the day together, avoiding all others. They did not speak many words, instead preferring the shared silence of their thoughts.

"You're leaving?" Dace asked softly.

"Yes," she replied. "I still have much to learn, and somewhere," she sighed wistfully, scanning the horizon, "he is out there, or she—as it might be this time. I don't know if what we had before will be renewed, but I must know before all is done."

Dace nodded. "I'll be sorry to see you leave," he said. His voice was very soft, and he too stared into the distance. "I have a duty to perform, and those who look to me for guidance. If it were not for them…"

She turned to him and silenced him with a kiss. "I know," she said. "I know. You have not seen the last of me, Dace of Nexus," she whispered. "When you are standing in your garden among the trees, and you hear a rustle of wings, or the cry of an owl, think of me. One day you will do so, and I will be there."

He grabbed her then, drawing her close and kissing her hungrily. They melted together in that one long moment and then, with the very cry of which she'd spoken, Lilith melted from his embrace.

Powerful wings stroked the air and she rose into the sky, falling away to a small speck against the brilliance of the afternoon sun.

Dace stood for several moments staring after her. The owl's cry echoed in his mind as he turned back to the city, and the world, smiling.

About the Author

David Niall Wilson is a USA Today bestselling, multiple Bram Stoker Award-winning author of more than forty novels and collections. He is a former president of the Horror Writers Association and CEO and founder of Crossroad Press Publishing. His novels include This is My Blood, Deep Blue, and many more. His most recent published works are the collection The Devil's in the Flaws & Other Dark Truths, the historical fantasy novel Jurassic Ark—a retelling of the Noah's Ark story... with dinosaurs, and the recently released novella When You Leave I Disappear. David lives in way-out-yonder NC with his wife Patricia, thirteen cats, and a chinchilla named Pook-Daddy.

Curious about other Crossroad Press books?
Stop by our site:
http://www.crossroadpress.com
We offer quality writing
in digital, audio, and print formats.

www.ingramcontent.com/pod-product-compliance
Lightning Source LLC
Chambersburg PA
CBHW030304200626
46816CB00002BA/754